EMMY

IN THE

CAFE

EMMY

IN THE

CAFE

K.A. YOUNG

Printed in the United Kingdom

First Printing: May 2024

ISBN - 978-1-7392465-9-4

To my mother for always supporting me.

CHAPTER ONE
EMMY IN THE CAFE

JANUARY 1997

Fred Marsh had invited a new employee to work at Marsh's Manor. And not just a regular employee, either. The newest addition to their "family" would now be their new manager.

They managed themselves just fine, in Emmy's opinion, but it wasn't as if her uncle asked her for it.

Fred chewed the last bite of his food and addressed his family again. As he looked around the table, he made eye contact with each of them.

"This could be a wonderful change, bringing someone in," he continued.

Emmy gritted her teeth.

EMMY IN THE CAFE

As he eased out of his chair, Emmy and Noah moved to help him. He wavered for a second and waved them away before he settled on his feet. He favoured his left leg as he turned and collected his crutches from beside him.

Noah sank back in his seat, his brow creased as he watched his father. His sister Lucy sat beside him. Her glazed eyes stared at a spot on the beige wall over Fred's head. But Emmy sat rigid in her seat, with her eyes drilled into the side of her uncle's head.

"Once I come back to work, I won't be doing the job full time," he sighed. "We need more staff. You can't continue like this. It's not right to ask that of you. Both of you deserve a life elsewhere. With Tania working weekdays, you'll have more time for yourselves now."

He propped the crutches under his arms and rested his weight on them. "Besides, it'll do the business well to have fresh blood." He studied the three of them still seated at the table.

Noah grunted as he stood, a head above Fred's natural height. Side by side, Fred and Noah were 'before' and 'after' pictures of each other. They shared the same sharp features, the same dark, heavy brow, curly dark hair and warm, tan complexion. They even had the same slouch. Their mannerisms were even the same. Yet, there were slight differences between them. They were both of different heights. While Noah was tall, young and sturdy, Fred was short, older and wiry.

"I think it's a good idea, Dad. Tania and Andrea mentioned wanting more time away." Noah leaned over the table to collect the dirty dishes and cutlery before he took them into the kitchen. After a few seconds, the sound of rushing water reached their ears. Fred looked at the two of them.

Lucy leaned back in her chair, stretching her legs out underneath the table. She, too, shared a strong resemblance to her father and her brother, though her facial features were much softer and expressive, like Emmy's.

"It's not like you need the extra help, though," she mumbled and stretched her arms over her head, her back arching like a cat's. "Emmy and Noah don't mind. Well, Emmy doesn't. Do you?"

The faint scent of her perfume mingled with the air as she leaned in to get a better look at Emmy. Before Emmy could speak, Lucy continued.

"And I wouldn't mind working there, too. Like, as a more permanent thing." She added. "It would be nice to have extra money on the weekends, so take on more shifts during the summer holidays."

Lucy gave him a small smile, her eyes wide and hopeful. Fred studied her for a long moment before he nodded. "You can work weekends for a few shifts. We'll reassess in a couple of months. If you do well, I'll see about getting you a permanent job."

Lucy smiled and jumped out of her seat to hug her dad. "Thanks," she sang, squeezing her dad around the neck, giving him a kiss. "I'm gonna go. I'll be in my room if you need me." She turned and left the living room. Her footsteps thundered against the wood as she ran up the stairs. The sound filled the air, joining the sound of running water from the kitchen.

Emmy turned her attention back to her uncle and crossed her arms over her chest. "We don't need anyone else." She snapped. Her voice was louder than she intended, and she flinched at the sound.

"Speak for yourself!" Noah yelled from inside the kitchen.

Emmy rolled her eyes and leaned forward on her elbows. She stared at her uncle, her eyes pleading with him. "I can run things. Let me take over."

Fred sighed again and slid out of his seat and limped away from the table, toward the hallway. "You do enough shifts already. It'll be easier this way, love. Why don't you enjoy this? Most people would be happier if they had to work less. Oh, and I'm not docking your pay if that's what's worrying-"

"That's not the problem." Emmy mumbled. She raised her voice louder. "I'd be great as manager. I have nothing but time." It annoyed her he would think money was her priority. Her reason for working at the cafe wasn't money. In all honesty, she could've found another job. She stayed because Fred needed both her and Noah at the time to help him.

And he still did.

"Well, then... take that time for yourself. Do part time. Consider going to university or taking a course. You can change your mind."

Emmy averted her eyes and frowned at her hands, resting where her plate had been. She brushed her hand over her right sleeve. Her fingers itched to pull at the frayed edges, a result of years of picking at the hem.

"No, I already said that I wasn't going."

She considered going to university to study after leaving sixth form, or taking a course to teach a language or... something. But that was three years ago. And she was fine where she was.

Fred looked at her for a minute before he answered. "Suit yourself." He sounded tired and weak, and guilt trickled like ice water down her spine.

She gave him a hollow smile. "But you're right. About taking more time off. I'm sure it won't be that bad to have extra help."

He gave her a hesitant smile before limping out of the room.

Emmy watched him leave. She listened to the sound of his uneven footsteps as they faded away. Seconds passed, sounds faded, replaced by a creak, then silence. Emmy sighed and deflated in her chair.

She didn't want to sound ungrateful or to cause him stress. But bringing in someone else to run the cafe was going to cause more problems than it solved.

Fred had broken his leg a week before while mopping the floor of their kitchen. Emmy had been at her parents' house in the middle of a two-week visit to celebrate her 19th birthday.

Knowing Fred's history with broken bones, his accident didn't come as a surprise.

Without Emmy and Fred, Noah acted as manager for what seemed like the longest two weeks of his and Emmy's lives.

While Emmy was with her parents, he had to run the cafe with his younger sister, Lucy, doing the odd shift. She had been working after school, while their other employees, Tania and Andrea, took extra shifts to help.

Emmy on her first night back home, Fred announced the new management.

With Tania's son starting nursery in a couple of days, he had changed her shift so that she'd be working with Emmy and Noah on the weekdays. Andrea and their new manager would work on the weekends.

The plan was for him to help them run the cafe in Fred's absence and even after he healed.

Instead of Emmy.

Emmy assisted in cafe management for two years. It was far from unfamiliar territory, so it was a little insulting. But she couldn't complain that he hadn't put her in charge.

At least, not to anyone else.

Her uncle believed the new employee would liven up the place.

Emmy agreed. But not for the same reasons.

She took in a long breath through her nose and exhaled. After a few seconds of quiet, she rose from her chair with a loud scrape. She left the dining room with Noah still standing in the lit kitchen.

That night, her mind whirled as she paced the length of her room. Her uncle's words were like a thick fog stuck in her head, even as her head hit her pillow and she fell asleep.

Emmy woke the next day in a soured mood with a throbbing headache.

Bright light poured through the windows, and the cold air crept into her room under her windowsill. It bit at her exposed arms. The clock on her bedside table beeped while it displayed 6:30 am, bright red on its screen.

Emmy groaned and flipped the covers off, fighting her sluggish muscles. Switching off the alarm, she rubbed her arms and bolted from her room, heading downstairs to the dim kitchen.

She padded around the kitchen and made herself a bowl of cornflakes before she collapsed into one of the dining room chairs.

Emmy hated early mornings, but they were normal for her job, so she did her best not to complain.

Moments later, Lucy strolled in and smiled as she dropped into the chair beside Emmy. "Morning."

Emmy raised an eyebrow. Lucy's hair was a nest stuck on top of her head. She passed a hand through it and her fingers caught on the tangles. Her eyes were still bleary from sleep and surrounded by dark circles.

"Mm," Emmy mumbled around a spoonful of cornflakes. Her eyes dropped to stare at the emptying bowl, the lids closing every few seconds.

Lucy rested her arm on the table and her chin on her palm. She drummed the fingers on her other hand on the table, gazing at Emmy with lazy interest. Emmy raised her head and scowled back at her, fidgeting in her chair. "What?"

"I heard you pacing in your room last night. What's wrong?"

Emmy swallowed another spoonful and shook her head. "Nothing."

Lucy raised a brow at Emmy. "Is something wrong?"

"No." Emmy snapped.

Lucy leaned back, her eyes narrowed. "Fine." She got up from her seat and headed into the kitchen. Emmy stared down at her bowl as she swallowed another spoonful around the lump in her throat.

Forty minutes later, Emmy, Noah, and Lucy were ready to leave. They waved goodbye to Fred lying on the living room couch before Emmy closed the front door behind them.

She pulled her coat tighter around her against the chill of the outside and followed Noah into the car.

The clouds overhead hung grey and dismal as Noah steered the family car down the bleak, damp streets.

Ten minutes later, they had arrived at Lucy's school, a symmetrical group of dull grey, bricked buildings.

The school underwent substantial changes within the past five years. It was a very different place from the school Emmy and Noah had attended.

It was a miserable, cold Thursday. Lucy's school at this early hour of the morning was empty. From where she sat in the car, Emmy watched a small girl carrying a bag twice her size on her back, with a lunch box in her hand. The little girl scurried through the main entrance of the building into the empty hallway.

Emmy dragged her attention away from the girl to look at Lucy. She had been babbling about the workload of her physics class.

"Have fun. Learn things." Emmy said, nodding towards the building. Even to her own ears, her voice sounded bleak.

Lucy smiled at her in the mirror. Her eyes lingered on Emmy before she slipped out of the car. "I'll try if you do." She sang.

"At least try not to come back stupid," Noah called from the driver's seat. Lucy's mouth curled into a smirk. "I promise nothing." She laughed.

Noah waved goodbye to Lucy in front of the school and drove off to the cafe.

They arrived outside of the two-storey brick building in Patton's Place. The wooden plaque on the front marked it as Marsh's Manor in black, handwritten script. The cafe sat on a corner of a block of stores, nestled along a side road.

Noah unlocked the front door and held it open for Emmy. Noah promised to return before he left, letting the door swing shut behind him.

Going to the off-licence before opening had become his ritual for the past two years.

She liked the quiet his absence brought. Just her, alone in the cafe.

Emmy looked at the worn furniture. In the room, there were old, cream-coloured, patterned couches bordering the edges. Scattered around the room were sturdy wooden tables. The biggest feature was an enormous stone fireplace with a metal grate standing at the rear of the cafe.

She ran her hand over the worn arms of the couches as she passed, rubbing the frayed woven material under her fingertips. She crossed the floor, reached the cafe's back, and lit the fireplace.

The fire's warmth filled the landing, yet the January chill remained in the air and followed her inside. The cold seeped into her body, making her sluggish and clumsy. Straightening her back, she began working.

Her mind cleared as she took down the chairs from the tables and wiped them clean. She brewed coffee and heated baked goods in the oven. She marched up the stairs to the second-floor landing and began taking down chairs from the tables.

As she worked, dull winter light filtered in through the large glass windows along the front of the cafe. It landed on the hardwood floors and spilt over the worn wooden tables and chairs scattered across the wide room.

She worked quickly. Only when she had finished all her tasks and had time to think was when she noticed the heaviness she was feeling earlier had come back.

Noah returned ten minutes later, still five minutes before the cafe opened. He tossed her a bar of chocolate as he passed, and she thanked him before her mind wandered again.

EMMY IN THE CAFE

The new manager arrived the day after tomorrow, leaving the two of them alone for only a few more days.

At 8:30, customers rushed in, and the bell over the door ringing like a battle horn.

In stormed office workers, ordering coffee to wake them up before they had to catch a train or fight through traffic. Some were parents who had just dropped off their children at school.

Regular customers arrived, following their routine, ordering their usual, and socialising with familiar faces.

The noise and chaos was comforting to Emmy. She revelled in the adrenaline it brought her. Noah took the orders with a patient nod, while she served them with bright smiles.

Just before 11 o'clock, the bustle in the cafe had eased. As the morning rush ended, the quiet returned, giving her more time to think.

Emmy stood behind the counter, with a pensive expression on her face, listing reasons it was counter-productive to hire someone new.

She swiped the sponge once more over the cafe counter, wiping away left-over sugar and coffee granules. While she worked, Emmy wondered once again what the new employee would be like.

Would he be tidy? Would he be on time? Easy to work with?

From what her uncle had said, he lived far enough that he wasn't familiar with the area. "Local, but not too local." He said.

Whatever that meant.

There was a gasp and a sharp tinkling that cut through the hum of the cafe as a cup shattered on the floor. Emmy looked toward the noise and saw Mrs Martin sitting by the front windows. The large plant she sat next to almost swallowed her as she stared with horror at the broken remains of her teacup on the floor.

Mrs. Martin, a regular at Marsh's, was extremely skittish when spoken to by Emmy or anyone else at the cafe. She was tiny and round and reminded Emmy of a turtle, because of the large green coat she always wore, which swallowed her up. Her head was the only thing peeking out from the mass of green. On top of her head, she wore a green woollen bundle pulled over her wiry hair.

Mrs. Martin disliked making a fuss or attracting anyone's attention, especially when there was a crowd in the cafe. The older woman looked up at Emmy, appalled and apologetic.

Emmy beamed at her as she rushed over with a dustpan and brush to pick up the pieces of the broken cup.

"Don't worry about that. I'll clean it up," Emmy reassured her as she picked up the pieces.

"I'm so sorry." The older woman whimpered. She wrung her hands together and began muttering more apologies that Emmy brushed off.

"It's fine.... Noah?" She called over her shoulder to her cousin. He glanced up while cleaning a table. "Can you get Mrs Martin another cup, please?"

She turned back to the woman. "Peppermint, isn't it?"

Mrs Martin nodded, and Emmy's smile widened. "You can have this one for free."

The woman smiled. "Oh, thank you, Emmy."

"It's my pleasure," Emmy replied.

Noah led Mrs Martin over to the counter to get another cup of peppermint tea, while Emmy disposed of the broken cup pieces before she returned to wipe the spill.

While cleaning, she heard laughter across the room. As she turned around, she spotted her friends chatting on the couches by the cafe fireplace.

They had strolled in an hour ago, welcomed her back from her holiday, and as always, claimed the couches by the window.

Tilda lay draped over one arm of the armchair closest to the large window that dominated the wall. Her thick dark hair and her long limbs dangling like the branches of a willow tree. A wide t-shirt hung from her frame, while her leggings clung to her legs. Her striped socks were visible just above her white running shoes. Her pointed nose raised to the ceiling and her round eyes fixed upwards towards the group, her hands gesturing now and then as she spoke.

Maelie was on her right, reclining against the couch, her tangle of red curls spread out from under her beanie. She had a notepad on her lap and a beaten book gripped in her hands. Her fingers brushed the sides of her book as she rotated it, her usual scowl fixed in place.

Henry sat across from her on the opposite couch, looking ragged and breathless as always, his light hair sticking up in all directions. He leaned over the coffee table and dragged the notebook from Maelie's hands. Still sweaty from his morning run with Tilda, despite the weather. His t-shirt clung to his back as he moved. Whatever he said next made the group laugh and Maelie snatch her book back out of his hand. She kicked her foot out at Henry, and Tilda cackled.

Katherine sat to Henry's right. On the top of her head, her dark hair was curled and pulled up in an elaborate bun. She smirked as she smoothed her dark woollen turtle-neck dress down. She crossed her legs, before her sharp voice cut through the laughter like a knife, quieting them in an instant.

Emmy stood, surveyed the room, then checked the clock. It was just after eleven. She knew from experience that it would be quiet until around half twelve when customers arrived for lunch.

She stood up, walked to the kitchen, and deposited the dirty cloth. As she exited, Katherine looked up in her direction and waved her over to them.

Tilda's face brightened as soon as she saw her, and she sat up. "You're back!" she squealed. "Don't leave us for so long next time." She reached out and wrapped her arms around Emmy. "But, fortunately, you've come back at just the right time."

Maelie hummed in agreement, stretching her legs out in front of her. "Yeah, Aiden and I need your help for our film project coming up."

Emmy tensed and prised Tilda's arms from around her. "You don't need to film me, right?"

"Might do. We'll let you know,"

Tilda waved impatiently. "Yeah, yeah, that's great, but I was talking about me. I want to go on a date."

"With who?"

Tilda shrugged. "Anyone. And I would love for you to find me a boyfriend. Whenever you're ready."

Emmy looked around at her friends, puzzled. "Why are you telling me? Go find someone."

Tilda made a face. "I want you to set me up with someone."

Henry leaned toward Emmy. "You should. She needs all the help she can get." He muttered.

"I caught her checking out a mime once." Maelie added, clicking the button on her pen. "Said his soul really spoke to her."

"So, there're worse things than her ending up alone."

"I am right here," Tilda said, deadpan. "And that's not even true."

She was right. They didn't. Tilda would date a guy she liked. To everyone else, they were a strange couple, as nonsensical as an engineless car. In a month or two, they would break up, and Tilda would spend two weeks complaining before moving on.

No one knew anything about Tilda's standards. Her type would change from month to month, but never mentioned her preferences in a boyfriend. Or even what had gone wrong between them? No matter who she chose, they always helped to form a weird, unlikely, and ultimately doomed couple.

"What else is there to get?" Maelie's voice was dry and crisp, as she twirled her pen and wrote in her notebook. "You can't see an idiot coming from a mile away, but they can see you."

Emmy fought back a smile and perched on the left arm of Tilda's chair. "She's not that bad," Emmy reasoned as she patted Tilda's shoulder. "Some of her dates have been...nice."

Everyone but Tilda grimaced at her words.

Katherine picked up her cup and brought it to her lips, her sharp eyes focusing on Emmy over the brim. "You could set her up with someone at the party. You'll have a clearer head than her."

Tilda sprung back to life. "This." She gestured to Katherine. "This is all I wanted. Just someone with good judgement, with me, when I'm looking my best, surrounded by people looking their best. People looking for new... friends."

Emmy frowned, and she turned her attention to Katherine. "What party are you talking about?"

"My party. The one I'm throwing? Tomorrow?"

Emmy gave a small scoff and massaged the back of her neck as she rolled her shoulders. She had a backache. "Another one? Why?"

Katherine's brow furrowed for a second before it smoothed out. "Oh, right! You weren't there when we decided on it, were you? You were at your parents' house, right?"

Emmy rolled her shoulders back again, against the tension stored there. "Yep. So?"

Katherine nodded. "We're having a welcome party for your new boss at my house. Just so everyone can meet him in an informal setting. You know, get to know him before he starts his job. From what I've heard from Fred, he sounds as dedicated as you. He already has a few ideas he wants to try. I think your uncle might have picked the perfect person for the job."

Emmy's shoulders stiffened, but none of her friends were paying close enough attention to notice. She rubbed her neck again. "Have you spoken to him? The new guy?"

Katherine nodded. "He seems nice enough. He's a little quiet."

Noah slid into view and took a seat next to Katherine, crossing his legs by the ankles. "So, what are we talking about?" he asked.

Emmy glanced at Katherine. "We're having a party for the new guy."

"Bellamy? I had forgotten about him."

Emmy's mouth dropped. "You knew about the party for...Bellamy, the new manager? That's his name?"

Noah nodded slowly. "Yeah, didn't you know? Dad mentioned it yesterday, didn't he? I remembered him saying his name."

Emmy shook her head. She had a hard time remembering the details of her uncle's speech, but she was pretty sure she would have remembered that piece of information.

"Well, yesterday was the first I heard about him."

Noah sank back into the cushions with a heavy sigh. "Look, the party will still be fun. It's been a while since we had one. Who did you invite?"

"Just a few people. Our friends..." Her phone chimed, and her eyes widened a fraction as she looked at the screen.

She froze as she read it, and when she turned back to Emmy again, her eyes were pleading. "Em, I need a favour. Can you take care of the food? I have got nothing myself yet because I've been too busy. I was going to get something today, but..." She raised her phone. "Now I have something to do. Please?"

Emmy met her eyes for a second before she looked away, as the familiar guilt crept up her spine. "I'm sorry, but I can't. I-I can't."

Katherine frowned. "Why not?"

Emmy's fingers fidgeted with her left sleeve. "It's too soon. I don't have enough time. I..."

"Emmy! I need your help with this. It's important. Please?" Katherine pouted at her.

Emmy raised her eyes to the ceiling and sighed. She knew Katherine too well to believe she could say no. "Fine! I'll do it."

Katherine gave her a satisfied smile and clasped her hands together. "Good. I appreciate your help."

Henry sank into his chair. "Great. So, what are we eating?" "And what time are we all meeting here?" Tilda added. "And will there be alcohol?"

Katherine flicked her hair over her shoulder. "The party starts at 8:30 pm at my house tomorrow, but we're meeting at 8:00 here first, at closing time," Katherine said, looking at Emmy. "It's just a few friends from around. And no alcohol." She shrugged. "I already asked my dad about using the house and he said it's fine. Well, he's fine with it if we clean up. And leave all his alcohol alone. That was the deal." A reluctant rumble of agreement rippled through the group.

Emmy looked at her watch and stood from her seat. "Well, fine, but better get back to work. Noah?" She called over her shoulder. He unfolded himself from the chair and followed her back to the counter.

Noah and Emmy left their friends as the two of them returned to business. Once they were out of earshot of the group, Noah leaned over to Emmy and whispered. "Are you sure you can get everything together by tomorrow?"

She bristled. "Of course I can."

Noah held up his palms. "Alright, then. I was just making sure. Would you like help with that?"

Whenever Katherine planned an event, Emmy was always the one who had to organise the food and drinks. It had been like that for years. Emmy shook her head. "I'll be fine."

Noah looked unconvinced. "It's a lot to do. And there's not much time. I can help."

"It's only a few friends."

He scoffed. "Better to be safe than sorry."

She deliberated for a few seconds before a customer entered the cafe; the bell signalling his arrival. With no time left, she agreed.

At eight pm, Emmy and Noah closed the shop to the public.

Katherine, Henry, Maelie and Tilda were all long gone. As Maelie and Henry dragged Katherine out of the front door, yelled out the details of the party. She had already given Emmy money for the food. She said that she didn't mind whatever food they decided on, but that they should bring plenty of it.

Noah sent a text to Lucy to tell her about the change in plans. She arrived at the cafe at half-past four, with the ingredients Emmy had asked for, then set out her physics books on a table next to the counter and camped there until closing.

Once the shop was secure and tidy, Noah slumped into the seat he had occupied and crossed his legs at the ankles. "What are we getting? Or making? Are we making sandwiches or something?" He glanced at the shopping bags Lucy had brought.

Emmy settled down opposite him. "Bit of both."

They had already written the list of necessary things, but they still needed to buy a few extras. Emmy debated baking from scratch, but it seemed like too much work. Her silence earned her a frustrated look from Noah.

"Well?"

She looked up and snapped. "Kitchen. Now."

***

The next day, Emmy woke more rested than she had been for the last few days. It was a relief that came from finishing a task, and she welcomed it like it was a warm blanket.

She and Noah had spent a few hours last night putting together the food for Katherine's party. Lucy had her opinions whenever she wanted to procrastinate on her homework.

Early on, they all decided that only Emmy would do the important tasks. They decided this after Noah burned the first batch of store-bought pastries. He had mistakenly left the oven on high and left it after a fight with Lucy. Emmy had snapped at the two of them, scaring them out of the kitchen.

Even with her help, nothing they made was up to her normal standards.

Katherine always gave her more notice before something like this. But this time she had dumped it on her at the last minute.

Fred rang half an hour into their task, demanding to know why they and Lucy weren't home yet. Emmy had explained their involvement with Katherine's party as she pulled a batch of pastries out of the oven.

Four hours later, Fred called again to remind them to lock up when they were leaving. By then, they had four dozen pastries and snacks stuffed in the cafe's fridge. After his baking disaster, Noah had volunteered to buy the drinks and the rest of the snacks the next day.

When lunch arrived the next day, Katherine marched in wearing a light blue dress with a dark blue purse and a matching coat and shoes. Her heels clicked on the floor as she closed in on Emmy.

"Well?" she demanded. "Why haven't you called me? I was waiting for you to call and tell me what's going on."

"We've been busy with the food and work," Emmy muttered.

Katherine looked expectantly at Emmy. "So? What's happening? Is everything sorted?"

Emmy's shoulders tensed again. "Everything's in the kitchen fridge. We made some pastries and sandwiches and stuff. Noah's gone out to buy drinks and more snacks."

Katherine raised an eyebrow, glaring down at Emmy. "That's it?" She moved around Emmy and stomped into the kitchen. Emmy bristled but didn't bother to follow her, choosing to root herself in the same spot she stood and waited. She heard the heavy refrigerator door open.

There was a loud rustling, and then the door slamming back louder than it had opened.

Katherine appeared at the doorway, looking disgruntled, but managed a weak smile for Emmy. "Not your best work, I'll admit. But... good enough, I guess."

Emmy's face grew hot and her hands clenched in frustration.

"I could have done more with extra time. Why didn't you tell me earlier? Why didn't you call me while I was with my parents? You always want my help, so why didn't you call the moment you decided to throw this party? I didn't know about any of this until yesterday."

Katherine pulled back, crossing her arms over her chest, her purse under her left arm. "I thought you could handle this for me. It's just a small favour."

"Small? You call organising food for a party last minute 'a small favour'?"

"Kind of. And you should've said something if you couldn't do it."

Emmy scoffed. "I did it. You didn't care. But I still did my best with the time you gave me."

Katherine deflated, averting her gaze and anxiously fumbling with her purse. Her gaze fell down to her shoes, and Emmy looked in the same direction. They were expensive. That's as much as Emmy could tell about them, but she knew it must have been if Katherine wore them. Quality was always very important to Katherine.

After a brief pause, Katherine let out a sigh and lifted her head. "Look, I didn't mean to sound ungrateful. I'm sorry. It's very... stressful."

Emmy's shoulders slumped as she nodded in agreement. The argument had invited an uncomfortable wave of guilt. "It's fine. I'm sorry... I snapped. What's stressing you out?"

Katherine made a face. "It doesn't matter... It's fine. Don't worry." She turned away, burrowing in her purse and pulling out her phone. "Can you get me a coffee?" She called as she walked away, heading to the upstairs landing.

Motionless, Emmy stood by the counter, staring after her friend as she walked away.

When she had made the coffee, Emmy picked up the mug, jerking it towards her quicker than she intended. The cup was overfilled and as she picked it up, coffee spilled onto her hand and down her shirt.

As the hot liquid made contact with her stomach, Emmy cried out in pain. She pulled her top away from her skin, picked up a pile of napkins. She cleaned spilled coffee off the mug, then placed it on the counter.

Emmy glanced down at herself and she saw the coffee had soaked the middle of her mint green top. She moved towards the counter, trying to hide the stain from the view of the customers, but it would still be noticeable if she stepped back.

Just as she faced the kitchen, the front door swung open, bringing in a gust of cold air, and a tall young man of her age entered. Despite him only wearing a simple t-shirt, coat, and jeans, he exuded confidence. He was unfamiliar, which was an intriguing and unexpected twist.

Emmy was torn between helping a customer and dealing with the stain, but she chose the former. She greeted him with a smile, hoping he wouldn't notice her stained top as she moved closer to the counter.

He scanned the room briefly, but his attention halted when he saw her. He smiled and closed the distance between them, settling on the other side of the counter. "Hey." He had a deep and calming voice. Leaning in her direction, he pressed his hand firmly on the countertop.

"Hi. What would you like? Tea, coffee, hot chocolate?" Her hands twitched nervously as she gestured towards the counter.

"I'm not here for the food. I'm meeting someone." He glanced down at the watch on his left wrist. "I'm looking for Katherine Parson. My name's Bellamy Vella."

CHAPTER TWO
EMMY IN THE CAFE

"You're Bellamy? You're the new employee?" Emmy stared at him as the enthusiasm drained out of her voice.

The coffee-soaked clothing clung to her stomach. She crossed her arms over her mid-section to hide the stain, repositioning herself closer to the barrier between them. It was lower than her waist and she had to stoop to cover herself.

Emmy pressed her lips together and gave him a tense smile. The corners of his mouth turned up, his eyes sparkling.

"Yes," he answered, his voice smooth as velvet. "So, you've heard of me? Good. I hope I meet your expectations." He joked.

Emmy fumbled for words, but found none. She had prepared herself for his arrival. Or at least she had tried. But when she imagined him, he was someone small, twitchy, and pushy, trying to take charge.

Emmy admitted to herself that this man was not what she expected. She looked him over again.

His mouth had a soft smile and his eyes were a warm chocolate brown with a playful glint in them. His slightly curled hair was a few shades darker than his eyes. He wore a sensible, nondescript grey coat and under that, his clothes were as plain, but they looked well kept.

He seemed calm and sturdy. Someone you can depend on. Not someone quick to anger, but someone who can be level-headed amid chaos and destruction.

She could only hope.

Bellamy leaned back on his heels and buried his hands in the pockets of his coat, towering over the counter with little effort. His eyes on her, he waited for her reply.

Every moment she stood there, the damp fabric grew colder and wetter against her stomach. "Mm."

She retorted. She had forgotten what he said, and she might lose her voice if she tried to speak.

The weight of his stare was a heavy, stifling cloak draped over her. It made her shift her weight from one foot to the other. Emmy needed to get to the kitchen without him noticing the stain.

She didn't realise she had stopped breathing until he removed his glance from her to look around the interior of the cafe and she inhaled sharply.

There weren't many customers left occupying the tables in the afternoon. There was a gentle hum in the air along with the warm, sweet smell of pastries. The feeble sun peeked in for a few seconds before retreating.

When Emmy remained silent, Bellamy returned his gaze to her and continued. "It seems like a very... welcoming environment. Andrea and Tania were friendly when I spoke to them. So were Lucy and Noah."

Emmy had nothing to say, so she kept her lips pressed together and her face neutral.

He couldn't have picked a worse time to visit. Noah was nowhere to be seen, and she wasn't prepared to meet Bellamy.

"Well, I'm Emmy. I work here too. Have you... did they tell you about me? About me working here?"

He nodded politely. "Yeah."

Emmy's expression became stoic as she focussed most of her attention on trying to keep her stoop behind the counter. She tucked a stray curl of hair behind her ear, but it sprang loose. She pulled at it again and hooked it around her ear. Reluctantly, it remained in place, but began curling away from her ear as soon as she let go.

Bellamy's mouth had the hint of a smile, and he continued. "Uhm, Noah mentioned you. You're Noah and Lucy's cousin, right? He said you were staying with your parents for your birthday. And, happy belated birthday, by the way. It's nice to meet you. I've heard only good things."

Emmy smiled weakly, searching for something normal, welcoming, or at least something intelligent to say.

Her brain decided on none of the three.

"So, you've been here... before now?"

Again, he nodded, watching her squirm with amusement. "Mr Marsh... Fred invited me to see the place when he gave me the job. I got to meet everyone else at the cafe. Except you."

Emmy forced herself to make her expression open and welcoming as she rubbed a knot at the back of her shoulder. "Well, it's nice to meet you, too."

She brought her hand down and began pulling at the hem of her top. She decided it was best to keep quiet if she had nothing to say and hope that he'd settle for nods and smiles.

Bellamy chose not to push. He leaned against the counter, his eyes glinting in the dim light, taking another glance around the room. "I guess it's a good thing that we're having this party," he smiled at her again.

"That's why you're doing this, isn't it? To introduce me to everyone."

Emmy pressed her lips together. Her pleasant expression melted away as his words registered. "So, you heard about the party too?"

Had Katherine told everyone else but her?

Bellamy's brow creased, but he shrugged. "Katherine suggested throwing a party while I was here. I said no, but she insisted."

This time, Emmy gave him a genuine smile. "She does that a lot."

He chuckled. "Fred said a party would be great. He thinks Katherine could make a living organising parties."

"Yeah, she does that, too."

He smirked at her words and extended his hand forward across the counter. Emmy glanced at his hand briefly before clasping it in her own right hand. His grip tightened around it. It warmed her small, moist hand, and she could feel the sticky coffee congealed between her fingers and his.

She pulled her hand away, taking a step back from the counter, flexing her fingers as he frowned at her.

"Sorry," she muttered. "I spilled some coffee."

His eyes dropped lower, and she followed his gaze to the stain on her front. "I can see that."

Emmy's cheeks heated, and she stepped further away. "Just wait here."

She ran to the kitchen and grabbed a cloth from by the sink. She returned and grabbed his right hand, wiping the wet cloth over his fingers. His hands were larger than hers and much stronger.

She was in the middle of wiping at the mess when she noticed his gaze. She looked up and saw him watching her.

"Sorry," she repeated, dropping his hand like a stone. "I-"

"Emmy? Where's my coffee?" Katherine's crisp voice cut through the air between them, and before Emmy could reply, Katherine marched down the stairs. As she moved toward them, the steady click of her heels pierced the air. Emmy picked up the cup from the counter and handed it to her as she reached them.

Katherine took the cup, but her focus drifted to Bellamy, who stood behind Emmy. She paused for a moment before recognition dawned on her face and she gave Bellamy a welcoming smile.

"Hello, Bellamy."

The young man had turned his head to Katherine, his smile mirroring hers. "Hello. I'm not too early, am I?"

"No," Katherine said. "You're right on time. This," she gestured to Emmy, "is Emmeline Marsh, but everyone calls her Emmy. You've heard of her, haven't you?"

Her tone had changed to one familiar to Emmy. Her voice was now commanding and filled with authority.

"We've met," Emmy interjected. Katherine frowned at her and she elaborated. "Just now. We introduced ourselves."

Katherine nodded as she clasped her hands together in front of her and kept going, undeterred. "I told her about you yesterday. About how perfect you'll be for the position. You'll give Emmy a run for her money."

Emmy froze at Katherine's words and her cheeks flushed with annoyance, but Katherine didn't notice.

She gave Bellamy a polite smile and clasped his arm, leading him away from Emmy. She directed him to the couches by the fireplace, her grip discouraging him from looking back, as Emmy trailed along behind them.

It was typical of Katherine to take charge, but today Emmy wasn't in the mood. She usually ignored her, but everything she had said today was a smack to the face. Though she knew it wasn't on purpose, it did nothing to soothe Emmy's mood.

"So," Katherine began, not bothering to look back at Emmy. "We're having the party tonight; it'll be at my house. A few people are coming. It'll be a great bonding experience. Emmy even made snacks."

The last part was dismissive.

Bellamy glanced back at her over his shoulder, and Emmy gave him a small smile.

As Katherine and Bellamy settled into their seats, the front door opened again, blowing more icy wind into the cafe. Noah shuffled in, wrapped up in his coat and weighed down by two armfuls of overstuffed bags. Henry and Aiden, the last member of the group, followed him.

Aiden was shorter than Henry, even with his perfect posture. He wore his dark brown hair trimmed lower than when Emmy had last seen him, but she found the haircut suited his sharp face.

The boys looked frozen as they shivered in place. They had bought packets of crisps and chocolate, bottles of wine, spirits and cans of beer that poked out from inside their bags.

In Aiden's bag, she saw a packet of pink and white marshmallows peeking out from under the rest of the food.

"You bought marshmallows?" Emmy asked, pointing at the bag. He gave her a lopsided grin.

Burrowing into his bag for a few seconds, he pulled out the packet and tossed it to her. She grabbed it out of the air and opened it. Taking out a pink marshmallow, she sank her teeth into the soft, squishy surface.

"Thanks. I haven't had these in ages."

Henry lifted his bags higher in the air, drawing them to her attention. "We bought a bunch of things we used to eat in school. Sour sweets, too. I got a box of fancy chocolates. For you, as a late-birthday-and-welcome-back present."

Emmy beamed, chewing another marshmallow. "A present you're going to help me eat, you mean?"

He scoffed. "Of course."

Aiden frowned at the two of them. "I did not realise we had to give you more presents? I gave you one already, remember? Do I have to get you another?"

He looked from Emmy to Henry. "Then where is my extra birthday present? My birthday was after hers!"

"No. You don't have to get me another present." Emmy insisted.

She remembered exchanging gifts with Aiden before she left. She had given him a hard drive since he had run out of space on his computer, and Aiden had given her books on the Renaissance, the Roman Empire and Tudor England for her birthday. They sat on her bedside table, waiting to be read when she had time to relax. She hadn't found time to read them, only flicking through a few pages.

Henry narrowed his eyes at Aiden. "We already gave you something. This is for Emmy's return home. If you get lost for two weeks, we'll get you a box of chocolates too."

Aiden relaxed, and his eyes shifted from Henry to Emmy. "I want to make it clear, if we were supposed to bring something else, that I helped him to pick that box out." He pointed at the chocolates in Henry's hands.

Henry nodded. "It's true. He pointed it out and everything."

Emmy rolled her eyes and ate another marshmallow while Katherine stared down at the food. "At least we have more options now."

Emmy ignored her and folded the packet of marshmallows. She walked to Noah and the boys and helped them with their bags. Noah smiled as he passed her one of his. "I called these two to help me. Sorry. We got carried away and kind of overspent."

Henry looked mischievous while Aiden's smile was smug, but none of them were apologetic. It was going to come out of Katherine's wallet, not theirs. If nothing else, Katherine would always pay them back.

She helped them to rest their bags on top of the couch opposite Bellamy and Katherine.

"Is this all for me?" Bellamy asked, staring at the overflowing bags. "I'm touched."

"Yes. But you have Katherine to thank for this," Noah replied, dropping his bags on the couch next to him.

Aiden turned towards Katherine with a deep bow. "Our gracious Queen Katherine requested we give you the star treatment," Aiden said to

Bellamy, glancing in Katherine's direction as he rose from his bow, his nose up in the air.

Noah and Henry chuckled, but stopped after one glance at Katherine. Noah sent her one last look as he took the cans and slipped into the kitchen.

Katherine glared at his back as he left before she turned to study Aiden. The temperature dropped and everyone else shifted in their seats. There was a stillness to Katherine's expression. The focus in her eyes made her look like a cobra poised to strike. Aiden stared back, unconcerned, refusing to break eye contact with her.

After a tense pause, Katherine's jaw clenched, and she crossed her legs. She sat back in her seat with a huff, and the tension broke its hold on the group.

With one last glance at her, Aiden lifted his bags and piled them on the seats of the couch before he sunk into the seat opposite Bellamy. He leaned across the table, extending his hand over it.

"I'm Aiden." He said.

Bellamy took his hand and shook it. Aiden motioned to his left, to Henry as he deposited his many bags on the couch with the others and dropped into the seat next to him. "And this is Henry." Henry waved his hand at Bellamy in greeting.

"I'm Bellamy," Bellamy announced to both of them.

By the time Noah had returned, Aiden, Henry and Bellamy were deep in conversation.

Katherine was staring off into space during the exchange. Once Noah returned, she shifted in her seat to face both him and Emmy as they wrestled the rest of the bags on Emmy's couch and slumped on it next to her.

"Is everything sorted now? The food and drinks?" Katherine whispered.

Noah nodded and stifled a yawn. "Yep. We got everything that we needed. So, I'm going to rest now. And eat. I have had nothing for an hour."

He pulled out six packets of crisps from a bag and, with a warning; he tossed a bag to each of them. His throw to Katherine was skewed, going past her head and landing three feet behind her.

They sat on the couches surrounding the coffee table, the heat from the fireplace warming them, as they sat squeezed in between the bags. They ate and chatted about the busy weeks they had.

The cafe was silent and almost empty, the only chattering coming from their group.

Emmy sat in silence after she finished her packet. She crumpled it in her hand and watched as Bellamy interacted with everyone else. They all liked him. She must admit she liked him too until she realised who he was.

Now, she wasn't so sure.

He seemed pleasant, but she couldn't gauge his personality. He was polite and formal and answered every question she asked him. Still, he didn't give more information than was necessary.

He claimed to be excited about working in the cafe, but Emmy had doubts about his authenticity. He sat rigid in his seat, despite his relaxed expression, which led her to believe that he wasn't as comfortable as he pretended.

Emmy collected her resolve and lifted her chin to speak to Bellamy. "Did they give you a tour last time?" She asked, nodding her head towards her friends.

Bellamy shook his head, crumpling his empty crisp packet in his hand. "No, they didn't."

"Well... would you like me to show you around the area... before the party? I was thinking of going to buy chips."

"Okay then. Let's go." He got up from his seat and waited as Emmy collected her coat from the back of the cafe before they marched out into the biting, frosty air.

Outside was a sharp contrast to the dull warmth of the cafe.

In the freezing wind, a few people fumbled around the empty streets.

Emmy could see her breath drift out in front of her. She wrapped her coat tighter around her and set off in the shop's direction as Bellamy fell in step beside her.

Emmy glanced over at him as they walked, keeping her gaze on his shoes. She was uncomfortable looking at him.

"I'm sorry," she muttered at the ground. "Katherine's... difficult sometimes, but she means well. And... Aiden and Noah like to provoke her."

"It's fine." He answered. "You don't have to apologise."

Emmy shrugged. "It's more of an explanation. They're great. Just big kids."

Bellamy nodded and stared ahead. Emmy waited for him to say more, but he remained silent.

Before she spoke again, they passed an old and dusty looking store. It was one which Emmy liked to browse when she was younger. She paused in her step and looked through the glass at the display. There were old books, worn cabinets, broken tables and odd ornaments crowding the tiny space.

Bellamy stood beside her, gazing out the window. "It's a second-hand shop." He stated.

Emmy looked up at him, not sure what had just happened. She crossed her arms as she replied. "I like the things they sell. I've gotten books and other bric-à-brac too. And they're very cheap. You don't want to go inside?" She gestured to the door.

His brow creased, and his jaw tightened as he took in the shop's front. "No."

His refusal surprised her. "There's nothing wrong with it." She said, as she took half a step toward the door.

Bellamy nodded, his eyes on the display. "No. But we came for chips."

He turned and walked ahead a few steps, pausing for her to join him. She pulled her coat tighter and walked to meet him, and they fell back in step with each other.

Emmy continued to point out more of the shops that lined the road, but with less enthusiasm now, as they walked along the street toward the chip shop.

She could not tell what he may be interested in, so she described the contents of every shop they passed.

Bellamy was attentive as she continued to show him the sights. He asked her questions while she pointed out favorite places. Somewhere during the walk, he relaxed.

It was on their way back, bags of chips in hand, when she began asking him about his home life. She had decided that it was best to take advantage of his lowered defences while they were still outside and amicable.

"Uncle Fred says you have to travel from a fair distance." She said, biting into a chip. She wasn't looking in his direction, but out of the corner of her eye, she saw him falter in his step.

"Yes." He hesitated. "It's a bit of a trip, but it doesn't matter."

He seemed reluctant to speak about it.

"Do you still live at home?" she pressed.

"Yes, with my mum and my sister." His voice was curt, leaving no room for conversation. A few minutes ago, he was very relaxed. Now he was withdrawing from her again.

"Well," she continued. "I live with my uncle and cousins most of the time. But I've been with my parents for Christmas, from the 15th of December until after the 2nd of January, so we have Christmas, New Year's Day and my birthday rolled together."

She was desperate to keep him talking, out of fear that he would clam up. Something told her she won't get another chance if he did. "My parents sent me to live with my uncle and cousins years ago because I spent a lot of time here. School was here. My work's here. So I just moved in with them."

"If it's so far away, why did you go to school here?"

"My family lived nearby but had to move because the house had structural damage. We lived with Uncle Fred for a few years. We bought a new house further away from here. The first year was tough because I was travelling back and forth. My schoolwork suffered, so I moved in with Uncle Fred."

Emmy looked at the pavement in front of her, this time hoping Bellamy won't question her further. She caught him looking at her again, out of the corner of his eye.

He was silent for a moment before he spoke.

"The chairs in my home are second hand." He murmured.

Emmy looked up at him in surprise. She had assumed he was going to press her on her school days, not open up to her. His behaviour at the second-hand shop made more sense now.

"I bought some of my books from that store. Uncle Fred also bought a painting there which he has hung in the living room." She offered.

Bellamy nodded, and this time he kept his attention on the pavement in front of him. His shoulders had slumped a fraction as the tension lifted. "How long have you worked here?"

Emmy shrugged, avoiding his gaze. "At sixteen, I started doing a few shifts at the cafe. My uncle gave me a job with Noah at eighteen. I put off going to university for a year. He needed me, so I stayed here. Now, he has you."

The last part sounded much more bitter than she had intended. Bellamy's only response to that was to bury his hands in his pockets, and he remained silent for the rest of the walk.

They arrived at the cafe a few moments later, escaping the biting wind outside. It was empty apart from her friends. The weather was keeping intelligent people indoors, as coffee wasn't a necessity on a late Friday afternoon.

The others surrounded them as soon as they returned to the couch. Emmy didn't look at Bellamy as they began passing out the food. She sat as far away from him as she could, avoiding any eye contact.

They seemed to get along, but now she was unsure. Perhaps she told him too much about herself.

When most of them had finished eating their chips, Aiden cleared his throat and addressed the group. "Alright. So Tilda's picking up her brother after work. Mae's at the library, so they'll get here a little before seven." He stretched out his legs in front of him and crossed his ankles, lying back against the back of the couch.

Emmy recalled Aiden mentioning that he and Maelie had to work on a project together for their media class, which neither of them liked to talk about, so it was a safe bet to say it wasn't going too well between them.

"Great, they can help us set up," Katherine stated, leaving no room for arguments. Aiden narrowed his eyes, while Henry rolled his.

"Hey Kat, did Emmy show you the food we made?" Noah asked, his mouth full. He swallowed and licked his thumb and forefinger.

Katherine, who hadn't opened her packet yet or touched her chips, smoothed out the packaging while he spoke, a look of disgust on her face at his lack of manners.

"Yeah, Emmy showed me what you did." She answered. Noah frowned at Katherine and looked at Emmy for answers.

Emmy did not want to talk about it, so she rolled her eyes at him, deciding to keep her mouth shut for a quiet life. Not satisfied, but unwilling to pry, Noah relaxed in his chair, his keen gaze shifting back from Emmy to Katherine.

Once they had finished eating, Noah and Emmy called their extended break to an end, despite the lack of customers, and excused themselves from the group. Emmy passed the opened packet of marshmallows to Henry. "Here. You have them." She said.

Henry thanked Emmy and shoved the marshmallows into his mouth while Katherine stared at her phone, checking for messages.

As soon as they were back in the kitchen, Noah rounded on Emmy. "Why did she say it like that?" He whispered in her ear.

"She's acting like this was something we just threw together."

"It was something we just threw together."

Noah's back straightened and his face hardened. His eyes, dark and piercing, turned to drill holes in the door, as if he could see Katherine on the other side.

"We made the food. What else did she want?"

"She didn't seem happy." Emmy sighed, bracing herself for his reaction. Noah's patience, as far as Katherine was concerned, was wearing thin.

Each of their friends dealt with Katherine in their own way. Tilda and Henry made jokes. Maelie was sarcastic, Aiden provoked her further and Emmy tried her best to ignore her. Noah, though, had a low tolerance for her criticism and was, along with Aiden, the one most likely to pull her up on her attitude.

His head snapped back in Emmy's direction, and she drew back from him. She could see the irritation burning in his eyes and the tension along the line of his jaw. "Impressed? Impressed? We... we worked hard rushing to make the food ready on time and she's still not happy, is she?"

"I thought you said we didn't rush the food."

Emmy tried some light humour to defuse the situation, but Noah waved her away, his voice rising with his temper.

"We did the best we could, with the time she gave us and everything still turned out fine. The sandwiches are delicious - because of my sandwich-making skills and nothing else. The stuff you made is even better. And that's because of your expert cooking abilities. Did she taste any of it? Did she say thanks? Of course not!" He shouted.

Emmy sighed, rubbing her forehead and hoping the mess, the pain, and the headache will vanish. "She says it wasn't up to my standards. But she had a point. I have done better."

Noah frowned. "No, you were great. If Queen Katherine wants something better suited to her 'refined' tastes, she should have done it herself." He turned and headed to the door.

Emmy's eyes widened, and she grabbed his arm in a panic, pulling him back. "Where are you going?"

Noah raised an eyebrow. "To tell her to apologise to you." Emmy's grip on his arm tightened.

"Don't say anything!" she hissed. "It doesn't matter. Katherine's just under pressure, so leave her." Emmy begged.

Noah gazed at her, puzzled. "Under pressure with what?"

Emmy shrugged. "I didn't ask, but we know she works hard. She helps her mum with events, and she takes over and organises things for her. She puts a lot on herself."

"And so do you. So do the rest of us." He shot back. "Why does she get to treat us, her friends, like lackeys? All we try to do is help lighten whatever 'pressure' she put upon herself, you know, despite her attitude. We don't attack her."

Emmy didn't have a suitable answer for him. Emmy agreed with him but she wanted it to be over without a fight.

Emmy knew Katherine worked hard for her mother's estate agency and never complained. She took her stress out on her friends instead. Katherine's exacting attitude toward them annoyed Emmy. They worked too, and they didn't snap at their friends when they were stressed or tired.

Arguing with Katherine exhausted Emmy. It was as if she had never taken a holiday.

"Just forget it for now. If she does it again, we'll tell her to the top."

Her answer didn't appease Noah. In fact, he grew angrier, but made no further move to force the matter.

After a while, Noah's muscles relaxed, and Emmy let go of his arm.

"Thank you." She whispered.

The front door opened, so they both went out to serve the next customers.

After another quick debate, Emmy and Noah decided it was best to close an hour earlier, since the cafe remained quiet for most of the day.

The pause allowed her to contemplate her day. She had to admit Bellamy wasn't like she first assumed, and their walk had removed some issues she had about him coming to work at Marsh's Manor.

She watched him as he became more and more relaxed as the evening wore on. He had taken off his coat and rolled up the sleeves of his black shirt, and seeing him at ease among her friends was as if he had always been a part of their group.

Around five o'clock, Bellamy drifted over to sit in front of Emmy at the counter. His mood appeared much lighter as he folded his hands on the counter in front of him, smiling at her.

Emmy, surprised, paused from wiping the counter to look at him.

Earlier, he had not attempted to speak to her since they returned from their walk, only glancing in her direction whenever she spoke. She assumed she had somehow upset him.

"Can I get you something? Any drinks or... something to eat?"

Emmy wasn't sure what else to say to him beyond that. He had spent the evening talking to Aiden, Katherine and Henry, but she hadn't listened to what they said, so she couldn't use any of it as a conversation starter. She rubbed her fingers together, realising that she could still feel the coffee on her fingers even after she had washed it away.

He shook his head. "No. Thank you." He watched her, leaning back on the stool with a faint smile on his face.

His expression showed no anger or annoyance, only humour and interest.

So, apparently, he had found her amusing.

"First you take me on a tour, now you offer me coffee. Are you always this polite with everyone? Or just customers?" His eyes sparkled with mischief, but his face was void of any other emotion. "Or am I just lucky?" He joked.

Emmy's face heated. "I try to be polite to everyone I meet. In and out of work."

"So, you're being nice because of your job. And everyone else? Are they being nice for their jobs, too? So far, everyone has been great."

Emmy shrugged with a little effort. "You heard what Noah and Aiden said. This party is for you. Katherine organised it for you. So, of course, we welcomed you. You're the guest of honour."

"So, is this party an... inconvenience?"

She scratched at the countertop. "No, it's just that Katherine dictating how we should welcome you can really be annoying."

"I see. Noah said you were a bit like her, too."

Emmy clenched her jaw, her eyes moving to find her cousin. Noah was dashing around the upstairs landing, clearing away plates, his back towards them. She glared at him before looking back at Bellamy. "What did he tell you about me?"

She wasn't half as irritating as Katherine, not what anyone said, but it didn't paint her in the best light.

Bellamy drummed his fingers on the table. "That you're a workaholic like Katherine. That sometimes you go overboard. He said that your uncle made sure you took a break during Christmas and for your birthday."

Emmy gripped the cloth she was holding and scrubbed the counter harder. "You say that like it's a bad thing. I just care about my job. And it's funny, but it includes customer service."

"Most people enjoy having days off. Especially at Christmas and New Year, even when it's busy."

"Well, I like my job. I enjoy working with my family and seeing my friends." She squirmed under his scrutinising gaze as he studied her. To him, she must sound dull. She was but, it still stung.

It was a little like she was trying to prove that she mattered. She felt the same about Katherine.

He looked at his folded hands. "Your uncle said you ran this place on your own."

"I still do." She shot back. "I can handle anything that happens. I've done it before."

"I'm not doubting you, but Fred gave me the job as your boss to watch over you, and I'd like the chance to do it well."

"You will be our manager, yes, but we'll still be the ones running the cafe. We know where everything is and we've been here for much longer than you. We know the customers and they trust us. It's been that way for years."

Bellamy met her eyes. "Sometimes change is good."

"And sometimes it's unnecessary."

The words came out before she could stop herself.

She wasn't usually rude to people, and she hadn't intended to be until she opened her mouth.

Bellamy's eyes shone in the dull light. "I didn't mean to upset you." He admitted. "Fred said the place won't be what it is without you. He knows you work hard. He doesn't want us to rely too much on you. Don't worry, I intend to work just as hard as you."

Emmy fidgeted and looked at the table to avoid his eyes. She felt even more ridiculous than before.

He sighed and leaned back, giving her a strained smile. "I get the sense that you don't like me. Or not happy to have me here."

She raised her eyes to stare at him, and he met her eyes evenly.

Emmy didn't know what to say. She didn't enjoy having him there, in her cafe. It was stupid the way she felt, but she couldn't explain her feelings to him.

She did like him a little more after their walk, but she hadn't changed her mind about having someone else running the cafe. It was just how she felt, and she was terrible at hiding it.

She tried to speak, to say something polite, but before she could utter a word, he interrupted.

"What can I do to fix things?"

His bluntness took her by surprise.

"My uncle leaves me in charge. Always has. So it's just... strange..." She paused.

He waited for her to continue.

She pulled up the corners of her mouth in a feeble smile. "Look, I don't hate you... I'm just not fond of the situation we're caught up in... I'd like to get to know you. I want you to feel welcome here."

The words sounded robotic and forced, but it was true. She wanted the words to be true. It wasn't his fault she felt the way she did.

"But?" He whispered.

"But, what?"

"You want me to feel welcome here, but...?"

Emmy blinked at him, searching for a reason etched on his face. A reason she shouldn't trust him.

She breathe deeply and shook her head, passing the cloth once more over the counter. "But nothing. I hope you'll fit in and make some friends."

"Well, I hope by the end of the year, we'll be friends."

He reached out his hand toward her again, this time as a peaceful gesture.

For the first time since she met him, she thought it was possible that they may become friends.

A genuine smile appeared on her face as she leaned forward to accept his hand.

"A year's a long time."

CHAPTER THREE

TILDA IN THE CAFE

Tilda parked her car just outside the university library and sighed as she sat back in her seat. She squirmed when sweat trickled down the back of her uniform. It has been a long day at the gym, and she was more than relieved for it to be over. Well, for work to be over, at least.

After a few minutes, Maelie opened the passenger door of the car and climbed in. Tilda shivered as the cold air rushed in behind Maelie.

"Hey," Maelie greeted her as she threw her bag into the back of the car.

"Hey." Tilda sighed, and rubbed the top of her arms, just under the short sleeve of her t-shirt. Maelie clicked her seatbelt into place and glanced at Tilda, pushing her hair back from her face. Tilda heaved another sigh, wiped away the sweat from her forehead, and loosen her hair from a tight ponytail. Maelie continued to stare expectantly until Tilda turned and stared back blankly at her friend.

Maelie raised an eyebrow. "What's wrong with you?"

"Sore. Sweaty. You know, the usual."

The headrest creaked as Maelie tilted her head back against it. "And that's why I hate the gym. I don't enjoy getting sweaty."

Tilda scoffed and rolled her neck. She tried to imagine Maelie in one of her classes. Heckling everyone from the back, perhaps. "You hate a lot of things."

Maelie gave a short laugh at her friend's irritation, then sank into silence.

Tilda settled back in her seat with yet another heavy sigh and started the car. She pulled away from the pavement and began driving toward her brother's school.

They drove in silence for a while, before Tilda grew tired of it and asked Maelie about her trip to the library.

Maelie, however, did her best to dodge Tilda's questions. Tilda tried to get her to speak, but with little success.

"I'm good. Don't worry about me." She mumbled, pressing her head into the headrest of her seat.

Maelie only spoke to say hello to Tilda's younger brother, Matt, as he climbed into the back seat of the car.

When they picked him up from school, he said little beyond a greeting to them both, before he too fell silent. He was even less talkative than Maelie, which rang alarm bells for Tilda.

As soon as they arrived at Tilda and Matt's house, Matt jumped out of the car and ran ahead along the stone path that led to the dark green front door. He'd spoken little to Tilda lately, and she was getting concerned.

Tilda's father was sitting in the living room, watching an old black and white movie, when Tilda walked into the house. Matt had already disappeared upstairs. Tilda waved to her father as she ran past the living room and skipped upstairs.

"Dad. Hey. Mae's with me. Say hey, Mae!"

"Hello, Mr Myles," Maelie called as she followed Tilda.

"Hello, Maelie." He replied as he drew his attention from the TV. "How's your mum?"

"Glad I'm out of the house!" Maelie yelled back as she followed Tilda upstairs.

They slipped into Tilda's bedroom, and Tilda grabbed her dressing gown. She ran to the bathroom to have the quickest shower ever in memory, while Maelie battled through the piles of clothes and exercise equipment on the floor to get to the bed, where she collapsed.

When Tilda stepped out of the bathroom and returned to her room, she found Maelie lying sprawled on her bed, staring up at the ceiling with dull eyes. Her hair was spread out around her on the bed, like liquid fire, and she reminded Tilda of a tragic painting that she studied in an art class or seen on the wall of a museum.

Tilda was sure that none of Maelie's problems were as dire as they seemed.

As Tilda searched her room for her make-up, they discussed how best to approach her brother. Maelie proposed violence to his toys to get him to talk, but Tilda refused.

"Fine. Well, you can forget about asking me for help. Ever. I mean, what's the point if you're always going to ignore my suggestions?" Maelie mumbled, picking at her fingernails.

"I'm still waiting for you to come up with a decent idea," Tilda muttered.

She fished out her giant bag of make-up from inside a drawer and crossed the room to rummage through her wardrobe.

With a grimace, she grabbed the nearest item of clothing she could find. Her panic increased once she realised there wasn't anything she wanted to wear. She was not bothered about what she wore, and would have been fine with wearing something casual, but she had a feeling that Katherine wouldn't be.

If she turned up in a t-shirt, old jeans and her favourite trainers, Katherine wouldn't let her through the door. It wasn't hard to imagine Katherine leaving her outside on the porch with a sandwich and a drink.

She wondered if she should call Emmy to ask her about what she should wear, but she doubted she would be any help.

No, Emmy would just tell her whatever Tilda wanted to hear.

Emmy was more likely to repeat someone else's opinion rather than give one of her own. Maelie would be the better choice to ask for her opinion, and she had already clarified that she didn't care either way. She was too busy lounging on Tilda's bed.

Tilda turned to her. "Do you have any other ideas? About Matty? I mean, he hasn't even done anything wrong, so scaring him won't help. It'll just make things worse."

Tilda pulled out the first dress she could reach, preoccupied by her concern about Matty. Her fingers brushed the material for a moment and she made a silent promise to wear it, no matter what it was. Though she had already glimpsed that it was yellow, and was pretty sure she knew which dress it was, so it wasn't much of a gamble.

Maelie sat up on the bed, her red curls spilling around her shoulders, a heavy sigh escaping her mouth. "No. But I guess you could just try talking to him."

Tilda shook her head. She threw her dress on to the bed, and her eyes met Maelie's. "I think he just misses Mum. I wouldn't know what to say to him about that."

It's been just shy of a year since Matt and Tilda's parents divorced, and no one was ready to talk about it.

Tilda sighed and pinched the bridge of her nose, feeling guilt wash over her. She wasn't sure what to say or to explain how the split made her feel, so she doubted her eleven-year-old brother could. Besides, she didn't feel like she was ready to explain those feelings to him, either. To anyone.

She used to spend her Saturdays with Matt. She would watch movies with him, take him to the park, and sometimes just drove him around whenever he felt restless. That tradition faded away as she began spending less time with him because of their parents' divorce.

Maelie grimaced, staring at her lap. "Well, just give him sweets and hugs. Or something. Say something nice and comforting. Like, you're there for him, or that it's normal to be sad." She shrugged, "But be persistent. Make sure he knows you care. All that mushy stuff. He's just as stubborn as you." The last part was a mumble under her breath.

Tilda tilted her head to the side to glare at Maelie. "What's that?" She snapped.

Maelie lowered her eyes to the bed and picked at the bedsheet covers. "Nothing."

Tilda scoffed and headed to the bathroom to change out of her dressing gown and into her party dress. When she returned to her room a moment later, Maelie was still sprawled on the bed.

Tilda eyed Maelie's clothes from where she stood, her nose wrinkling.

"Are you going to wear that?" She asked, pointed at the baggy t-shirt and jeans Maelie wore. The girl raised her head and stared at Tilda's dress, appraising it for a second. "Yep."

Maelie would happily provoke Katherine at her own party, but it was different for her. Sure, Maelie was smaller than her and Katherine, but Tilda couldn't imagine Katherine being able to leave her on the porch.

Maelie would break in through the back door. Or Aiden and Henry would find a ladder and sneak her in.

Tilda nodded. "Alright then." She walked back to her wardrobe and pulled out a t-shirt and jeans.

Maelie smirked as Tilda slipped back into the bathroom.

When she was finished getting dressed, Tilda strolled out of her bathroom, pulling her hair out from under the collar. She walked past the bed and out of her bedroom door. Maelie's eyes followed her lazily as she walked down the hall, pausing outside of Matt's room.

His door was on the left of the hall, opposite the bathroom. He had plastered old stickers on the wood of the door. Someone must have scratched some off 'Matt', as he grew in and out of trends.

She knocked on the wood. "Matty, it's me. Can I come in?" She called.

The door handle turned, and the door creaked open. Her brother stood just inside the room, staring up at her. She smiled down at him, feeling a strange sense of pride that he had grown so much, and was looking more and more like her each day.

He had her dark hair, her eyes and her owlish expression. She could even see that they had the same frame and in a few years, he'd be tall, like her and their dad. His head had already reached her shoulders.. He opened the door wider to let her have a glimpse of him.

His room behind the door was, she was disappointed to note, much tidier than hers. He had scattered his toys around the room, on the shelf above his bed, on the top of his wardrobe and on his desk, but each of them looked like they belonged where they were placed. He displayed on a shelf opposite his bed a toy their grandparents sent for him from Singapore.

Matty was standing in the middle of his room on his dark blue rug, already dressed for bed in his pyjamas. His top had a logo from one of his favourite TV shows printed on the front and the bottoms a similar recurring pattern, but his sleeves were already too short for him and his ankles were visible underneath the hem of the legs. He'd been insisting he was too old for the branded pyjamas and maybe he was right.

He had outgrown them.

"Are you going to that party?" He questioned. She told her father about the party the day before and though Matt was present in the living room, playing a game on Tilda's old laptop, she didn't think he paid attention to what was being said.

"Yes. I'm going with the others. It's for the new guy at the cafe. I told you about him, didn't I?"

"I heard you talk about him." He muttered and sat down on the edge of his bed. He had made his bed, but the sheet was creased in the middle and her old laptop was on top of the covers.

Tilda followed him into his room and sat down next to him. He didn't object, so she pressed on. "How about... this weekend, we go see a movie? We haven't done that for a while." She mused.

He shrugged. She waited for him to say more, but his eyes remained fixed on the rug at their feet. "Or if you don't like that, we can do something else. Like, go to the park?"

"What are we going to do for your birthday?" He mumbled.

That was the question that she'd been dreading for months. She knew they must discuss it sooner rather than later, but the selfish, immature part of her- the major part, to be honest- hoped she could move out before that happened. Or they could just coast and pretend everything was fine.

In a couple of months, it would be her first birthday since their family separated. They held together just long enough for Matt's last one, but no one said anything about what would happen for his birthday this year. It's been a struggle for the two of them to adjust to moving from one parent's house to another in between terms, but this was different. This was the first time they would celebrate a birthday without both parents being present at the same time.

She knew she couldn't avoid the question for long, but she still didn't have to answer it tonight.

Tilda shrugged. "I don't know." She whispered.

Matt nodded his head in silence, and she moved closer to him, pulling him into her arms. She didn't know what else to say, but as he relaxed beside her, resting his head on her shoulder, and she placed her chin on his head, it didn't matter anymore.

"We'll watch movies all weekend, ok? Just you and me."

Matty nodded, and she hugged him to her tighter.

***

Tilda and Maelie arrived at the cafe a little after seven, with Lucy trailing just behind them. Tilda and Maelie had walked to the Marsh's house to meet Lucy. They had traveled with her, taking Emmy's party dress with them to the cafe.

Maelie threw her books somewhere into the back of Tilda's car. She was still wearing her tired t-shirt, with a sarcastic quote on the front that made Katherine raise an eyebrow when she saw it, and her frayed jeans.

Tilda's insistence on her wearing something else caused Maelie, who was by now tired of her pestering, to give her a colourful and definite response that left Tilda speechless.

Tilda picked lint from her dress as she took in her surroundings. She had buckled under the pressure and changed again into a blue dress that reached her mid-thigh.

The cafe was empty apart from their group of friends. Emmy, Noah, and Katherine sat on a couch opposite Aiden and Henry. Next to Katherine sat a tall, dark-haired boy in a black long-sleeved shirt. She and Maelie had not yet met Bellamy in person, but from the information she had dragged out of Noah, the picture she had of him differed from the reality. He was a lot better looking than she'd dared to hope.

Tilda smiled at Emmy when she saw her and pulled out a folded piece of green and black fabric and a pair of shoes, waving them at her.

"We grabbed you a dress. I think it's a dress. Well, Lucy did. And shoes. She figured that you'd be too busy to head back home, so she got something from your wardrobe on her way out."

Lucy gave Emmy a smirk before stifling a yawn at the last minute. Lucy yawned again, giving Emmy a cheerful and apologetic smile. "Sorry," she mumbled, "school's terrible. Dad told me to say hello for him and for us all to have fun, but that we shouldn't party too late."

Katherine, who sat motionless on the couch, sprang into action. "Of course. Bellamy, this is Tilda," Katherine gestured to Tilda, who beamed at the mention of her name.

Bellamy's answering smile was like the sun, warm and inviting to each of them.

"This is Maelie," Katherine gestured to the red-haired girl, who waved back. "And you've already met Lucy." She waved at the last girl.

Bellamy leaned forward, his arms resting on his knees. "I remember." He said to Lucy. "How's Physics?"

Lucy sighed, a faint smile on her lips, and she dropped on to the couch between Henry and Aiden, disturbing them. "Like pure torture. Thanks for asking." She glanced at Katherine.

Katherine rolled her eyes. "Emmy, we should let you get dressed." Tilda passed Emmy the dress and watched as she ran into the cafe's bathroom to change.

Noah, Lucy, and Emmy took his car with the food and belongings packed in the back. Maelie and Tilda took Henry's car and Katherine led them all in her own, with Aiden and Bellamy in the back.

Half an hour later, they arrived at the Parson's imposing house, nestled amidst other well-kept houses, with gates and shrubs decorating the fronts.

Some of the most expensive cars Tilda had ever seen were parked in front of the houses. Each house they passed differed from the others in its own unique way. The entire street seemed to exist in another era. They could not hear any traffic nearby, and only a few people wandered the street. The air was still once they turned off the busy main road, and all the ambient noises were overwhelmed by silence.

The house itself was a wide bricked building, with two storeys, surrounded by trees that scratched at the windows of the top floor, and a tall gate at the front. Katherine pulled her car into one space inside the two-car garage. Noah parked beside her, and Henry parked behind them on the stone driveway that led up to it.

They all clambered out of the cars, fumbling with the bags of food. Cold air snapped at them while Katherine unlocked her house. There was the sound of a click and the door swung in to invite them inside.

A pale grey carpet lined the hallway, surrounded by beige walls. There were pictures along the walls placed with care, the carpet was clean, and ornaments were in their place, clean and free of dust.

Tilda clamped her arms to her sides at the sight of an expensive-looking porcelain vase. She didn't know how much it cost, but it made her sick to think about it since she didn't want to find out the wrong way.

Once they were inside the living room, Katherine started giving them orders. She instructed Maelie and Henry to set up the music system, while the rest of them distributed the food and beverages onto tables around the room.

All of them apart from Bellamy.

He was 'encouraged' by Katherine to relax since he was the guest of honour.

In Tilda's opinion, Katherine's front room was perfect. The whole thing looked like a set piece from a department store. Two long grey couches dominated the room with a coffee table between them, and along the back of the room was a hardwood table next to a door that led into the den. Cabinets lined half of the back of the room, with windows and a back door that led into the backyard lining the opposite wall.

It made Tilda uncomfortable just by being there, even without a drink in her hand.

Tilda watched Katherine as she whisked around, straightening the tables and wiping away imaginary specks of dust.

"Do you need to complain so much, Kat?" Aiden snapped, dropping a bottle of fizzy lemonade down on the hardwood table.

"There's nothing wrong with paying attention to detail." She shot back.

Aiden pinched his nose and groaned to the ceiling. "No. But there's something wrong with shoving around your friends. We're not paid to work for you. We're not here for your entertainment."

Katherine scoffed, placing her hands on her hips. "And who have I been pushing around?"

"You pushed Emmy around," Noah announced to the room.

Everyone turned to stare at Emmy, who froze at the mention of her name. Her eyes widened, and her cheeks darkened. Five pairs of eyes moved between Aiden, Katherine, Noah, and Emmy.

Henry and Maelie watched for Katherine's reaction. Lucy and Bellamy hovered by the walls, out of danger. Tilda tensed where she stood. She wanted to help Emmy and deflect some of Katherine's rage. She moved a step closer to Emmy, but there was nothing to fear since Katherine seemed unfazed by Noah's words.

"We've already spoken about that. I admit it. I was a little short with Em, but we've worked it out already. Just this evening. Didn't we, Emmy?" Katherine's eyes fixed on Emmy waiting for her reply and Emmy nodded.

Emmy turned to glare at Noah, her round eyes burning holes in the side of his head.

Noah's jaw clenched, and he gave a bitter laugh. "You pushed her into working on your party when she didn't want to. You didn't even give her enough time to do it, then you complained it wasn't up to your standard. And you didn't even say 'thank you for all of your help, Emmy. I couldn't do it without you,' or something like that. Or even thank the rest of us for helping."

Katherine stiffened, and her face went blank as if someone had wiped all expression from her face. In seconds, her jaw clenched, and she picked non-existent lint off of her dress. "I just wanted... for this to go well. And without my house being torn apart, thanks."

Noah clenched his jaw again, but he dropped the argument. Aiden, however, refused to let go.

"Listen." He started. "Your house is fine. It's spotless. Perfect, even. I wish that this was my house already. And even if someone doesn't like your house, you'll be safe amongst friends. What little you have. No one will care what anything looks like. So stop fussing."

He grabbed a cold can of soda, opened it, and took a long swig. Katherine watched him with distaste. He stopped and look at her, his expression daring. "Keep going like this and no one will be left in the house in an hour with you pestering us. We'll leave."

Katherine's eyes narrowed to slits. Aiden glared back and placed the perspiring can on the wooden table. Everyone turned to watch them, but no one interrupted. Tilda could see Katherine clench her fists as she opened her mouth to speak. But before she said anything else, she turned and walked away from the group, leaving the rest of them to do their tasks in silence.

Tilda spotted Bellamy leaning against a wall near the glass doors that led to the backyard and meandered over to stand next to him.

She raised a hand in greeting, and he gave her a smile in exchange. "Tilda, right?"

Tilda nodded and beamed. "Yep. How are you doing? Scared of us yet? Ready to run?"

He pushed his hands into his pockets and sighed. "Not sure I could make it to the door." He leaned over to her and lowered his voice so only she could hear. "Is it always like this with them?"

Tilda glanced at Aiden, who was skulking in the corner, standing next to Noah. Both of them were staring down at a fuming Emmy. The small girl was hissing at the two of them, her curly hair flying around her head.

While they fought, Katherine ignored them all. She was organising and reorganising the food on the other side of the room. When she looked up, she began scolding Maelie and Henry as they fiddled with the speakers.

"Sometimes," Tilda answered. They clashed. A lot. They all did. But never like this. They all had their quirks, but Tilda was sure he'd learn to love them.

At least, if he learned about them over a period, not in one go, and only after it was too late for him to retreat.

"Well, yes," she admitted, "they clash. But it's never anything like this. It might be stress."

Bellamy shifted as he rested against the wall, his mood dimming. "Because of the party?" he asked. "It's just a party. If it was going to be this stressful for everyone, why do it?"

Tilda sank into the wall next to him. "No, it's not. It's no trouble." She inhaled. "I think most of this has nothing to do with you. Sorry. I just think everyone's excited. It's a lot of change."

Bellamy looked toward Emmy, and Tilda followed his gaze. Emmy was still hissing at Noah and Aiden on the other side of the room. Aiden put his arm around Emmy, attempting to calm her, but it aggravated her more. "Some people don't like change."

Tilda looked back at him. "Who? Emmy? She's a sweetheart."

Bellamy did not seem to agree. "Maybe. She thinks I'll take over, or something."

"Emmy...means well. She likes to take care of people."

In Tilda's opinion, sometimes too much. She knew Emmy since they were at secondary school, and she saw how she had changed over the years. At the start, Emmy never wanted to be part of their group, spending most of the time on her own. A few years ago, she grew more confident, thanks to her job at the cafe.

But the bad thing was, this new persona didn't seem to exist beyond Marsh's Manor.

"I'll admit that she might care a bit too much about what other people think. And she has a temper."

Bellamy scoffed, a smirk dancing along his mouth. "I'll say." He watched the minor argument on the other side of the room with interest.

"She bit my head off when I tried to talk to her today. But we made up. I think."

Tilda had noticed that Emmy seemed withdrawn when she arrived that evening. While the rest of the group were questioning Bellamy, Emmy kept her distance, staring off into space.

"You caught her by surprise," Tilda answered. "And I'll also admit that she's not fond of surprises. And I don't think it's fair that Katherine made her work all night last night to make the food. Now, Katherine isn't normally that insensitive, I swear."

Bellamy exhaled and rubbed his hand against his chin. They returned their attention back to Noah and Aiden as they attempted to calm Emmy down.

A few minutes later, the doorbell rang, and people trickled into the house. Katherine rushed out of the room to greet them.

Tilda sighed, her muscles still aching from her shift at the gym. She nodded to the door. "Let's get you meeting people. You don't want to only have us to talk to." She shuddered. "Imagine that."

For the next ten minutes, the doorbell rang non-stop as more people arrived and soon, over two dozen guests were milling around the house, while Maelie and Henry fought over the blearing music.

Tilda had peeled herself off the wall and led Bellamy across the room to meet the new arrivals to the party.

Tilda's workmates, Darcy and Will, arrived first, followed by a large group of Aiden, Henry and Maelie's old school friends. Tilda and Bellamy spent an hour talking and laughing with a group of people. The music was lowered to a hum in the background and there was a buzz of conversation in the air.

Tilda knew everyone there, but Bellamy was unknown and so desirable. To everyone else, he was a mystery and his newness made him the centre of attention. All of them were interested in meeting Bellamy, and he charmed them.

Out of the corner of her eye, she could see that Emmy was calmer and was dancing with Henry, the both of them in the middle of the room laughing like hyenas. Noah and Lucy were dancing in time to the music beside them, but Emmy and Henry were heckling their moves.

Tilda wanted to join them, but she was having a lot of fun with Bellamy, hearing all of his tales and telling him all of hers.

When she first met him, she thought he'd be like Katherine. But Bellamy was far from anything like her. He was funny and cute, too.

Her friend, Darcy, was in the middle of telling them about her hectic school days when Aiden wandered over to them. He was in a better mood than before, but she suspected the company he was in was the reason for his improved attitude.

He grinned at Tilda and Bellamy. "Having fun?" His voice slurred.

Bellamy grinned back, and Tilda nodded. "Yeah," Bellamy answered, "lots."

Aiden nodded, mulling over the information. "Good. That's good. Tilda?" He turned to Tilda. "Would you like to dance? I'm sure we can out-dance them." He jerked his head at Emmy and Henry.

Aiden extended his right hand toward her, and she took it. He led her over to where Noah, Lucy,

Henry and Emmy were dancing, and danced with Tilda, his movements slow and exaggerated.

"Nice moves," Henry called over his shoulder. He spun Emmy around once and they danced around Aiden and Tilda, moving in time with them while Noah and Lucy watched them. "How's everything?"

"Great," Tilda answered. "Everyone likes Bellamy, and everyone's having fun. But I still want you to set me up with someone." She turned her head and looked down at Emmy.

"Oh yeah. That." Emmy pulled away from the group. "Do you want to get a drink?" She asked.

Tilda nodded, leaving the huddle to follow Emmy. They walked over to the table packed with canned drinks and picked up one can each.

"So, I've been thinking... how about Sam?" Emmy asked. "I don't know him that well, but he comes into the cafe every once in a while, and he seems nice enough. Have you seen him yet? I'm pretty sure Katherine invited him."

Tilda tilted her head to the side. "Yeah, I did when he arrived. So? What about him?"

"How about you dating him? I think you've met him at the gym before, right?"

"Yeah. I have. He comes in a lot. About twice a week. He's got a younger brother and Matty hangs out with them a lot. We talk. But I think it would be too awkward if I dated him, though. I mean, imagine if it didn't work out. Things would be too difficult for Matty. I don't want that."

Emmy nodded and glanced out toward the crowded room. Tilda followed her line of sight. Bellamy joined the group they'd just left.

There was something soothing and likeable about him. He blended in with the rest of them, talking with everyone he met, ready to be accepted and liked.

"How about Bellamy?" Tilda prodded. She watched as he laughed with Henry and Lucy at something Noah said. She returned her attention to Emmy and saw that the girl was frowning at the scene.

Emmy shrugged. "What about him?"

Tilda turned to watch her friend, remembering what Bellamy told her before about Emmy. She reached out to tug at one of Emmy's curls and yanked on the end, stretching it out and drawing Emmy's attention back to her. "He says you snapped at him."

Emmy's eyes widened. "I... might have. But we're good now." She relented. She looked away from Tilda, down at the floor, rubbing her fingers together. Remembering the can in her hand, Emmy took a drink.

Tilda smirked and twirled the curl in between her fingers. "It's ok, you know." Emmy met her eyes, puzzled. "Not adjusting to change. I didn't."

Emmy scoffed. "It's not the same as a divorce."

Tilda's hand stilled in her hair. "So, you admit it? That you're not adjusting?"

Emmy took another gulp from her can before staring Tilda straight in the eye. "No, I'm not. But I will. Give me time."

Tilda knew Emmy for over eleven years. If there was anything that she discovered about Emmy was that she had trouble relinquishing control. The last thing she would do was give up control of the cafe.

She couldn't help but think that welcoming Bellamy into the cafe would take a little more than time.

CHAPTER FOUR

EMMY IN THE CAFE

Emmy squeezed past the other guests out of the den, cradling her can to her chest as she backed out into the living room.

There were people occupying every available space on the first floor. The party had been going on for more than an hour and the party was in full swing.

Someone opened the door of the den, a room that connected to the living room, and guests flocked in, ready to lounge on the expensive couches.

Why Katherine would suggest a party in her own house, considering how valuable everything was, Emmy didn't know. Though, she supposed no one would dare do anything to tick off Katherine. They all knew better.

Emmy shivered as she walked past the glass garden doors and an icy wind drifted in and bit at her legs underneath her dress.

Someone had left the backdoors to the garden wide open to let people mill in and out. The sky outside was an inky indigo, with splashes of pale grey clouds. It had gotten much colder since the time they had left the cafe, but that didn't stop people from going outside from time to time.

Most of Katherine's friends were in the den, with Tilda and Henry's workmates from the gym, while Aiden and Maelie's university classmates were with Emmy and Noah's old school friends in the living room.

Even Lucy had friends from her A-Level classes lining in the doorway between the two rooms.

Katherine had invited a few of each of their friends so that everyone had someone to talk to.

Tilda had moved from where Emmy had last seen her to stand at the back of the living room, slouching against the wall, near the entrance that led out into the hallway.

Her glassy eyes watched the guests as they gathered in the living room, when the music changed to a faster beat. She shifted her weight from one foot to another as she surveyed the room, her hands playing with the hem of her blue dress.

Emmy slipped in between the dancers and crossed the room to settle against the wall beside her. Tilda nudged her in acknowledgement.

"Hey, you. Again. I thought I got rid of you." She said, her voice heavy with sleep.

Emmy scoffed and nudged Tilda's side. "Thanks. That makes me feel so wanted. I just came to say hi. Again. But I could leave. Again."

Tilda shook her head. "No. Stay." She grimaced and wrapped her arms around Emmy. "Besides, who would you hang out with? Not Noah or Aiden. Not soon, anyway. And don't forget, we have Maelie and Henry fighting over the music. Lucy's over there somewhere, busy with her friends. And Katherine... is doing Katherine things. Trust me. I'm your best choice. And you're mine."

"It's not much of a choice," Emmy muttered.

"Tell me about it!" Tilda tilted her head to her right. Emmy followed her direction and spotted Katherine as she rushed out of the den and to the music system in the room's corner, where Maelie and Henry, now joined by Aiden, were fighting over the music.

The song that had been playing came to an abrupt halt, and another one played in its place. The new song sounded like a different person had taken over the music, and from the gestures Aiden, Maelie and Henry were making, that was what had happened.

Tilda watched, a sluggish smile on her lips as Katherine closed in on them. "There's no saving them now. Best not to disturb them after what happened last time. They'll take you down with them."

Emmy scoffed. "And what else could they say to make things worse?"

Tilda shifted her position and folded her arms over her chest, watching their friends fight with amusement. "Don't ask. But if you want to find out for yourself, go on. I'll just wait here."

Tilda looked at her, hoping she'd go. Emmy ignored her and stayed by her side. Emmy was still furious with Noah and Aiden for dragging her into the middle of their argument with Katherine.

She knew Noah was trying to stand up for her, but she didn't need him to. Emmy thought she could handle Katherine, even if the rest of them didn't believe that she could.

"Yeah, well, I guess they were trying to help. In their own way. Noah, at least."

Tilda bobbed her head. "Aiden, too, I guess. But he's been annoying Katherine a lot. I'm not sure how he figured pushing her would help."

"You mean, more than usual?" Emmy asked, and Tilda made a face.

They turned to watch as Katherine joined the group and started arguing with them over the music. Katherine wrestled Maelie and Aiden from the speakers, but Henry had slipped past her and began fiddling with the music.

Although the music was loud enough to drown out most of what they said, Emmy could hear a few less than pleasant words from Katherine and Maelie returned a few colourful ones of her own.

"I guess it's getting to Katherine." Tilda sighed.

"More than usual?" Emmy repeated.

Tilda gave Emmy a bleak smile. "Even Katherine has her breaking point."

She ran a hand through her hair and sighed. The corners of her mouth twitched up and her eyes glinted with mischief. "You know, we should find someone else for you to talk to. Bellamy, maybe?"

Emmy made a small noise that sounded to anyone like agreement, hoping Tilda was just making an offhand joke and not an actual suggestion.

As they watched their friends all bicker with one another, a tall, slender girl with shoulder-length dark blonde hair walked over to join her and Tilda. She had a heart-shaped face and electric green eyes that probed for answers to questions she hadn't even asked.

Darcy Taylor worked with Tilda at the gym. Emmy wasn't that familiar with her, but she knew about her outgoing personality from Tilda. Emmy had met her a few times before while visiting Tilda at Patton's Place Leisure Centre. She liked Darcy well enough from her own experience with her, but Darcy still seemed more like Tilda's friend than hers.

Emmy spent very little time at the gym. Tilda had always insisted that they work out together, but she wasn't a fit person, and she didn't consider embarrassing herself in public for an hour a week could change that.

"What are you two talking about?" Darcy beamed as she picked up a can from a table next to them and joined them against the wall.

Tilda straightened the minute she saw her, her eyes still burning with mischief, and she gave Darcy a sly smirk. "Emmy was just going to help me find a date. Weren't you, Em?"

Emmy froze for a moment before her promise to Tilda came rushing back to her.

Darcy turned to look at Emmy, raising a straight eyebrow. "Who do you have in mind? I have a few suggestions of my own." She said. The glint in her eyes was playful.

Emmy shrugged a shoulder. "No one yet." To be honest, Emmy had little interest in setting up Tilda with anyone. Dating wasn't something she had any experience in, so she was pretty sure she was the worst person for the job of matchmaker. Tilda didn't appear to think so, however.

Regardless, Emmy was also pretty certain that the act of Tilda asking her for her own opinion was just a habit by now.

Even if it had no real influence over what she did, Tilda would still ask, though she would do the exact opposite or end up ignoring her suggestion altogether.

But Tilda had asked her, and she couldn't say no.

Emmy scanned the room with pursed lips, waiting for inspiration to hit, and her eyes landed on a familiar face on the other side of the room.

Eric was a friend of Henry's. The two of them worked out together and afterwards, they would come into the cafe to grab something to eat. Again, he wasn't someone that she knew very well, but she remembered talking to him a few months ago, the day they had both dropped by the cafe for coffee and pastries after their jog.

He was tall. Taller than Tilda, with short brown hair and a long nose. He slouched against the small table as he stood, bending down to accommodate his shorter friend.

"How about Eric?" Emmy suggested, nodding in his direction. "He goes to university with Mae and Aiden. He works out at the gym, too. I think Henry is already pretty friendly with him."

Emmy figured he and Tilda would make a pleasant couple. He was always kind and respectful whenever she spoke to him.

"He's cute," Darcy admitted. "And hilarious. And, like Emmy said, he enjoys working out. Oh, and he loves movies, like those sci-fi ones you like. Yeah, he'll be perfect for Tilda." Darcy looked at Tilda, the glint in her eyes growing with each word.

Tilda leaned back and tapped her lip, opening her mouth every so often to bite the nail. "Sure. I remember talking to him with Henry a few times. He's got good taste in films." Tilda looked down at Emmy. "You have the final say on this, though... so we all agree?" Both girls stared at Emmy, waiting for her decision.

Emmy paused for a second. She knew Eric had gone to university with Aiden and Maelie on the weekdays, studying film and during the weekends he went to the gym to train with Henry.

Tilda liked films; Tilda liked the gym. As far as Emmy could tell, they seemed like a good enough match.

She may not have known much about relationships, but she appreciated Tilda's faith in her judgement.

She glanced once more in Eric's direction and nodded in agreement.

Tilda's shoulders relaxed, and she smiled at Emmy. "Right, so... aren't you going to speak to him first? See if he's interested? I'd do it, but I don't want to look too desperate. Please?"

Emmy stiffened. "What? How is it going to look better coming from me?"

Tilda gave her a sheepish look. "Well, don't tell him. Suggest that he speak to me, I'll handle the rest."

Emmy drew in a long breath and sighed.

"Fine." she grumbled. "I'll speak to him."

"Just don't be too obvious!"

"Me? Never." She muttered and set off to find Eric, leaving Tilda and Darcy alone.

The man in question had disappeared from her line of sight and she scanned the room, raising up on her toes to see over the heads of taller people.

As the party intensified, Emmy moved through the living room and into the den, out into the hallway, mingling with the friends she met, a can still held in her hand.

She passed Katherine on her first circuit, smiling at her guests, like the excellent hostess she was. She had given up fighting with Maelie and Henry. Her shoulders were rigid and climbing up toward her ears, but none of the tension showed on her face.

Emmy walked on, stopping to chat with more familiar faces than she knew, before leaving them to the music.

Faster, popular songs followed slow indie songs. The violent changes in the music were rather telling. They proved that Maelie and Henry hadn't yet agreed on what they should play.

As Emmy strayed into the den, Aiden and Noah roped her in to playing a few card games with them, before she halfheartedly returned to her search. The boys had figured the best way to make it up to her was to beat her in almost every game. Allowing her to win would imply they considered her incapable of winning on her own, and they couldn't have that.

Emmy would have preferred that they just let her win.

On Emmy's second circuit of the downstairs rooms, she spotted Tilda again. This time, she was alone and standing in a corner by the kitchen with a phone receiver pressed to her ear. It was all most ten, and so Emmy assumed she was calling her brother before bed.

She couldn't remember the last time she had seen Matty, but from what little Tilda had said, Emmy supposed Tilda had spent little time with him either.

Emmy took a sip from her can, pulling her thoughts from the siblings, and moved on with the search.

As her eyes scanned the room, she thought about what Tilda told her about Bellamy. She saw Tilda and Bellamy getting along before, and they seemed to make a decent couple.

Bellamy was opening up to Tilda. Anyone could see that from the way he spoke, his movements were much more unrestrained, and he smiled more. It had been like pulling teeth to get him to talk to Emmy, but he seemed to get along with Tilda.

Tilda had noticed her reaction and Emmy felt exposed by just how easily she had read her. Did she know her so well, or was Emmy too obvious? If the latter was true, she wondered what Bellamy must think of her.

As if she drew him to her, Bellamy stepped out of the den and into her line of sight. He wasn't facing her direction. In fact, he hadn't even noticed her. He was too busy staring at the sky with his shoulders hunched over.

She hesitated in place for a second, debating whether she should talk to him. Emmy realised he was a nice guy, so why did talking to him make her nervous?

She had meant what she said to him in the cafe, that she wanted him to settle in, but a part of her was still reluctant to accept him as part of the 'family'.

She watched him walk out through the glass doors and out into the garden.

Emmy brushed her hair back as best she could, then followed him to the door. She leaned out of the threshold and spotted Bellamy standing just outside the door on her right, still staring at the sky.

"Hey." Her voice was small and sharp out in the still air.

Bellamy lowered his head, turned and when he realised who it was, he smiled at her. "Oh, hey."

Emmy raised a hand and pointed out to the garden. "You don't mind if I join you, do you?" She asked.

Bellamy shook his head. He shoved his hands into his back pocket and gave her a warmer smile. "No. Come on out."

She stepped out into the frosty air and stood next to Bellamy, surveying the work of art that was Katherine's backyard.

The garden was impeccable, much like everything else in Katherine's house. There were fresh flowers lining the edge of the garden and a patio in the middle of it. A few feet away stood a tall tree looming next to the house. A few people were standing outside, immune to the night air, while sipping from cups and cans, talking to each other.

She shivered as an icy breeze blew past them, swirling her dress around her legs. "Are you having a good time?"

"Yeah. Henry introduced me to some people he trains at the gym, and I got to meet some of your friends from your old school."

Emmy gave him a half-hearted smile and ran her fingers around the side of her can. "Oh? What did they say?" She whispered, her voice heavy with cynicism and apprehension.

Bellamy's eyes narrowed in suspicion. "They just asked me questions. About myself, my friends, family. Why? Did you figure they would say something else?"

Emmy shrugged and turned her head, looking away from him and back inside the living room, where the party continued.

Bellamy talking to her old school friends made her uneasy. School hadn't been the best years of her life. She had changed a lot since then and she didn't want Bellamy to hear more about what she was like before.

"I don't know." She said, with an effort to sound light-hearted. "But I wouldn't trust anything they said. Most of them lie. A lot."

Bellamy pushed his hands into his pockets and rocked back on his heels, his eyes facing up to the sky. "If you say so."

Emmy circled the rim of her can with her index finger. "It won't be all laughs. When you find out that this is them on their best behaviour. They get worse the longer you know them." Her attention was drawn back to Maelie and Henry fighting over the music. That was something she was used to. The arguing.

"Well, everyone's been welcoming. So even if it's temporary," Bellamy turned to her and rested his shoulder against the back of the house, gazing down at her. "I appreciate everything you and your friends have done."

Emmy's cheeks heated, and she stared off to the side, at the tall tree towering beside the house, to avoid his eyes.

"It's nothing. I'm glad you like them. That makes things easier since they're always at the cafe." She tugged a curl behind her ear and took a sip from her can.

"Well, now what about your friends?" She questioned. "Your family? You said you live a little further away from the cafe, so is it going to be difficult for you and your friends to find time to meet up?"

Bellamy shrugged, crossing his arms over his chest. "Yes. I have to travel a bit. Er... I don't have many friends. But I still hang out with the ones I have, when I have time. Even if it's rare. Anyway, I prefer to stay in, if I can help it. Though that doesn't always work out." The crease between his brow deepened, and he avoided her gaze.

Emmy could relate. She wasn't the most outgoing, so she would not punish him for being the same.

"Are you busy a lot, then?" Emmy tensed as the last words left her mouth. It sounded more probing than she had intended.

From his posture, it seemed Bellamy thought so too. Bellamy's spine tensed, and he shifted on the spot.

He drummed his fingers on the side of his arm and eyed her. "I guess. I spend most of my time looking after my little sister, Janey."

"Oh?" Emmy asked. "How old is she?"

"She's seven."

"Oh. Tilda has a younger brother, Matty." She stated. Emmy had hoped to change the subject to something else, and to do it a little smoother, but that didn't seem to go as planned.

He looked puzzled for a moment as he took in what she said, before he nodded. "Oh." An awkward silence fell between them, but Emmy continued.

"I remember when he was little, a toddler, and he would always run after Tilda and me whenever we would leave the room. He was so sweet. Still is. But I haven't seen him in a while."

Bellamy looked down at her and smiled. "Janey used to do the same with me. She thinks she's all grown-up for that now, but still has a bunch of stuffed animals on her bed."

Emmy smiled with him. She shivered again, and this time Bellamy led her back inside, to the warmth of the house.

They walked through the garden doors, exchanging family stories with one another. As they talked, the song that had been playing ended and another, faster song began, and more people milled into the living room, drawn to the music.

Emmy's head snapped up, and she scanned the faces in the crowd, her neck craning to get a better look at the entrance. Bellamy watched her, amused, and he picked up an unopened can from the table packed with drinks.

When she didn't find who she was looking for, she leaned over to Bellamy, turning her face to him, and raised her voice over the music. "Have you met a guy named Eric, yet?"

Bellamy frowned as he looked down at her, breaking the seal on his can. "Uh, yeah. Henry introduced us. He's over there, by the doors." He pointed toward a tall figure, standing by a tall plant and a smaller table by the doors that led to the den. As soon as she saw him, she recognised him as Eric, talking to another shorter guy that she couldn't place. The crowd of people coming in and out of the den, helped to hide them from view.

Emmy raised her hand above the crowd and waved in his direction. She caught his gaze after a few seconds, and he waved back before he returned to his conversation.

She smiled to herself, relieved to see the end of her pursuit standing by a plant and looked back at Bellamy. He was watching the exchange with a blank expression, his dark eyes intent.

"Tilda asked me to match her up with someone." She shrugged and drained her can. "They'd make a good match, wouldn't they?"

He raised an eyebrow at her and lifted the corner of his mouth into a smirk, but his eyes were dark and piercing.

"Huh." He mused. "Get into your friend's business a lot, do you?"

Emmy narrowed her eyes. He gave her a broad, toothy grin. He was about to say more, but before he could, she gave him a pinched smile.

"No, I don't. Now, excuse me. I have people to meet." She turned and hurried off to meet Eric.

Eric had just finished talking to his friend and was hovering over an empty plate, watching a high stakes card game in the den.

"Hey, Eric," Emmy called as she approached.

He looked up at the sound of his name. When he saw who it was, he grinned at her. "I haven't seen you in ages."

She grinned back at him and shrugged her shoulders. "I've been around. Having fun?"

"Yeah. Great food. Great music. Great company. What's not to like?"

Emmy smiled and gestured over to Noah. He was talking to Henry by the hallway, near to where Maelie and Tilda stood with Darcy.

"You can thank Noah for the sandwiches, and the snacks. He's proud of them. The sandwiches."

"It was a good sandwich." He nodded. "Hey, I saw you talking with Bellamy. I met him earlier. He's a cool guy. I guess I'll be seeing him at the cafe with you and Noah soon. When does he start?"

"Tomorrow." Emmy looked down at her empty can, rolling it in between her fingers. "Everyone likes him."

"I can see why."

Emmy smiled again, but this one didn't reach her eyes. She was getting tired and wanted to move the conversation along. "He has a younger sibling, like Tilda. By the way, have you spoken to her tonight?"

"Tilda's here?"

She nodded once and pointed to Tilda, still standing in the corner.

Eric followed her finger in the direction she was pointing, and recognition entered his eyes the moment they landed on Tilda. "I haven't seen her in ages, either. I keep missing her at the gym."

"Well-" Emmy stopped speaking when she sensed someone behind her. She turned her head in surprise and saw Bellamy standing next to her, his smile fixed back in place. "Hey, Eric. Emmy." He nodded to her once.

Lianne, one of Katherine's friends, was with him. She was a tall, curly-haired girl. When she caught sight of Emmy, she smiled at her.

Emmy gave her a confused half-smile. Lianne turned to Eric, and they both smiled at one another.

Bellamy looked down at Emmy. "Do you want to dance? And talk. Just for a minute." He held out his hand toward her. She glared down at it as if it would bite her. "I wanted to say something, something that won't make you mad. Hopefully."

"I was just talking to..." She looked at Lianne and Eric. They were standing a little away from them, already talking to each other and acting as though they were alone. She didn't know exactly what had happened, but her confusion was being replaced with annoyance.

She had only left Bellamy a short while ago, and in that time, he somehow spoiled her plan. How had he gotten to Lianne so fast?

She turned to scowl at him, but his expression was open and patient. "Would you like to dance?" He repeated, softer this time.

With one last look at Eric and Lianne, she gave a frustrated sigh that was closer to a growl, and took Bellamy's hand. He held it and led her to the centre of the living room, where they danced. It relieved her that the music was fast and upbeat and not slow and romantic.

"How did you find her so quickly?" She hissed as he spun her away.

"I didn't. She came to me, and we came over to join the two of you. Why do you think I did something?"

Emmy frowned,. "One minute I was talking to you about setting up Tilda with Eric, and the next thing I know, you showed up with Lianne out of nowhere, and I mean nowhere at all!"

"I told you. She showed up, and she was watching Eric for a while, then asked me about you and him. Then she came over. I followed her, but I had nothing to do with it. She likes him, I guess."

Emmy glanced back and saw Eric and Lianne laughing with one another. She rolled her eyes and turned her attention back to Bellamy. Once again, he was observing her.

"What?" she snapped.

"You were trying to set him up with Tilda?"

Emmy nodded. "Yes. Was. I said I was, didn't I?"

"Why?"

She rolled her eyes at the question. "Because she asked me. I've already told you so."

Bellamy didn't answer her. He only shrugged, but she didn't expect him, of all people, to elaborate.

The music kept playing. For half an hour, all the songs that played were upbeat and fast, which she appreciated.

As they continued dancing, Emmy relaxed, and her annoyance with Bellamy and the situation decreased with every spin he made.

Every time he spun her, he gave her a terrible pun as an apology for ruining her mission, which led to her having to fight back the laughter at his poor jokes.

He kept spinning her around and twirling her back into his chest until, with a flourish, he spun her wildly and she giggled helplessly.

When the song finished, she was out of breath, but happy.

In the middle of the room where she stood, she could feel eyes staring at her. She turned until she saw Tilda and Maelie watching them, and whispering to each other. She pulled away from Bellamy, planting her feet on the ground. He looked puzzled, but she gave him a small smile.

"I am sorry about before. With Eric." He whispered.

She shrugged. "It's alright."

She couldn't muster any genuine feelings about losing Eric.

Emmy wanted to say more to Bellamy, to keep their conversation flowing, but she wasn't sure what to say. "I'm having fun." She admitted.

He smiled. "Well, there's an accomplishment." He tilted his head in the den's direction. "Do you want to play cards? Board game?"

She looked past him, into the den where groups of people were playing both card and board games, surrounded by spectators. People were taking winning a bit too seriously, if the shouting coming from the Monopoly table was any sign. "Fine." She agreed with a sigh and followed him in.

***

A few hours later, the party came to an inevitable end. Bellamy was much better at card games than he had let on, and he had beaten Emmy in two games of Crazy Eights.

All the guests were gone, leaving Emmy, Bellamy, Noah, Henry, Lucy, Tilda, Maelie, Aiden and Katherine in the house.

Just as they began clearing up, Katherine wished Bellamy a good night and ushered him out of the front door. They all yelled their goodbyes before the door closed between him.

Aiden huffed as soon as the lock on the front door clicked. "And why do we have to stay, and he doesn't?"

Katherine place her hands on her hips and glared at Aiden. "Because he's the guest. We threw this party for him. It's good manners."

Aiden scoffed. "You threw this party. We showed up. But fine, we'll do it your way."

He glanced at the stairs that led to her parents before he skulked back into the main living room. He was struggling with whether he should push Katherine further, now that her parents were home. The rest of them followed him, with varying levels of complaints, though not loud enough for Katherine to overhear.

They each began sorting the remaining food and drinks into groups, deciding who would take what, and reorganised Katherine's house, bringing it back to its original state.

Emmy lay in bed that night, unable to go to sleep. She had been restless since they came back home. Every time she was close to sleep, Bellamy's face would pop back up in her mind, no matter how hard she tried to push the image away.

All she could think of was how warm his hands had felt in hers as they danced in Katherine's living room.

CHAPTER FIVE

MAELIE IN THE CAFE

Maelie arrived at the doorstep a little after two in the morning, her hands numb from the cold, and her eyes shutting down from fatigue.

She turned back and waved to Henry, still sitting in his car, waiting to make sure she was safely inside. As she shut and lock the door, he started the motor and with a loud purr, his car pulled away from the curb and drove away.

Standing in the hallway, she felt a rush of heat swaddle her. That was nothing new. Her mother always kept the house toasty when one of them was at home. Maelie's cheeks burned, and she rubbed her hands to warm herself faster.

Beth's voice floated out from the living room into the entrance to greet her.

From the sound of it, she was speaking to someone on the phone.

Maelie followed the sound and found her mother in the living room, reclining on the white couch that took up most of the space in the room. An image was frozen on the screen of the large TV, showing a movie Maelie didn't recognise.

Beth took the phone from her ear as Maelie entered to give her a beaming smile as soon as she saw her standing in the hallway.

She pressed a button on the handset with a loud beep and placed it down on the couch next to her. "Mae! Did you have fun with your little friends?"

Maelie shrugged out of her coat and hung it on the coat hanger as she kicked off her shoes. She dragged her beanie off her head and her red curls fell in a tangled mess around her shoulders. She stuffed the beloved beanie inside her coat pocket as she walked down the hallway to greet her mother.

Her socks dragged against the tiled floor as she trudged over to Beth. Sitting on the arm of her mother's chair, Maelie leaned over to peck her on the cheek.

"They're not little." She countered as she pulled back, stifling a yawn. "And yes, we had a lot of fun... But that's enough about me. How was your day? Or your night? Did you do anything exciting while I was out?"

Beth laughed and patted her daughter's knee. "Yes, I watched a few movies I've been wanting to see. The ones you didn't want to see. It was nice having the telly all to myself for an evening. Oh, and your aunt called, talked my ear off in the middle-"

A yawn burst from Maelie's mouth and Beth's eyebrows raised high on her forehead.

"Sorry," Maelie mumbled around another yawn.

Her mother smiled. "As long as it isn't me, that's boring you. Go on, darling. Go to bed." She patted Maelie's leg. "Your dad left for his shift already. He said to tell you he sends his love."

Maelie smiled, her eyes dropping closed even as she tried to focus on Beth. She rose from the chair, giving her mother one more kiss on her cheek. As she left the room, her mother unfroze the television screen and continued the movie.

Maelie dragged her feet upstairs to her room, pulled off her shoes, jeans, and her top, leaving them on the floor of her bedroom in a pile.

She grabbed an old t-shirt from her wardrobe and pulled it over her head before she collapsed on top of her bed.

Just before she fell asleep, she dragged the covers out from under her and realised that she was still wearing her socks.

She took them off and threw them in the general direction of her pile of clothes.

She had just enough time to pull the covers over her before her heavy eyes closed and she fell asleep.

The next morning, Maelie woke up with her head underneath her pillow and her right foot hanging out from under the covers.

She pushed herself up to look at her phone sitting on her bedside table as her phone rang, loud and shrill.

Emmy had called Maelie, telling her to meet Emmy, Noah, Tilda, and Aiden at the cafe at twelve noon.

She was still exhausted from the night before, and since it was Saturday and she didn't need to go to uni, Maelie wanted to stay in bed today. But she doubted she'd be left alone.

After she got dressed, she skipped downstairs to the kitchen. Once she had finished the tea, toast, and eggs her mother had made for her, Maelie grabbed her bag, kissed her mother goodbye, still bleary-eyed and half asleep, and headed off to Marsh's Manor.

She entered the cafe twenty minutes later, her muscles still aching from her walk. As she stepped into the warmth of the cafe, she spotted Emmy and Noah in their usual Saturday seats, in a secluded corner of the cafe.

Emmy looked harassed and grumpy, staring at a steaming cup in front of her. Noah sat beside Emmy, his eyes closing every few seconds before they snapped open again.

Andrea, one of the weekend employees, was already standing behind the counter, serving the customers, looking far more alert than the other two.

Maelie greeted Andrea before she joined them at their table. She dropped her bag on the chair next to Noah with a loud thud, and the noise startled him awake. Emmy jumped up out of her chair in fright, scowled, and settled back into her seat once she saw the source of the noise.

Maelie smirked at Emmy, taking in her red watery eyes. Emmy and Noah both seemed to have trouble seeing her.

She pulled out a dense book from her bag and dropped it on the table with another dull thud on the wood. She reached inside her bag again, and this time she fished out her notebook and pen and placed them next to the book.

"Hello, Mae," Emmy mumbled, her eyes glassy and staring at Maelie, but not seeing her.

Maelie waved a heavy hand at her. She dragged her hat off the top of her head and dropped it on the table with the rest of her things. "Did you two have lots of fun last night?" She chirped.

Emmy looked peeved, but her lips lifted into a smile.

"Tons." Noah nodded, even though Maelie thought he hadn't been listening. Neither of them said anything else.

Maelie exhaled and smiled at their misery, happy that at least someone felt worse than she did. She looked around at the cafe. It was empty, but that did not surprise her.

Despite it being a Saturday, it was bleak, and only after 10 in the morning, so, she expected all the sensible people with sensible friends, would still be asleep in their warm beds or wrapped in their dressing gowns, sipping steaming cups of coffee. At home.

As Maelie looked around the room, she searched for the newest employee.

She saw the usual workers, but they were old news. She was rather looking forward to seeing Bellamy take orders in an apron. Her eyebrows furrowed as she realised she couldn't see him in the open room.

"Hey!" she said, tapping Emmy on the arm and jolting her awake. "Where's Bellamy? Isn't he supposed to work today?"

Emmy rolled her bloodshot eyes. "He's upstairs." She stabbed a finger toward the stairs beside them.

"Someone called?" Bellamy's voice drifted down ahead of him as he walked down the stairs from the second landing.

He stopped in front of Maelie, paying no attention to the other two at the table.

Unlike Emmy and Noah, Bellamy looked fresh-faced and alert. His clothes were on straight and unrumpled, though his hair appeared tousled. The two-hour head start Katherine had given him had put him in better shape than Emmy and Noah.

His eyes were bright and focused. Emmy sighed and Maelie pulled up one corner of her mouth in a lazy smile.

"Just me. I was wondering if you were here yet and if you were doing better than these two." She waved at a drowsy Emmy and a sleeping Noah.

Bellamy eyed them. "I'm doing fine. I've been here since 8:30. Though, I got more sleep than these two. They were like this when they came in." He said. "And how about you?"

Maelie raised her eyes to the ceiling as she thought. "I'm tired," she admitted, "but I had a good time last night. Well, as great a time at a party, where the host forces you to clean up at the end."

They hadn't even made that much of a mess, but Katherine made certain they fixed the living room to look as it did before the party. She also lectured them after they found a wine stain on the rug. Things had devolved into another fight between Katherine and Aiden. With Katherine's parents just upstairs, it had been the quietest shouting match Maelie ever saw.

Bellamy frowned, but before he could ask, she held up a hand to stop him. "Please don't ask. The whole thing was ridiculous enough the first time. If I have to repeat it, I will have to hit my head against a wall."

Bellamy chuckled, but didn't push any further. "So, what do you want? Tea? Coffee?"

"Here," Emmy grumbled, a disgruntled pile in her chair, shoving the steaming cup in front of her to Maelie's side of the table. "The usual."

She glanced up at Bellamy for a second, out of her bloodshot eyes. "If you're still offering, I'd like a cookie and ten cups of coffee. But let's start with one. Milk and two sugars."

Bellamy smirked and left to get her order.

Noah yawned, staring at the side of Emmy's head. "At least you were nicer this time." He turned his head toward Maelie, swiping at his eyes with the palm of his hand. "When we got here, he said, 'good morning' and she bit his head off. Although," he added, "she could have just been mad about losing a few games to him last night."

Emmy groaned into her hands. "I didn't! And that's not why!"

"You did! And It is."

"I lost a few games to you too, remember?"

"I remember, and you still snapped at him."

"I just said there was nothing good about this morning unless you were lucky enough to get a decent amount of sleep."

"You could try going to sleep earlier," Maelie smirked.

Emmy's head snapped towards her.

"Don't start. I am not in the mood." She barked.

Maelie giggled and took a careful sip from her cup. "Is this the charm you used on Bellamy?"

Emmy sighed again, the air rushing out of her in a huff, leaving her deflated and lifeless.

"How come you're not shattered?" Emmy wailed, rubbing her eyes. Her eyes were even redder now, tears spilling down the corners.

Maelie shrugged and fiddled with her bookmark lodged at the back of her book.

Though tired, the amusement Maelie got from seeing Emmy like this was enough to distract her from her own exhaustion.

The bell over the door chimed, drawing their attention to the newest customer to walk through the door. An older woman walked in, her handbag hanging from the crook of her elbow.

She walked up to the counter as Bellamy greeted her.

"Good thing you got extra help today." Maelie nodded to Bellamy as he spoke with the customer. Andrea stood next to him, bustling away behind the counter. "It would have been hell if you had to work alone." She waved her hand in Emmy's direction.

Emmy's mouth pursed, and her eyes narrowed a fraction as they moved to find Bellamy. The woman Bellamy was talking to laughed out loud, and Bellamy joined her before she found an empty table.

The night before, Tilda had blabbed to Maelie about Emmy and Bellamy's rocky relationship. They were spying as Bellamy walked over to talk to Emmy, Lianne, and a guy who looked familiar.

Maelie was sure that the guy was a friend of Henry's, but she was positive that Lianne was one of Kat's stuck-up friends.

She had a fuzzy memory of Lianne standing next to Katherine in her expensive blouse and trousers, towering over Maelie in her high heels.

She also remembered Henry talking about the same guy and the way Lianne's eyes lit up when she saw him.

Tilda had told Maelie all about Emmy's meddling, including her disappointment.

Emmy seemed to like Bellamy, but Maelie knew that when it involved the cafe, she became territorial.

She never liked to accept help for anything, and that puzzled Maelie. Emmy was happier muddling through on her own. Even if it took her ten times longer.

Maelie remembered the day she had met her. It was at the cafe, of course. Tilda had introduced the two of them, and Maelie had thought that she was a lamb, but sometimes she wondered otherwise.

Maelie was convinced that Emmy enjoyed playing the martyr and just allowed people to push her around, but there were other times Emmy can be very stubborn.

"Give him a chance, Em." Maelie insisted. Emmy's eyes wandered back to Maelie. She wasn't sure if Emmy was listening or not until she gave Maelie a nod.

The door opened again, blowing in Aiden, and a reminder of the cold. He looked tired. His eyes were squinting as he tried to focus on the group, as he lumbered over to greet them.

"It's too early for this," He groaned as he sank into a chair beside Maelie.

Emmy stared at the ceiling. "If you were nicer to Katherine, she might have let us go sooner."

"I wasn't being mean…"

Emmy scoffed. The sound was loud and crude. "You weren't trying to be nice. You know what she's like, so why provoke her?"

Aiden brushed his hand over his messy hair. "I wasn't trying to provoke her. I just wanted her to be kind and nice and honest with us. You know, like a friend. You know that she's using us, don't you?"

Despite his tiredness, there was steel in his eyes as he glared at the rest of them. "She's trying to make a point with us."

Maelie frowned and looked at Emmy to see if she heard the same. The other girl had paused out of curiosity and was staring at Aiden. "What do you mean?" She asked.

Aiden leaned forward in his seat, his forearms resting on the table. "She's throwing these parties to make a point. Not for fun. Or for us. I think it's for her. This all might just be practice for her. She told me she threw a party for a co-worker of her mother's last month. They were getting retired or something. Or having a baby. Or it could have just been a weekend thing. I don't remember."

Maelie sat up in her chair, her fingers tracing the edges of her book. "Sure, but so what? What does that have to do with us?"

Aiden raised his eyebrows at her and stared at her. "She wants to throw parties for events. Like an actual job."

Emmy closed her eyes and rubbed at her forehead. "That's not a bad thing. So, what if she does?"

Aiden scoffed and shrugged. "Of course, you wouldn't have a problem with that. You don't know when to relax, either. But normal people can tell when someone is burning themselves out. And from the looks of things last night, she intends for all of us to go down with her."

Maelie thought for a moment. She had always known Katherine was a control freak, but she thought the party would help her wind down.

She didn't always get along with Katherine. They all had issues with her, but Emmy was ashamed that Aiden, argumentative Aiden, was a better friend to her than they were.

Noah shifted in his seat, shaking off the sleep, though his voice was still thick with it. "Why didn't she ask us? We would have helped her if she needed it. We would have helped her with other parties. She could have just said, instead of shouting at us."

"She thought we wouldn't agree." Emmy retorted.

"Agree with what? Her throwing parties?"

Emmy frowned, her eyes unfocused, but this time from thought instead of exhaustion. "Isn't she's supposed to be working at her mother's estate agency? I think that's the plan, anyway. Where's the party planning coming from?"

Maelie dropped her book back on the table. "That's what I want to know. Next time we see her, we can ask. We'll just be nice about it." She looked pointedly at Aiden.

"Fine, fine. But at least we know." Aiden countered. They all muttered their agreements and silence fell among the group.

Maelie sighed, dug into her bag, and pulled out a pack of cards. "It's still pretty early, but since we're here, let's play. Aiden? Emmy? Noah?"

Aiden looked as though he had almost fallen asleep with his eyes open, but he blinked, and the fog cleared from his eyes. He grinned. "Sure. What do you want to play?"

Two hours later, Maelie had beaten Aiden in three games of Crazy Eights, Aiden had beaten her in two and Emmy had taken up fuming on her side of the table after it became clear she was terrible at the game.

They started playing poker, but Emmy did no better at that either. Noah had fallen asleep in his chair with his head slumped on the table.

Bellamy dropped by to watch the game whenever business became slow. He didn't join in since Emmy still seemed upset with last night's outcome. With every trip to their table, he became more amused by the game and the foul language that had trickled out of Maelie's mouth and the insults Aiden hurled across the table.

But none of it seemed to amuse him as much as Emmy's reaction to the game.

She had proven herself to be even more adept at swearing than Maelie, something that surprised all players involved. That only made her an ideal target for Bellamy, who had taken to teasing them when they lost, fuelling their rage at the game and each other. He stood nearby, leaning against another table. He looked carefree, his eyes shining as he watched them.

When he came back to the table after another lapse of customers, Emmy threw him a dark look before returning her attention to the game. "I think we should play something else." She pouted.

Maelie and Aiden laughed. Their voices rang out together like the loud chimes of bells. "That's only because you're losing." Maelie sang.

Aiden nodded, not looking up from his cards. "If you were winning, you'd bite our heads off for suggesting something so ridiculous."

"I wouldn't!" She snapped, slouching in her chair.

"Yeah, you would." Maelie chuckled, keeping her eyes on the game.

"Don't be a hypocrite, Emmy." Aiden chided. "People don't like hypocrites. I don't. What about you, Mae?"

"Nope. Or a sore loser." Maelie added. They both roared with laughter as Emmy pushed back her chair. They flinched, but she ignored them.

"I'm going to get a drink." She announced with a huff. "Does anyone want one?"

Aiden paused and looked up at her, pretending to be alarmed. "From you? Now?"

Maelie picked at the sleeve of her top, pulling it over her hands for warmth. "I would love one, Emmy, but my mum always told me never to take a drink from someone I've just pissed off."

"Sounds like excellent advice." Aiden nodded.

"I would never poison you. I'd never do that to you." Emmy's tone was indignant, but only half-heartedly. There was a sly edge to the tone that made her sound insincere. "Besides, I don't have poison."

"I guess you could-" Maelie started.

Aiden kicked her under the table, and Maelie wailed in pain. "Don't give her ideas." He hissed. "I still want to eat from here."

Bellamy made a sound that sounded like a chuckle. It changed into a cough, however, when Emmy turned to glare at him.

"Don't you start." She growled.

He folded his arms over his chest, trying to hide a grin. "Wouldn't dare. How about I get you another coffee and a muffin, on the house?"

Emmy made a sound of agreement, got up from her chair, and walked past him toward the kitchen. He followed Emmy, moving away from their table after her.

"Hey," Maelie whispered to his back. Bellamy turned around and raised an eyebrow. "Don't provoke her too much in there," she gestured toward the kitchen. "Too many weapons."

Bellamy's smile widened as he walked off towards the kitchen.

Maelie returned her attention to Aiden and debated for a long moment if it was a good time to talk about their project.

There had been some arguments between them in the last few weeks, most of them focused on their project. She didn't want to talk about it, but she supposed they had to.

She watched Aiden over her cards. "Now, about our project. I've been thinking-"

Aiden groaned and focused his attention on his cards. "We've done enough. It's best to just keep it simple."

Maelie and Aiden were doing a film project for their class at university, which they had to finish. They made a short film with Henry as their lead actor. All the filming was finished and Aiden had worked hard to edit it in a week.

The result was astounding, in Maelie's opinion, but she still felt that there was more to do. This was where they clashed. Aiden thought they were just about finished with the project. Maelie disagreed. They still had their other coursework, documenting the entire thing to complete.

"Just two hours! Give me two hours of your time, Aid. I'll fix everything." She pleaded.

"Fine. But only if you do everything. I'm sick of that video."

"Great! I will. Promise." Maelie declared. She was tired of the project too, but she felt they had a very good chance of getting a top mark if they just did a little more.

She looked back at the kitchen door and wondered how Emmy and Bellamy were getting on. "Do you think he likes her?"

Aiden raised an eyebrow and looked toward the kitchen after them. "I wasn't sure Em would like him taking over her space, though."

Maelie nodded. "Me neither. I think she's coming around, though. It's nice to see her enjoy herself. Would be nice if Kat did too."

Aiden scoffed. "You'd have better luck asking an actual cat to go fetch."

Maelie shrugged and got up out of her seat. "Let's not worry about that now." She put her cards face down on the table and pointed at Aiden. "Don't you dare peek!"

Aiden held up his free hand in a placating gesture. "Fine. Where are you going?"

"Food." she said, pointing at the counter. She frowned at him, still doubtful he wouldn't peek at her cards, but trusted him as she wandered over to the counter to order a sandwich to go with her coffee.

While she waited, voices drift out from the kitchen. She wandered closer to the door and propped herself against the wall, hoping to eavesdrop.

She heard a kettle bubbling and the tinkle of cutlery being moved around. The sounds of a busy kitchen.

"So, you're in a good mood this morning." Bellamy drawled.

Emmy scoffed. Her voice was heavy, with not only sleep but resentment, more so than it had been while she was at the table. "You haven't seen me in the mornings. You don't know if this is normal for me."

"Well, I will now. Are you always this grouchy?"

"Only when I'm up late the night before."

The sound of the fridge door opening reached Maelie's ears.

"So, you'll be a ray of sunshine on Monday?" Bellamy asked.

"Yep. I always am. No need to worry about me," Emmy snared.

"Good, because on Monday, I want you to show me what you do here. When you order stock things like that."

"Or I could simply do it like I did before. I already know how to do my job, thanks."

Bellamy hummed, amused. "I thought we were getting along. The last time I saw you, you were having fun. What did Katherine make you do after I left? Or did something else happen after the party?"

There was a heavy silence while both Maelie and Bellamy held their breath, waiting for Emmy's reply.

Maelie was sure that if she could see her, Emmy would be fiddling with the sleeve of her top, looking anywhere but at Bellamy.

Emmy wasn't normally this antagonistic, and Maelie knew it was because of Bellamy.

Her tone was sharper whenever she addressed him, though Emmy seemed to be in a worse mood today. Last night, she had been dancing with Bellamy and laughing. Now, this morning, she was ready to rip him apart.

It couldn't just be a lack of sleep because Maelie had also been there after the party cleaning up.

"Nothing. I..." Emmy mumbled, and Maelie was afraid she'd miss the rest.

"You what?" Bellamy asked.

Emmy huffed. "Just a bad dream. I just need coffee."

"You had a bad dream? About what?"

"Nothing... I can't remember."

"Well, which is it? Was it about nothing, or you don't remember?"

Emmy groaned, and the sound of her voice grew closer to the door.

"I don't remember it. It just kept me up and I couldn't go back to sleep."

"Huh... and I thought it was because of something I did."

"Why? I never said I was mad at you."

"No, but you're attacking me as if I gave you the nightmare."

A stifled, humourless laugh rented the air. "It had nothing to do with you. Nothing at all." Emmy's voice had risen in pitch and Maelie's suspicion with it.

Did it have something to do with Bellamy? They had been dancing together the night before and nothing had happened between them to make her this on edge. Unless...

There was silence between them for a few seconds more, and Maelie wondered if they were going to walk back out of the kitchen before Bellamy answered.

"You know, with the way you're acting, anyone would think that you dreamt about me." His voice had lowered and become more serious, as if he was compensating for Emmy's raised pitch.

Emmy huffed again, and this time when she spoke her voice had returned to its normal level. "Well, they would be wrong, wouldn't they?"

Would they?

"If you say so," Bellamy answered.

"Look, I'd feel much better with sleep and peaceful dreams," Emmy promised.

The kettle clicked off as it finished its job, and Maelie listened as one of them poured the boiling water.

Maelie knew she had eavesdropped as long as she could and that any moment now, Emmy and Bellamy might walk through the door. She turned and drifted over to the counter as if she had been there all along.

Andrea had left her sandwich sitting on the counter, and Maelie picked it up as she retreated to Aiden and her chair.

He raised his eyebrows as she sat back down. "So? Did she kill him?"

Maelie dropped her sandwich on the table and picked up her cards. "No, she didn't. But I wouldn't worry about him."

"Why not?"

Maelie scanned her cards again. "It's like water off a duck's back with him."

Maelie wasn't sure if she should mention the rest of the conversation. Aiden would jump to the worst conclusions and tease Emmy about it in front of Bellamy.

Maelie thought Emmy was lying about her dream, but it was for the best to not draw any more attention to the situation.

The door opened once more, and Tilda came rushing in, flustered and sweaty, wearing running gear. She looked around the empty cafe and spotted them in their usual spot. The door opened again, and Katherine entered wearing exercise clothes too, but unlike Tilda, she looked relaxed.

"Hey. Ooh, game, okay, well... wait." Tilda wheezed.

"Words, Tilda, use your words," Maelie said, leaning back in her chair.

"Good day. Great day. I went jogging with Kat." She waved at Katherine. "Anyway, where's Bellamy?

I wanted to ask him if he wants to go to the cinema tomorrow evening."

CHAPTER SIX

EMMY IN THE CAFE

Emmy's fingers slipped on the cold metal of her key as she pushed it into the lock. It made a satisfying click, and she swung open the door to let in Noah and herself.

The warm air from the house hugged her as soon as she stepped inside, and she sighed, feeling her body relax for the first time in hours.

Noah stretched as soon as the door slammed shut behind them and he yawned widely in the quiet hallway.

"I'm going to sleep for the rest of the evening." He announced, stifling another yawn.

Emmy rolled her shoulders as she peeled her coat off and hung it up on a peg. "It's not like you've been doing anything else for the past few hours."

Noah had slept through most of their games and hadn't even budged an inch when Tilda and Katherine arrived, although Tilda did not lower her voice.

Tilda had jolted him awake only after she ruffled his hair and though he claimed he was now wide awake, his eyes had remained glassy.

Noah gave her a lazy smile that didn't clear the fog from his eyes and hung up his coat on the peg next to hers. "True, but it didn't help my neck."

He rubbed the back of his neck and walked into the living room; Emmy followed as she undid her ponytail and raked her hands through her curls.

Fred was sitting in the living room, his foot propped up on the couch, watching a documentary. Wild cats prowled across the screen, stretching in the sun. On the coffee table, between him and the TV, was an empty plate with a knife and fork resting on it and a mug that once held what she supposed was tea.

Noah collapsed into the seat beside his father, crossing his legs by the ankles, and yawned into the crook of his elbow. "Hey, Dad." He mumbled.

Emmy leaned against the wall behind Fred and folded her arms, watching as the screen showed a family of cubs wrestling with each other.

Fred tilted his head toward his son, not taking his attention from the TV. "Noah. Emmy. You two back already?"

Noah yawned again and nodded. "We were there for the entire day. Or didn't you notice? We came back because we needed some sleep."

Fred nodded. "Before you do... Emmy, can I speak to you for a minute?" He turned around in his seat to meet her eyes, resting his arm along the back of the chair.

Emmy exchanged a puzzled look with Noah. "Sure. What's wrong?" She couldn't imagine what he could want to tell her now, but it sounded important, and that made her uneasy.

He drew in a long breath, as if he were bracing himself for her reaction. That did nothing to calm her nerves. "Nothing's wrong. It's just that... I need you to work on weekends, starting tomorrow. You'll be swapping shifts with Andrea, so instead of working with Noah, you'll now be working with Bellamy."

Emmy felt as if someone had slapped her. The heat was rising in her cheeks and she felt annoyance building up inside her.

Emmy crossed her arms over her chest, unwilling to believe what he had just told her. "What about Andrea? She works on weekends."

Fred nodded. "She has been wanting a change in shifts, so she could have shorter stints at the cafe on the weekdays and see her children on the weekends. I told her that when Bellamy got here, we could see about changing her days."

Emmy rubbed at her red eyes and rolled her shoulders back. "Sure. I'll do it." She replied. Even though she knew he wasn't asking.

She hoisted her bag over her shoulder and marched upstairs into her bedroom.

Emmy scowled as she stalked through her bedroom door, and threw her bag by it, causing everything to rattle around inside, as it crashed, and flopped on the floor. She ignored the alarming noise and sank onto her bed.

Emmy, exhausted from partying last night, had hoped she could sleep in tomorrow.

Well, no chance of that happening anymore.

Tilda had woken her up early in the morning and asked her to gather the group to meet around twelve. She then strolled in forty minutes late, grinning from ear to ear without an apology. All she had said was that she had gone jogging with Katherine.

She was closely followed by Katherine, who looked bright-eyed and refreshed.

Tilda then asked Bellamy if he and his sister wanted to go to the cinema with her and Matty the next day.

In less than two months, it would be Tilda's birthday and she wanted to make sure it went as smoothly as it could with her family apart. Tilda hoped to make things easier for Matt by getting him to bond with Bellamy's sister.

She asked her friends to help arrange a party for Matt when his birthday came around in December so that he could at least have an enjoyable day to remember.

Everyone had said that they would do what they can to help Tilda, and she had collapsed in relief, promising to hold them to it when the time came.

It hadn't taken her long, however, to bounce back, and within half an hour, she was chattering with Bellamy about their siblings.

Emmy wasn't sure how they had bonded so quickly in one night, but she supposed it was nice that he was blending into their group so well. From all the jokes he had made at Emmy's expense in the past four hours, it seemed like he already felt at home.

Emmy wished she had stayed at the cafe just a little longer. She still had a lot of fun, even with Bellamy teasing her.

No one would have guessed from the glare she gave him every time he spoke, however.

He continued to poke fun at her for the rest of the day, but after a while, she stopped feeling annoyed at him and felt a flutter in her chest whenever he looked in her direction.

She supposed that was just annoyance, but it no longer felt like that. This was something different. Attraction? of course not! Maybe she felt attracted to him because she dreamt about him last night. She noticed, though, that the more she was around him, the more the strange flutter in her chest increased.

Maybe she was closer to accepting him into the family than she thought.

She still wasn't happy about the change in her schedule. Even if she was fine with working with Bellamy, she wasn't fine with that.

Despite what everyone thought about her being a workaholic, she loved her free weekends.

On the weekends, she could relax with her friends, something that might not happen as often as she would like anymore.

When she worked there during the week, her friends would come in after their shifts and their classes and lounge around the cafe while she worked, but the weekends were the days they would hang out in other places like the mall, or some sophisticated restaurant.

She loved the place like a second home, but if she was honest, she loved how it brought her closer to her friends.

She had wondered if she could exist outside of Marsh's Manor, and she wasn't sure, even now, if she could answer that with confidence.

With the way things were going, it didn't seem likely.

The distinct shrill ring of her phone by her bed startled her. Emmy reached over and answered the phone. It was her mother.

She hadn't heard from either of her parents for a few days, but her mother, Lisa, always called Fred every other day to check that Emmy was okay.

"Emmy?" her mother's voice called.

Emmy smiled at the sound and the comfort it gave her. "Yeah, I'm here."

"Oh, good. How are you and Noah and Lucy doing? How was your day?"

Emmy shrugged into the empty room and sighed. "Oh. I'm fine. I'm good. Everyone's good." She paused for a second and her mother waited for more.

Emmy inhaled heavily, deliberating on what to say. "Uh... Did Uncle Fred tell you... we have a new employee? Bellamy? He's... um... new. Our new manager."

There was a tense pause on the other end of the phone, and Emmy wondered for a second if she had cut the call off. She looked down at the phone receiver but she could still hear noise at the other end of the line.

Her mother exhaled. "Your uncle mentioned him this morning. He said that this... Bellamy started work today. That's good, isn't it? You work too hard. I told Fred that he needs to stop relying on you so much. I even asked if he would think about changing your shift. Did he tell you about that?"

Well, now Emmy knew the reason for the drastic change in her shifts. She had her mother to thank for that.

Her mother had always had some objection to how much time Emmy spent at the cafe. Every time Emmy mentioned working overtime, her mother always fussed and tutted and complained about why she shouldn't.

Emmy massaged her forehead. "Mum! That was you?"

"Yes, this way, you'll have time for other things." Lisa's voice was heavy with meaning. She paused, and when she continued, her voice became much more tentative. "I was thinking... have you thought any more about going to university this year?"

Emmy moved her hand down to pinch the bridge of her nose and took a deep breath, her shoulders slumping forward.

This wasn't the first time they had this conversation. Emmy thought it was over when she declined the first time. She felt sure she had explained her reasons for her decision much better the second time, but seeing as she was having the third conversation about this, that didn't seem to be the case.

"I've told you, I don't want to go."

"Why not? It'll be good for you. I was talking to Sandra and her daughter-"

"Mum! I said I don't want to go."

"You can't just stay working with your uncle for the rest of your life, can you? You can't work there forever. Where do you see yourself going?"

"I don't know what I want to do. I just don't think that university is for me."

"Well, why don't you stay with me and your father for a little while? You're not in school anymore, so that shouldn't be a problem. You don't need to stay there."

Emmy lowered herself onto the end of her bed. "I like it here."

Her mother sighed. "Your room's still here whenever you want it. If you want to move back."

"I know," Emmy whispered, running her hands over her bed covers.

"We love you, and we just want you to go out and do something with your life. You have so much talent."

"I'm glad you think so. I like to think so too."

Her mother chuckled. "I'll talk to you later. Bye, sweetheart. Love you,"

"Love you too. Bye." Emmy pulled the phone away from her ear and ended the call. She sighed and lay back down on her bed, feeling uneasy.

She had thought about going to university, but could not decide what she would do after that. The whole thing seemed too complicated and not worth the bother.

Besides, she was happy here. Wasn't she?

****

The next few weeks passed swiftly, and by the sixth week, Bellamy had riled up Emmy so much, she felt like killing him.

At first, the weekends Emmy worked with Bellamy went without problems.

The first weekend Bellamy allowed her to take charge of running things. She told him what to do, and he followed her instructions.

Nothing too drastic had happened at first, and the second and third weekends were the same. Bellamy continued to follow her instructions.

It was a Sunday morning, at the end of Bellamy's fourth week, when their problems began.

The sound of his smooth, calming voice drifted up to meet her as she came out of her bedroom, rubbing the sleep out of her eyes. The sleepy haze had yet to clear from her mind and the sound of his voice in her home, while her bare feet dug in the hallway carpet, confused her.

When she could place the voice, she dipped back inside her room to grab her brush and dragged it through her hair, hoping to tame it. It helped very little. In fact, she looked worse. At least her bed hair looked like she didn't care about his unexpected arrival, but she had brushed it to look like this. Sighing, she wrestled her hair back with a hairband as she followed the sound of Bellamy's voice downstairs to the living room.

She walked in and found him sitting in the middle of the living room on the couch, surrounded by Lucy, Noah, and Fred. Lucy sat with her feet curled up under her, staring at Bellamy. Noah was reclining on the armchair opposite them and Fred was in an armchair next to him, with his injured leg propped up. They had been chattering with one another but paused when Emmy entered.

"Emmy, look who stopped by," Lucy chirped, presenting Bellamy with a wave of her hand. "He's picking you up for work. Isn't that nice?" She leaned forward and picked up a plate of toast resting on the coffee table and handed it to Emmy.

Bellamy turned to look at Emmy as she sat down next to Lucy. His eyes scanned her clothing before returning to her face. Emmy pulled at her worn pyjama bottoms, embarrassed. He was smartly dressed, clean-shaven, and his eyes alert as always, while she looked dishevelled and in need of a shower.

She picked at the toast on her plate, ripping it apart. "That's nice of you."

"He's here to pick up a set of keys for the cafe," Fred said, his voice still heavy from sleep.

Emmy pulled her gaze away from her plate and looked at Fred. "Why? Why is that necessary?"

Fred turned to Bellamy, his voice encouraging. "Bellamy should have a key, so he doesn't have to wait for you to arrive. When it was you and Noah, it made little sense for you two to have separate keys, but with Bellamy here, I don't see why not? He could open up before you arrived if you wanted a lie-in."

It wasn't a question. No one was asking her for her opinion. It was a done deal. All she could do was sit, nod, and chew, so she did.

The idea itself wasn't ridiculous. In fact, Emmy thought it was quite sensible. Bellamy was the manager and would be in charge, not just in name. It made sense for Fred to want him to have better access.

What bothered her, however, was why Fred asked Bellamy here before work at 7:15 in the morning.

"Well, that seems like... a good idea, but you didn't need to get him here so early." She answered, her tone measured. She turned to Fred. "It's not very fair, you know. Asking him to come over before the cafe opens. He could have slept in longer."

Bellamy smiled and leaned forward, resting his arms on his knees. "It was my choice to come over. I woke up early, so I thought I could pick up the keys and drive you to work this morning."

"Oh..." So, he was to blame. She rubbed her eyes and stood up from her seat. "I suppose I can eat on my way to the cafe. Give me ten minutes and I'll get changed."

"We'll be here." He answered. She placed the plate on the coffee table before she turned and left the living room, retreating to her bedroom.

Fifteen minutes later, Emmy came back downstairs, dressed, her skin still damp from her shower. Her clothes stuck to the damp middle of her back as she moved, which made her grumble under her breath. Everyone was still sitting in the living room when she stuck her head around the doorway.

"I'm sorry for making you wait." She said, glancing at the clock. "I'm ready. Let's go."

She grabbed her leftover toast and together, she and Bellamy left her house. She turned back to wave goodbye to Fred, Noah, and Lucy as they climbed into Bellamy's car. Bellamy started the car and drove away as they headed towards the cafe.

They drove at a steady pace. Emmy rolled down the window and inhaled a lungful of the morning air as buildings sped past them.

The air was much more forgiving and much warmer than when Bellamy first arrived.

As he drove, Emmy folded her piece of toast in half and took a bite. Her eyes felt heavy on her face and it was a struggle to pay attention to where they were going. Though Noah had made this run himself more than a hundred times before, she wasn't a fan of early mornings.

Bellamy glanced at her and watched her as she ate. "How are you?"

She swallowed the bite. Bellamy always asked that question every morning at the cafe. She wasn't sure if he asked because he wanted to know, or if he was trying to be nice. Either way, she always told him the same thing, true or not. "I'm fine."

He nodded and returned his attention to the road ahead. Her conversation with her mother ran through her head. If she was going to improve her relationship with him, she would have to open up to him.

She hesitated for a second, chewing to give herself time to think before she continued. "I spoke to my mum yesterday. She wants me to go to university." She tried to sound indifferent, though she waited for his reply.

Bellamy kept staring forward at the road, and for a second, she thought he wouldn't answer, but after a few seconds more, he did. "Are you going to go?"

She shifted in her seat and stared at his profile. "I don't know."

He frowned at the road. "Why not? You're working less now that you work on the weekends."

She took another bite and chewed it. When she finished, she looked up at him and shrugged her shoulders. "I'm not sure."

She wasn't sure why Bellamy was pushing her in this direction. Had he been talking with her mother? No, but he had been talking to her uncle.

She ignored his question and asked him one of her own she had been meaning to ask him. "So, how was the cinema? When you went with Tilda and her brother? I forgot to ask."

The day after they went, Tilda had dropped by her house and told her all about it. She gushed about what movie they went to see and how well Matty got along with Janey.

From the way she spoke, Emmy had wondered if Bellamy had even gone with them. Tilda had neglected to even mention him until Emmy asked.

Bellamy, himself, hadn't mentioned it at all.

He smiled at the memory. "Janey loved it. I didn't. It was some animated film."

Emmy narrowed her eyes. "You don't like animation?"

Bellamy's smile widened. "Sure. My sister just loves them more. And the soundtracks. Just wish she'd love singing lessons just as much."

Emmy smiled at his words, silently agreeing with him, and the rest of the day drifted by uneventfully.

Drawbacks arose in the weeks after, when Bellamy started taking charge of opening up. It started as a subtle changes. Tiny changes that anyone else might not have noticed, but Emmy did.

Instead of following her instructions, he started working on his own, dealing with the actual work while sending her off to do other things. Minor things, like wiping down tables and tidying napkins.

He acted as if she was the one who was the new employee, and he was the experienced one.

Emmy tried to not think of it as a slight. He thought he was doing her a favour.

He had said the day that she met him he would work just as hard and even harder at the job. Perhaps this was just his way.

He tested her patience further when, in his sixth week on a Sunday morning, the third customer of the day entered.

Mrs. Martin had scuttled into the cafe a little after 9:00. She sat down in her usual seat and Bellamy went to serve her.

A few minutes later, Mrs. Martin was laughing, her voice like tinkling glass hitting the floor.

Emmy watched as they chattered and in the few minutes she watched them, she saw Bellamy charm Mrs. Martin, and the woman responded with a radiant smile. Her smile wasn't the brittle one Emmy was used to, but a sturdy one plastered to her face.

For as many years as she had worked there, the woman had never been as friendly to Emmy as she was being to Bellamy. She had been too nervous to do so.

Watching him at work was unnerving. His whole demeanour had changed in front of the customers. The polite facade he had worn when she saw him greet Katherine was in place and even more insincere, but more charming. He served every customer with a bright smile and a patient manner.

It was nauseating.

Mid-day, they had their first actual clash, when they had to decide on how best to get rid of the pastries. They were on the verge of becoming stale and they would need to discard them. Emmy wanted to bring them forward on the display, while Bellamy wanted to sell them at a reduced price.

She rubbed the bridge of her nose, irritated. "Bellamy, we're selling the pastries at the same price. It's what we always do."

Bellamy folded his arms over his chest. "People are more likely to buy them if they're discounted. Everyone likes a bargain."

"You can't make them buy something they don't want. Most people that come in here are regulars and they buy the same thing every time. There's a woman named Patricia who always buys peppermint tea and a tuna melt. And there's a man, his name's Kevin. He would order tea and a muffin. People like routine."

Bellamy shrugged. "They might like to try something new."

"Or maybe they won't." She responded.

"That'll be up to them." He shrugged again.

Emmy gritted her teeth and left him to it. Since he was so intent on having his way, he could do it himself.

She resolved to work on her own in silence for the rest of the day after that, but Bellamy had other ideas.

While the cafe was still quiet, he tried to make conversation with her whenever she passed him. When she kept her answers short and continue with her tasks, he would ask her to elaborate.

"So, you've known everyone for ten years, right?" Bellamy had asked her about how she met each of her friends. From the questions he asked, she could tell that he already knew enough about her and, most likely, from Tilda.

"Yeah, about that, I guess. Tilda and Katherine from school, but Tilda knew Maelie through their parents. Maelie's mum worked with Tilda's dad. And Aiden and Henry knew Noah from around. I don't know about that, but we would all meet up in here." She waved a hand around at the open space. It had been the first time she had any real friends or felt she belonged to a group. The cafe itself was the house of their friendship, where it began.

Bellamy took in the information and opened his mouth to ask her yet another question, when the bell over the door rang and a group of girls came in and sat down, laughing with one another. Katherine's friends. Emmy had never been so relieved to see them. Bellamy had taken to getting to know her better, while they had free time.

Bellamy turned to the group of chattering girls, who greeted him cheerfully. They had been at Katherine's party, avoiding the other guests the entire night. Bellamy greeted them as if he were also acquainted with them.

Emmy sensed an opportunity to escape and took it, retreating upstairs while Bellamy served the newest customers.

The cafe emptied just before they closed the shop. They closed earlier on Sundays at 7:00. Emmy cleared the tables while Bellamy closed the shop and began washing up the dirty dishes. She stacked the plates one on top of the other and carried them into the kitchen to Bellamy. He took them with a throwaway thanks in her direction and washed the plates.

"Could you go into the back and check the stock? We might have to order some more supplies." He called, looking up at her from the soapy dish in his hand.

It was a manager's job to manage the cafe and all, but somehow it fell to her. The not-manager.

Emmy wanted to tell him she had checked, and that everything was fine, but she didn't bother.

She turned and went to go to the back of the cafe to check what needed restocking.

After a few minutes of counting the stock, she felt a presence behind her. She turned to see Bellamy standing behind her, looking up at the shelves over her head.

"I'm already doing what you asked." She snapped, more forcefully than she had intended.

Bellamy didn't even bother to look down at her and somehow, that made things worse. "Good. Just making sure you can reach the shelves." He said.

Emmy's cheeks heated, and her jaw clenched as she fought the urge to turn around and confront him.

He paused for a beat before he continued. "Or that you don't trap yourself in here. Again."

The word "again" sat in her brain, and none of her other senses wanted to obey her. She couldn't take in anything she saw or heard. Who would dare mention what had happened?

"Who told you?" she hissed. "Noah, or Aiden?"

He seemed to love to tease her. To wave a red flag in front of her and rile her up.

Instead of finding her temper scary or concerning, her temper amused him. Bellamy's voice dripped with delight. And she didn't need to see him to know that he was smiling from ear to ear.

"Lucy."

Over a year ago, there had been an incident that Emmy never wanted to remember when she had been trapped in the room for over forty minutes. Noah had gone off to another shop and left Emmy there alone.

Without checking to see where she was, he accidentally closed the storeroom door, locking her in.

Emmy nodded and turned around, fuming, a harsh breath escaping from her mouth. "Why?"

His smile grew as her patience ebbed. "Why what?"

"Why did she tell you?"

Bellamy shrugged and folded his arms over his chest. "I guess she thought it was a funny workplace story I'd like to hear about my new employee."

"It was one time, and it was Noah's fault." Emmy protested. "I was in here and I was trying to get to the stock behind the door... and Noah... he pushed the door, and the door shut... I wasn't even in there that long." The forty minutes had felt like forever, but she would not give Bellamy more ammunition.

"Sure. Whatever you say." Bellamy nodded. His eyes moved to a spot over her shoulder and she turned to see a crowded shelf.

"This should be over there." He said, and he reached a hand over her left shoulder. She flinched and turned to see him reach up to pick up a can on the shelf behind her and move it aside. He moved past her and rearranged the shelf.

Emmy held her breath as he shifted the tins along, his hands moving to organise the tins and packages. She was close enough to smell his aftershave, and she realised she hadn't been this close to him since Katherine's party.

"I was going to do that." She bit.

He stopped what he was doing and backed away from the shelf. "Fine. Have fun in here. Yell if you need anything. Or if you get stuck." He said and turned to leave.

"Uh, thanks." She added, as an afterthought. He turned back, puzzled, before giving her a quick nod in acknowledgement and walked out. She waited until he was out of the storeroom before she turned her attention to the shelves.

She hovered in there, trying to extend the reasonable time she could spend in there by straightening the products on the shelves. But he had done most of the work.

Once again.

Tilda arrived at the cafe just after 7:40 in the evening, after her shift at the gym to pick Emmy up. She looked ragged, with her bag slung over her back and her hair coming out of her ponytail. Emmy dragged her off to a corner of the cafe and told Tilda about her day. She, however, saw nothing wrong with his behaviour.

"You're just mad because he doesn't agree with everything you say." She mumbled, dragging her hands over her face. "You're being too touchy and you're just looking for an excuse because you don't want to get to know him better."

Emmy barked out a harsh laugh. "I know him well enough. Not like you, but I've worked with him for weeks. He just wants to come in and change everything for no good reason. That is why I didn't think this," she gestured in his direction, "was a good idea."

Tilda tilted her head to the side, looking puzzled. "What has he done that's so bad? Is he rude to you?"

Emmy looked down at her shoes, scowling. "No."

"Is he making you do more work?"

"That's the problem! He keeps taking over and then changes things. I barely had anything to do. I take the orders and he makes them. He serves the food; I clean the plates."

Tilda stared at her. "That's called cooperation, Emmy! Normal people working with each other to achieve a goal." She sighed, and her shoulders slumped. "I know you are territorial and all, but you can't get mad at him for helping. Or for trying to be efficient and showing some initiative. He's just doing his job. A job he's paid to do. Is it so hard to relax and let other people help for once?"

Emmy picked at the string at the hem of her sleeve, avoiding Tilda's eyes. "If these other people are doing the job properly, then-"

"Emmy! Give him a chance. He works hard for his pay, not to rile you up. And then he gives his money to his mum, for bills and things. To help her out."

Emmy's cheeks heated, and she looked away from her friend. She realised she didn't know as much about him as Tilda.

Tilda yawned and rolled her eyes, stretching her arms above her head. "Anyway, did you know Katherine's taking us to a restaurant next week Saturday? We'll go after you two shut up shop."

Emmy nodded and tilted her head toward Bellamy. "Is he coming?"

Tilda shrugged. "Do you want him to?"

Emmy knew that under different circumstances, she would have liked Bellamy and that it wasn't fair to blame him for the change. He just had the misfortune of being the face of that change.

She inhaled sharply, straightening her spine. "Bellamy?" She called up to the second floor, where he was milling around. The man in question raised his head in her direction. "Next week, we're going to a restaurant. Katherine's treat. Would you like to come with us?"

Tilda stared at the side of her head in disbelief, but Emmy didn't let that deter her. Bellamy looked at Tilda for confirmation before he looked back at Emmy. "Ok, just tell me when." He answered and went back to whatever he was doing.

Tilda shook her head. "What are you trying to prove?"

"You just said I should give him a chance."

Tilda scoffed at her. "It seems like you're trying -and failing- to look like the bigger person."

Emmy rolled her shoulders back. "I am trying to get along with my colleague. Maelie said I should give him a chance, too."

"Alright," Tilda muttered. "We'll see how long this will last."

CHAPTER SEVEN
AIDEN IN THE CAFE

Almost two months had passed since Katherine's party, and Aiden had spoken little to anyone besides Maelie. He would have preferred not to speak to her at all if he could, though it meant he'd be staring at the blank walls of his flat for months.

Maelie, however, had made it her business to keep track of him.

She had decided that they were finished with their project, so Aiden had assumed, perhaps stupidly, that he was free, at least for a few more weeks, before their other deadlines were due.

At least that was before Maelie marched into his flat, just after nine, and sat him in front of his computer to complete their coursework.

The first year of university wasn't what he thought it would be. In some ways, it was better. But in other ways, it was way, way worse.

Aiden had more freedom than he had in the sixth form. He was living alone in a small flat. His parents made a deal to pay his rent as long as he came home for Christmas and the summer holidays, and he had money saved from the store job he had during sixth form.

Since he had no wish to cook a Christmas dinner for himself, he did not fight his mother on that one.

The downside was he lived on his own and so handled himself for the rest of the year.

The only reason he had lasted so long was because of Maelie and Emmy. Maelie reminded him of his deadlines and Emmy made sure that he ate.

They even teamed up a few times. Maelie dragged him to Marsh's to work on a project, while Emmy kept their table well-stocked with sandwiches, pastries, and coffee.

He supposed he owed them for that, if nothing else.

Aiden and Maelie were in the middle of working on their coursework, squeezed into Aiden's room in his tiny flat, when Katherine rang him.

She asked him if they had plans for next Saturday. He told her he didn't have any, and as far as he knew, Maelie didn't either. She then tells him that on the following Saturday she was inviting them all to have dinner at one of her favourite restaurants for Tilda's birthday. She finished by telling him she'd give them the details later, then abruptly hung up, leaving Aiden frowning at his mobile phone.

Maelie asked, "Saturday? Isn't that the 7th?"

Aiden thought for a moment and then nodded, and she scoffed. "What if I had things to do? She never asks! And Tilda's birthday is on the 2nd, not the 7th. Why not have it then? We could have been busy!" Maelie muttered, but her mind was clearly elsewhere.

She raked a hand through her tangled hair as she returned to her laptop, her eyes going back to the screen in front of her.

Maelie continued to tap away on the laptop, explaining how they made their short film and the techniques used to do it, and soon forgot to yell at Katherine.

Twenty minutes later, Maelie stopped typing to call a break for them both and wrestled her way out of his room to get lunch.

Aiden reclined in his chair and stared at the ceiling, waiting for Maelie to return from the restaurant with their food.

Aiden was thankful for the break. He'd tried to keep up with Maelie, but his mind kept wandering to what Katherine told him the night of the party.

Katherine had spoken about her plans for her career. But she had been avoiding him since that night and he noticed she seemed... embarrassed. But why?

Aiden teased Katherine from time to time, but he considered her a good friend. That was why he was even contemplating dragging himself to the restaurant when he should have been catching up with some sleep.

Perhaps he should have reconsidered.

***

The rest of the week drifted by as Aiden focused on his assignment. By Saturday, he was so fed up with doing coursework that he would have been happy to do anything else.

He spends the day in the cafe monitoring Bellamy and Emmy whilst they worked on what must have been the slowest Saturday that Aiden ever remembered in the cafe's history.

When Aiden strolled into the cafe after midday rubbing his hands from the cold, with his laptop in the bag strapped to his back, he found that there were only four customers inside. The reason for this was the horrible weather. The light filtering in through the windows was as grey and depressing as it had been all day.

Emmy and Bellamy looked up toward the door as he entered. They were standing behind the counter, a foot away from each other, their bodies facing each other. Both of them looked as though he had caught them in the middle of a fight.

Or just seconds before the physical fighting started.

Emmy pivoted toward Aiden and beamed, her face morphing with ease from a scowl to a smile. Bellamy remained blank-faced, still staring at where she stood.

"Aiden!" Emmy smiled, walking around the counter to meet him. "Did Maelie send you here? She told me you still have a lot of work to do. And that I should make sure you do it."

Emmy had pinned her curly hair on the top of her head and she wore a dull grey jumper. She flexed her right hand and Aiden saw that there was a fresh coffee stain on the sleeve.

He raised an eyebrow at it, but she shook her head. "It was just an accident."

She glared over her shoulder at the young man behind the counter, and he lowered his head. She turned back to Aiden and ushered him over to their table in the corner.

He let her guide him, looking back to see Bellamy leaning against the counter, looking as though he would rather be anywhere else but there.

Emmy pushed Aiden down into his chair and crossed her arms as she stood over him. "So, when do we get to see your film? I hear Henry's in it. Maelie's happy with it, so you must have done something right. Even Katherine's excited to see it."

Aiden raised an eyebrow. "Did she say that, or are you just assuming that's what she meant?"

Emmy shrugged. "A bit of both. She mentioned it in passing. In the middle of her plans for tonight."

Aiden scoffed. "Of course."

He pulled his laptop out of his bag and put it on the table. It made a loud thud in the still air. He scanned the interior. Everyone else was minding their own business. "Slow day?"

Emmy gave him a dismissive shrug and glanced at her watch. "You missed the morning rush. Don't worry. It'll pick up in an hour."

It was almost nine in the morning and while Aiden liked to sleep in; he knew he worked best in the early morning. In one corner of the room, near the window, he saw Eric and Lianne.

He stretched in his seat and leaned back to crane his head past Emmy. "Bellamy? Are you any good at coursework?"

Emmy bristled and stepped back in front of Aiden. "I am!" she exclaimed. "Ask me. Bellamy's got work to do."

Bellamy walked to the table and stood beside Emmy. "I don't mind. Besides, don't you have work, too?"

"I don't know, do I?" Emmy asked sniped.

"You can both help," Aiden interjected.

He didn't understand what was going on, and he didn't want to find out.

For the next hour, Emmy and Bellamy exchanged ideas to help Aiden. They told him what to focus on when writing his evaluations, and they even agreed with each other on a few points.

"You need to keep explaining why you did what you did," Emmy scolded, leaning over his shoulder to read the end of his last paragraph.

Aiden growled under his breath. "I already did! Look, it's here." He scrolled up and pointed higher to another paragraph.

Emmy pulled the laptop away from him and, scrolling back down, pointed at his newest paragraph. "You need to do it again. That was the story. Now this is the camera angles."

"But I mentioned it already," Aiden whined.

"She's right," Bellamy stated, as he cleared away the plates from a table behind them. He was craning his neck to look at Aiden's screen.

Emmy straightened her spine in surprise. "Thank you." She said.

"Well, you're right." He switched his focus from the computer to Aiden. "You need to explain your reasons. Do you want a higher mark?"

Aiden sighed. "What if we didn't have reasons? What if we just thought that it looked good?"

"Then lie!" Emmy hissed. Her hands snaked their way to his keyboard, and she began altering his paragraph.

Aiden turned to stare at her in disbelief. "Lie?"

He wasn't judging, he just wanted to make sure most of the blame was off him if Maelie asked.

Bellamy hovered over their table. He leaned down to stare at the screen over Emmy's shoulder. "Uh, I think what she means is that you should attribute meaning to your choices. I mean, you chose the angles because they fit, for a reason, so... you knew what you were doing. You just need to put it into actual words."

"Yeah, what he said," Emmy agreed, still typing away.

"I like that," Aiden whispered, staring at the two of them. He waited until Emmy finished typing before he dragged his laptop away from her... Or at least he tried to.

"Hey!" He protested once she slapped his hands away. "You don't even know what to write. You don't know anything about camerawork!"

"I know enough." She assured him as she continued to write. "I skimmed through your textbook and your notes. Maelie's notes. Why don't you read them? I don't understand. How do you know what to do without knowing anything?"

"It's a gift." He said as he tried once again to take the laptop back. She slapped his hands away and continued typing. Bellamy joined them and soon they fought again. Aiden gave up and sat back in his seat. He let the two of them fight over his work and hope they pieced together a decent grade for him.

Maelie, who was followed by Noah, arrived at five in the evening and was delighted to see how much progress Aiden had made.

He didn't bother to tell her he would have gotten further if it wasn't for Emmy and Bellamy fighting over his laptop to rewrite his essay.

Bellamy and Emmy closed the cafe after seven and together they all travelled to the restaurant in Bellamy's car.

The atmosphere inside the restaurant was warm and inviting. The lighting was dimmed and tinted blue, as if the restaurant was submerged underwater. Aiden's eyes adjusted to the darkness as he entered, and he glanced over his shoulder, making sure that Emmy, Noah, Bellamy, and Maelie were following behind. Emmy and Bellamy were still bickering with one another like they had done the whole day. Every time he saw the two of them, they bickered.

On the other side of the room, he saw the rest of the group. Henry sat opposite Tilda and Katherine in a large booth at the back of the restaurant, already waiting for them.

Tilda sat up in her seat as soon as she saw them.

"You took your time. We've been waiting for you to show up. I'm so hungry I could eat a horse," Tilda whined.

Aiden slid into the booth beside her as Maelie, Bellamy, and Emmy joined them.

"We haven't been waiting that long," Katherine insisted.

She had chosen the restaurant, Seashell, a favourite of hers and her parents. Aiden had to admit that Katherine had good taste. She could afford to.

"No one stopped you from eating," Henry said, folding his arms over his chest. He looked dishevelled and was ready to bite someone's head off. Or bite into something.

Tilda picked up a fork and twirled it between her fingers, her eyes hooded. "I couldn't eat without them here. Not at my birthday dinner." She pointed her fork around the table at the rest of them. "You don't think I have manners?"

Henry leaned back in his seat. "First, it's not your birthday, and you've already eaten your cake without us. And second? No, I don't think you do."

Tilda rolled her eyes. "It was a small cake and Matt ate most of it."

"He said you did."

"Well, he lied."

Maelie walked to Henry's side of the booth and tugged on his sleeve. "Hey, move! And stop talking about cake. I'm hungry."

Henry grumbled but shifted to the other end and allowed Maelie, Noah, and Emmy to squeeze in next to him. Aiden, Tilda, and Katherine moved down to their side to allow Bellamy into the booth.

Tilda leaned around Aiden and tapped Bellamy's shoulder. "So, it's been about two months, right? Since you started?"

Bellamy nodded. "About that, yeah."

Tilda grinned. "You're one of us."

Henry patted him on the shoulder. "It feels like you've been here for much longer than that. That's another reason for a celebration. Well, that and the fact that the cafe's still standing."

"Just about," Aiden muttered under his breath.

Emmy looked up from the table and Bellamy tensed, but Tilda and Katherine didn't notice any change in the atmosphere. Katherine clasped her hands together on top of the table. "Now everyone's here. Let's eat."

They ordered their food. Katherine encouraged them all to try the menu, but they stuck to what sounded the most familiar and the cheapest. They chatted amongst themselves as they waited. Once the servers arrived, they began shovelling food into their mouths, hardly speaking until they finished.

Aiden couldn't remember the last time he had eaten so well. Oh yes, he did. It was the last time Katherine paid for his meal.

"Thank you, Katherine. That was delicious." Tilda laughed. She stretched her arms above her head, groaning in her seat.

Katherine inclined her head like a queen and smiled. "You're welcome."

Everyone chimed in with their thanks, and Katherine acknowledged them with another tilt of her head. "You're all welcome. We should do this more often."

Aiden stretched. "As long as you're paying, I'm fine with that."

Katherine's lips curved upwards, and she picked up her mobile from the table. "I need to make a call." She stood up and slipped out of the booth.

Her phone had been beeping every few minutes and even when she wasn't looking at it, Aiden was sure that she wanted to check who was texting her.

Henry downed the rest of his drink. "Does anyone want something from the bar? I'll pay."

Tilda jumped up from her seat. "I do. Bell?"

Bellamy got up from his seat. "Sure."

Everyone got up out of the booth to let them out. Henry, Tilda, and Bellamy left the table and walked across the room to the bar.

Emmy took a sip from her glass as she, Noah, Maelie, and Aiden sat back down. She watched them over the rim as they went.

Aiden reclined in his seat. He stretched his arm out and wrapped it around Emmy, pulling her closer. "So, how's it going with Bell? I keep hearing you two arguing amongst yourselves. Tilda says you don't like the fact that he's doing your job better than you."

Emmy's eyes widened, and she turned to scowl at Tilda's back.

Tilda hadn't said that, but Aiden didn't need Tilda to tell him anything. Emmy was having trouble letting go of the reins of the cafe.

She shifted in her seat. "We're working out our differences."

He sat back and watched as Emmy drank the rest of her drink with something close to pride. The dark blue lights cast a grey tint to her skin. She placed her glass down next to her empty plate and smiled in satisfaction.

"See, I told you I could keep up."

The corner of Aiden's mouth twitched upwards. "I never doubted you for a minute. Mae's the one who did. And Noah."

Maelie took a long swig from her glass and shrugged. "I didn't think that was your style."

Noah folded his arms over his chest. "Neither did I."

Aiden pushed away his near-empty glass and looked to the bar, where Tilda stood with Bellamy and Henry. "It's good he's making friends." He said with satisfaction, gesturing toward them.

Emmy followed his gaze and scoffed. "It's easier for some." She frowned, her eyes unfocused.

Maelie raised her eyebrow at her. Aiden took a deep breath and rested his head back against the booth. "School can be tough. It just wasn't for you. University, however..."

Emmy groaned. "Not you, too. Who have you been talking to? My mother? Bellamy? Noah?"

Aiden exchanged a weighted glance with Maelie and Noah. "You wanted to go at one time, didn't you?"

Emmy rolled her eyes and pouted. "At one time, maybe. But..."

"But, what? You only stayed here because you wanted to help your uncle. Now, you've got the time. Why not join us?"

Emmy's eyes narrowed. Aiden could almost hear her thinking about it. At one time, Emmy had wanted to go to university to study history. She would have gone along with Maelie and Aiden, but her uncle needed her at the cafe.

Emmy opened her mouth and closed it. She looked lost and confused. It wasn't a look Aiden was used to seeing on her face. Emmy always knew what she was doing, even when the rest of them didn't.

The sound of heels clicking on the ground filled the air, and Katherine slipped back into the booth next to them.

"Who was that?" Aiden asked, motioning to the phone in her hand.

Katherine gave him a withering look. "You know, I didn't think this was your kind of place, Aiden. But you used a fork, so... well done, I guess."

Aiden shrugged. "I've been practising." He took a long sip from his glass. "Doesn't answer the question. One of your underlings?"

Katherine's eyes narrowed. He knew from the moment she hurled her first insult; she had no intention of telling him anything. He also knew that he wouldn't give up trying to find out what it was.

Emmy shifted in her seat and cleared her throat. "Aiden said that you're trying to get into party planning."

The statement sounded innocent enough to Aiden's ears, but it was like a call to battle for Katherine. She turned to Emmy and scowled.

"What do you mean 'trying to get into party planning'? I do plan parties.... Pretty well."

Emmy swallowed, and Aiden could see her shrink back. She wasn't in the mood to argue with Katherine this evening, but then no one could have predicted that this would be her reaction.

Maelie leaned around Emmy and faced Katherine. "Kat, leave her. She meant nothing."

Aiden placed his hands on the table and leaned toward Katherine. "Yeah, it's just a question, Kat. Why don't you like questions? It was harmless enough. What is the problem? We're just asking our friend about her life, her ambitions. Why are you so touchy?"

Katherine rounded on him, and her scowl burned. Aiden pulled back from her as if the heat from it scorched him. "Yes, I want to get into party planning. What about it?"

Aiden shrugged his shoulder. "Nothing. We just wanted to know why you didn't tell us."

Katherine straightened her spine. "It's got nothing to do with you. I don't have to tell you everything."

Aiden glanced at Maelie and Emmy. The two of them looked just as confused as he felt.

With anyone else, this would have been a simple conversation, but they were talking about Katherine. This appeared to be a delicate subject for Katherine, and since Aiden did not know how or where to tread next, he retreated.

"Forget it. It doesn't matter." He stood and waved his hand toward the bar. "I'll be back soon."

"Bring beers," Maelie called after him. He grinned over his shoulder as he sauntered over to the others at the bar.

Tilda grinned at Aiden as he settled next to them. She called over to the bartender and motioned to Aiden. "The same for him."

The bartender nodded once to her and pulled out a glass, and poured him the same amber liquid. He took it and sipped. It burned the back of his throat and trickled down to his stomach, warming him. "So, what are we talking about?"

Henry took a long sip from his glass and nodded toward Bellamy. "We're exchanging work stories."

Tilda and Henry talked about the customers they had to deal with at the gym over the last few weeks. Aiden was pretty sure that the two of them exaggerated quite a few of their tales, but Aiden was used to it, though it made their tales no less amusing. Aiden had nothing to add, since he didn't have a job. Bellamy, however, was notably silent.

Aiden turned to Bellamy, propping his chin on one hand. "And how is work going for you? Is our dear Emmy treating you well?"

Bellamy's eyes flickered as they glanced at Emmy, then darted back to Aiden. "It's going well. Can't complain."

Aiden leaned forward in his seat, maintaining eye contact with Bellamy. "Can't you? Please complain. It'll make you feel better."

Bellamy raised an eyebrow at him. "There is nothing to complain about. We clash, yes, because our opinion differs. It's nothing to worry about."

He rose out of his seat, leaving them to return to the others in their booth.

Tilda and Henry finished their drinks and returned to the table a few minutes later with Maelie's beers.

Aiden watched Katherine pay for their food at the counter at the far end of the room. He decided not to tell them what had happened with Katherine. Her work was a sore subject for her since it upset her so much. He hadn't expected her to lose her temper like that, but he was used to clashing with Katherine. There wasn't a week that went by without the two of them arguing about something or other, but it was never very serious.

Recently things have been worse. They seemed to aggravate each other far more than they did. More so than usual. So, he thought it was best not to mention her strange behaviour to Tilda and Henry.

He wasn't even sure there was anything to tell.

Emmy or Maelie could tell them if they wanted. Regardless, he would make sure it wouldn't be him who did.

Emmy joined him a few minutes after that, sliding onto a stool next to him. "We're getting ready to leave, so grab your things."

Aiden bobbed his head in agreement and left to go to the bathroom. When he came back, Katherine, Tilda, Henry, and Maelie were hovering by their table, talking to each other as they waited for the others.

Emmy and Bellamy were arguing with each other by the bar. As he got closer, their conversation became much clearer.

"I don't see why we have to." Emmy hissed, her hands planted on her hips. Bellamy crossed his arms over his chest as he stared down at her.

"Of course, you don't." He retorted. "But then, that's nothing new, is it? You love keeping everything just as it is."

Emmy bristled. "What's wrong with the way we were doing things? Tell me, why is your way better?"

"I never said my way was better. But even if I did everything your way, you still wouldn't be happy, would you?"

Emmy scoffed. "That's not true! Look, you were right about the pastries, it worked, ok? But this isn't necessary. You don't have to keep proving yourself-"

"Who said I was trying to prove myself?" He interrupted.

"No one. I just guessed. I-" Emmy stared past Bellamy and spotted Aiden standing behind them. Her eyes widened as she realised he had been listening to their exchange.

"We should go," Aiden drawled.

Bellamy turned to look at Aiden, his face flushed. His eyes looked bright with anger, or embarrassment, as they met Aiden's. Emmy seemed enraged, and she continued to scowl at Bellamy.

Aiden scoffed at the two of them. He slouched against the bar next to them and folded his arms. "Again? You two have been going like this since this morning. Aren't you done with whatever this is?"

Both Emmy and Bellamy looked away from him in different directions. Bellamy shoved his hands in his pockets and Emmy played with the sleeve of her top, staring at the coffee stain still there from her fight with Bellamy that morning.

"Let's go." Aiden continued. "You can continue your fighting or your flirting tomorrow." Their heads both snapped up in surprise at that. Emmy glanced up at Bellamy before lowering her eyes to the floor. He just stared ahead at Aiden, unmoving.

Emmy folded her arms over her chest. "We weren't…" she trailed off.

Aiden held up both of his hands in surrender. "Fine. Whatever. But some of us would like a bit of a rest from hearing the two of you argue all day."

Neither Emmy nor Bellamy looked at him after that. They both remained silent as they left the restaurant. The only regret Aiden had was that he had not said something sooner.

CHAPTER EIGHT

HENRY IN THE CAFE

As spring continued, the rainy days became more frequent. This made it more difficult for Henry to go out every day on his morning runs. It wasn't impossible, but the cold made his limbs move slower than he was used to.

The month of April began grey and bleak with the occasional ray of sunshine, which did little to warm up the days. On Thursday, the weather was mild, with lots of sunshine that warmed up as the day progressed. Aiden dropped by Henry's flat early that morning, eager to show him the final product of his and Maelie's short film project.

Henry had expected little. He wasn't an actor, and Aiden hadn't appeared to care much about the result.

He didn't imagine Aiden to be a very bookish person in a classroom, because he wasn't serious in any aspect of his life.

The film was much better than he had expected, which took him by surprise.

Maelie had filmed it while Aiden had edited with Maelie's input, with the end product being very professional.

The result had shocked Aiden when he first saw the end product for the first time. He had only seen the film in bits and pieces and through bleary eyes. He was sceptical when they first started, convinced it would be terrible, but Maelie pushed him to work on it more.

By the time they left Henry's flat that morning, he was praising himself for his genius.

Henry strolled into Marsh's Manor an hour later with Aiden trailing in behind him, still bragging about his editing skills.

They spotted Katherine, her dark hair curled, perched in one of the wooden chairs along the windows of the cafe. She was scribbling in a notebook resting on the table in front of her, with a mug, a planner, and her phone next to it. The rest of the cafe was empty.

Henry and Aiden exchanged a look between each other and, after a moment's hesitation, went to join her.

Katherine's eyes flickered from her notebook to them before her focus returned to her book. It was a new notebook with clean pages. She had folded it over and stuck a neon green tab at the top, marking the start of her writing. She held the new pages in her other hand as she flipped them over to write on the back.

"Good morning, you two. Is everything ok?" she inquired.

Henry pulled out the chair next to her and sank into it. "Yeah, it's great."

He leaned over to read what she had written on the page, but her right hand was too quick for him to read her cursive handwriting. It looked like a list or a plan from the bullet points and headings.

Her handwriting was elegant, flowing across the page. From where Henry sat, the words were unintelligible, but he could see that she had filled a few fresh pages already and it wasn't even ten in the morning. How long had Katherine been working on this? What was this?

"What are you doing?" He asked as Aiden pulled out the chair next to him and sat down, twisting his head to read over her shoulder.

"Working." She answered, her hand moving over the page as she wrote.

Aiden raised an eyebrow as she returned her attention to her notes.

Katherine finished the sentence she was writing and gave a satisfied smile. She packed up her things on the table, shoving them into the large, bottle green bag that was sharing her seat. "So, I thought we should all have a brief shopping trip."

Aiden crossed his ankle over his leg and leaned back in his seat. Curious, he fixed his gaze on Katherine. "Why do we need to go shopping?"

Katherine crossed her leg over her knee and sat back in her seat, her arms folded across her chest. Her glare was withering as she stared back at Aiden. "Anything you want. I'm not your mother. I just thought it would be fun. But don't come if you don't want to. I'm not forcing you."

Aiden shifted in his seat, staring hard at Katherine. Her gaze didn't waver. She raised an eyebrow, challenging him. He shrugged in defeat. "Okay. I'll come."

Raised voices drifted down from the upstairs landing and seconds later, Emmy and Bellamy appeared at the top of the stairs, their voices increasing in volume as they walked.

Emmy marched ahead of Bellamy, her curly hair flying out of her bun behind her. Bellamy sauntered down the stairs behind her, but his raised voice matched hers.

It wasn't unusual to see or hear them argue with one another these days. In fact, it had become a regular thing in the past months for them to fight about something, from who worked on the till to which customers each of them served.

What was a surprise was seeing the two of them together on one of their days off?

Henry thought that they would have preferred to avoid the other. He was wrong.

Katherine leaned over and whispered. "They came in after me and they've been arguing non-stop."

"Same as usual, then," Aiden muttered.

Emmy spotted them in the corner and crossed the floor to meet them. She settled in front of their table and Bellamy followed behind her, staring with fury at her back. "Morning." She chirped. "It's a lovely day, isn't it?" Her voice had gone higher and became fluffy and sweet.

Henry dragged his hand over his chin, feeling the stubble that survived his morning shave. "Is that why you two are here so early? Together?"

She glanced back over her shoulder at Bellamy and fidgeted with the end of her sleeves. She scrunched up her face. "We were just going over the takings. The cafe's doing well."

Aiden lifted his chin. "So why are you arguing?"

Bellamy took a step closer to the table and shoved his hands in his pockets. His face was a passive mask. "Emmy and I were just talking about how well the changes at Marsh's are going. Things just keep on improving. Right, Emmy?" He gazed down at her, his eyes sparkling.

Emmy raised her head to look at him and gave him a bitter smile. "Yes, they are. And it's all thanks to Bellamy." She turned back to the others and her voice returned to its normal pitch. "So, what were you talking about?"

Henry was sure the fight wasn't as good-natured as they were making out, but he was also sure it wasn't as serious either. They argued like Katherine and Aiden, and that was borderline flirting. But he didn't want to be the one to tell them that.

Henry scratched the back of his head. "Kat's planning a shopping trip."

Emmy raised her eyebrows in interest and glanced at Katherine. "Is that so?"

Katherine shrugged, a graceful gesture coming from her. "I need to go into town to buy a few things, so I thought we could all make a day of it. Everyone should be free. Tilda doesn't work today, and Noah starts a little later. Oh, and Maelie doesn't have any classes."

Emmy nodded. "Sounds good."

Henry saw Aiden's eyes focused on Katherine. "Just light-hearted fun, right?" he mocked.

Katherine ignored him and took out her mobile phone as Emmy and Bellamy settled at the table.

An hour later, Maelie, Tilda, and Noah walked in.

They all left the warmth of the cafe together, once everyone had arrived, and began walking down the empty streets toward the town's main mall.

Maelie, Katherine, and Noah walked in front, with Aiden and Henry behind, closely followed by Emmy, Tilda, and Bellamy.

Henry was thankful that the weather was improving, as a strong wind blew past them. It wasn't as bitterly cold as it had been for months.

As they walked, the mall loomed in the distance and the streets were filled with people.

Katherine slowed down, pulling the group to a stop, and looked over her shoulder at the rest of them as she tightened her grip on the front of her coat. "So, I thought that once we get to the mall, we could split up..."

Aiden grabbed his chest with one hand and gasped, his other hand held imploring out in front of him. "You're breaking up with us?" He wailed dramatically.

His face had shifted to a mask of sadness, but his eyes sparkled with mischief and his mouth threatened to tear into a smile. "What did we do? We can change, please. Just give us another chance."

Henry, Maelie, and Tilda snickered when Katherine shot him a venomous glare and he dropped the act.

"When we get to the mall," she continued, ignoring him, "We can split up into groups, to do our shopping. I need to buy some clothes and a few other things." She looked hesitant for a moment before she continued. "I need to buy a work outfit."

Noah's mouth curved into a smile. "You're working now? Why didn't you tell us? Where are you working?"

Katherine looked away for a second at the people milling around them, measuring her words.

"I have to organise an event." She whispered.

Henry had trouble hearing her and wasn't sure what he heard. Neither did everyone else, it seemed, since they all broke ranks and swarmed Katherine.

Maelie tugged at Katherine's sleeve. "What? As you a party planner, or event organiser? Did someone hire you?"

Katherine flushed under her makeup and tucked a strand of curled hair behind her ear. "Yes. They did. And now I need a new outfit. Or three. Maybe four."

Tilda rushed forwards, pushing past Aiden and Henry, squealing, and drawing people's attention to their group. She threw her arms around

Katherine's middle, lifting her on her toes. Katherine pulled away from her and straightened her hair and clothes, but Tilda carried on yelling. "Yes! Why didn't you say earlier? I would have dragged you there already. Mae! Emmy! Let's go."

No one moved, and everyone became silent. Tilda turned around and stared at Maelie.

There was a long pause and Maelie's jaw clenched as she poked the ground with her toe.

"I've got to buy some stationery." She grumbled. "So, I'm out. Sorry." She turned to Aiden and Noah. "You two with me." It wasn't a question.

Noah took a step back and nodded, dragging a hand over his face. "I have a shift later, so I've got to be back by 1 o'clock." He added.

Aiden scratched the back of his head. "Stationery, yes. I need some, too."

Henry, himself, understood Maelie wanting to stay out of Katherine's way and also why she wanted to keep those two away from her.

For a few months now, Katherine had been behaving unpredictably. One minute, she was ignoring everyone, then she was arguing and blaming everyone for the strangest reasons. And Aiden, most of all, would be the one that provoked her. It was best to avoid any instances where Aiden or Noah commented on Katherine's clothes. For everyone's sake.

Tilda rolled her eyes. "Cowards." She muttered. "Emmy, what about you?"

Emmy's eyes widened a fraction as Tilda drew the others' attention to her. She hesitated, and Henry was certain she would have run off if they weren't looking.

She fidgeted with the sleeve of her coat, her fingers picking at the edge. She looked down at the pavement, deliberating for a second before Bellamy spoke up.

"Henry said that he was going to drag me and Emmy to the gym," he began.

Henry froze at the mention of his name. He had no memory of this conversation at all.

He had never spoken to Bellamy about the gym. In fact, he was pretty sure he had never had a proper private conversation with him.

Both Katherine and Tilda raised an eyebrow at him.

Maelie, Aiden, and Noah didn't even look like they believed the lie. Emmy stared at him, her eyes pleading. So he nodded.

Bellamy continued. "Well then, we should buy workout clothes. I don't have any. Emmy, do you?"

Emmy shook her head. "No, I don't."

Tilda's eyes narrowed, but Katherine's expression softened, and she smiled at them. She looked at Emmy and then at Bellamy. "That's alright." She answered and turned back around, leading the group forward again.

Henry looked down at Emmy and she mouthed a silent thank you.

As they walked, the shops grew larger and more stores with popular brand names appeared. Once they arrived at the sliding glass doors, Maelie, Aiden, and Noah slipped away into the crowd.

"We'll be over here," Aiden yelled to them as he followed Maelie into a large stationery store. Noah followed them, ducking his head, hoping they would forget about him.

Tilda and Katherine paid them no notice as Tilda dragged Katherine off towards a clothing store on the other end of the mall.

"See you a lot later. We'll text you." Katherine called before the crowd swallowed her.

They left Henry, Bellamy, and Emmy standing in the middle of a crowd as they stared after their friends. Emmy relaxed, her shoulders drooping in relief. She turned to the remaining two and gave them a small smile. "So, what now?"

Bellamy pushed his hands into his coat pockets and shrugged as he gazed around at the stores over the heads of the shoppers. "I don't know. What do you want to do first?"

The wind swirled past them, through the sliding doors, as they stood by the entrance to the mall. Henry flexed his fingers. They were cold and numb, and they didn't feel as dexterous as they should have. He cupped his hands together and blew on them.

Light filtered in through the glass installed in the ceiling, from three floors up. The mall itself had three floors, with four escalators in the centre, two heading up to the different levels and two heading back down. Each floor had rows of stores, all of them filled with shoppers.

The escalators directly in front of them were packed with people as they wandered from store to store, bags in their hands, chatting with their companions.

Henry hadn't expected it to be so crowded, though it was a very popular mall, and hardly ever empty.

Emmy folded her arms and rubbed her hands along the side of her arm. "Thanks for that." She gestured in the direction that Tilda and Katherine had gone.

Bellamy looked down at her and his answering smile was faint, but it lit up his eyes. "It's nothing. I wouldn't wish that on my enemy."

She scowled up at him, but her gaze kept flickering away from his face, instead of making direct eye contact. "I'm not your enemy." She whispered.

"I know..." he whispered back.

"I know that sometimes I might act like it, but..." she paused.

"I know." Bellamy repeated, then gave Emmy another faint smile. This time, Emmy returned it.

Henry sighed and dragged his hand through his hair as he felt his frustration with the two of them rise.

He cleared his throat, instantly gaining their attention.

"Since you two are so interested in fitness," he began, leading them over to a store that he was very familiar with.

"Let's get you some shoes. Let's go." He continued, gesturing for them to follow him.

The store behind them specialised in fitness, with trainers and equipment. Out of the corner of his eye, he saw the two of them exchange a look.

They spent close to an hour in the store, as he talked Emmy into buying a pair of trainers, vowing that she would join him on a jog sometime soon.

Emmy made a face but said nothing as she took the shoes to the counter, so Henry took that as a sign of agreement. He couldn't talk Bellamy into buying a pair, however.

Bellamy was reluctant to buy anything, it seemed. He searched around with mild interest, but nothing seemed to hold his attention. No matter how hard Henry tried, Bellamy didn't budge on the matter. There was talk of actual fitness clothes, but neither Emmy nor Bellamy were that invested.

They left the store and wandered from the bottom floor and up on the escalators. Emmy huffed, frowning down at the shoebox in her bag.

"Henry, you don't expect us to come with you when you run, do you? I hate running. You know I do. Look, I don't mind the gym, but I don't think I could keep up with you. And I don't like running on the grass. Or in public."

Henry waved her words away. "You'll be fine. Don't worry about it. I'll help you out. After a few weeks, you'll get used to it and in a few months, you'll be a pro." He stated and patted her on the back in encouragement.

"A few months?" Emmy echoed. "You think that this will last that long? We'll go on a few runs. Three runs at the most, maybe, and then quit."

"I won't let you quit."

Emmy's eyes widened. "No, it's fine. You can let me quit. Please?"

Henry rolled his eyes. "No! Bellamy, how about you?"

Bellamy shook his head, gazing at the stores below them as they travelled up the escalator. "Exercising's not my thing."

Emmy narrowed her eyes at him, fuming with indignation. "And it's mine? Well, what is your thing? Running could be your new thing."

Bellamy smiled, not bothering to look at them. "I have a lot of things I need to do." His reply was vague. "I'll be too busy to run with you."

"We haven't set a date or time yet," Henry stated

The corners of Bellamy's mouth turned up. "I'll be busy. Besides, I only made that up to help you."

Emmy scoffed as she stepped off onto the second floor. Henry and Bellamy followed her, and she took the lead. "And look how well that worked out."

Bellamy looked down at her and laughed. "It worked out pretty well. Didn't you just thank me?"

She folded her arms. "Perhaps it was premature." She answered, fighting a smile.

"Blame him." Bellamy pointed at Henry.

Emmy's eyes flashed and her mood darkened. "If I have to do it, so do you."

Bellamy stepped away and pushed his hands in his pockets. "I told you. I have things to do. You know? I have... hobbies and friends to see."

Emmy's eyes lit up with curiosity. "Well, what do you do with your friends? You know, if they exist." She pressed. "What do you like to do in your spare time?"

Just as Bellamy was about to answer, they passed outside a bookstore and slowed down as Emmy's attention shifted to the display window.

Henry hadn't been in one of those since he left school. The books he bought then were always for school, classics that he had little interest in.

He didn't mind reading, but the books he enjoyed weren't ones that his teachers had thought suitable. He may as well just watched TV, in their opinion.

Any books he had needed, he bought online.

Bellamy nodded to the store in front of them. "I read. At least I can, and sometimes I do it as a pastime. And I like to play games."

Emmy pursed her lips. "The recreational kind or the ones that mess with people?"

Bellamy feigned innocence as he smiled back at her. "Both. But not as well as you. You seem to have a knack for card games that I just don't have."

They wandered in and out of stores for over an hour before they arrived on the third floor of the mall. This level was much quieter than the others, with very few people venturing up this high.

They passed a shoe store, and Bellamy slowed to a halt outside the window. Henry turned back to watch him. "Want something?" He asked.

Bellamy didn't reply, but walked into the store. Henry and Emmy followed him.

Bellamy was standing in front of the children's section, staring at a pair of polished black shoes.

Henry raised an eyebrow. "I'm not sure that they'll fit you."

"Do you want to get something for Janey?" Emmy asked, peering around Henry to look at Bellamy. Henry recalled Bellamy mentioning he had a younger sister called Janey, but he hadn't known she was this young.

He nodded and took the shoes to a shop assistant. Ten minutes later they were leaving the store with Bellamy holding a bag with a shoebox.

They wandered around the mall, drifting in and out of stores without a fixed destination.

Henry was just about to suggest they meet up with the others since Maelie and Tilda had sent Emmy a text to meet for lunch when someone joined them. It was Darcy, a colleague of his and Tilda's at the gym. She bounded up to them and smiled.

"Hey, I haven't seen you in a while." She said, looking down at Emmy. Emmy smiled back, fiddling with the bag in her hands.

"Yeah, not since the party. You should come by the cafe more often."

"I will. What happened with Eric? Tilda said that you never got to pair them off."

Emmy's eyes darted to see Bellamy and Henry's surprise. Bellamy shifted under Emmy's glare. She looked back at Darcy and gave a tight-lipped smile. "Bellamy got there first."

Both Darcy and Henry frowned, confused, but Emmy waved them away. It's a long story. Ask Tilda.

Henry and Darcy both nodded, though still confused. Henry turned to Darcy. "Why don't you join us for lunch?"

Darcy beamed. "I'd love to. Is that ok with everyone?" She looked from Emmy to Bellamy, searching for the answer in their faces.

Emmy nodded. "No. I mean, yes, come. Tilda'll love to see you. And Katherine's got some good news. Bellamy?"

"Yeah, sure." He answered, folding his arms over his chest, his bag still held in his hand.

Though she smiled, Henry was sure that Emmy wasn't happy about Darcy being invited to join them. He had known her long enough to recognise when her smiles were only to appease. They weren't like the ones she had been giving Bellamy most of the day.

Half an hour later, all four of them met Maelie, Aiden, and Tilda after drifting through the stores. Noah had already left to get ready for his shift, and Katherine had gone home to put away her new clothes.

According to Tilda, Katherine bought five different tops, three pairs of shoes, a skirt, and two pairs of trousers and she needed to figure out how her new clothes would work with her older ones. Henry thought that was unnecessary, but what did he know?

Tilda smiled warmly at Darcy, then led them to a fast-food restaurant on the ground floor at the back of the mall. They each ordered their meals and once they arrived, Henry stuffed his face. Emmy, however, had little appetite and only ordered chips and a chocolate milkshake.

It must have had something to do with Darcy monopolising Bellamy since the moment she arrived. They ate and talked, with Emmy's lack of appetite going unnoticed by the others.

It was almost 3 o'clock when they left the mall. After their meal, they called it a day and walked back to Marsh's Manor, where they parted ways. Darcy headed towards the bus stop. Tilda and Emmy left in Tilda's car, waving goodbye before Tilda drove away. Aiden and Maelie drifted down the street, ambling along and yelling their goodbyes over their shoulders.

That left Henry with Bellamy.

"So... what are you going to do now?" Henry asked, pulling his car keys out of his pocket.

"I have to pick up my sister from school," Bellamy answered.

Henry searched along the road for Bellamy's car. "Where's your car?"

"My mum has it, so I'll just have to walk."

Henry nodded. A brisk wind blew past them and he shivered in his coat. "Hey. What school does she go to?"

"Maple Wood Primary."

Henry pointed at his car. "I can drive you there and drive you two home."

Bellamy gave a dismissive shake of his head. "We live a long way off. It takes an hour to get there."

"That's okay." Henry dragged a hand over his chin, scratching the stubble. "I've got nowhere to be this evening."

Bellamy hesitated, and for a moment Henry thought he would decline again. Instead, he agreed. "Uh... yeah... thanks."

"No problem. Maybe you can join me and Emmy..."

"No chance."

They crossed the pavement to Henry's car and climbed inside. Henry started the car and pulled away from the curb before he drove them in the school's direction.

Henry knew the way to Maple Wood Primary School. When he was younger, his parents had thought of sending him there. They thought that would be for the best since it was closer to home, but he was happier where he was.

The air in the car was dense. Henry glanced over to see Bellamy staring out of the window of the car, watching as cars, buildings, and people turned to blurs of colour. They remained silent, though it was comfortable until they reached the school.

Henry pulled his car to park outside of the school under Bellamy's direction before he climbed out onto the pavement, the shoebox under his arm.

Henry watched as school children swarmed out of a glass door on the side of the building, and a young girl among the crowd broke free of the herd and rushed up to Bellamy.

He led her back to the car and handed her the box. Her face lit up as soon as she saw it. She opened the box and pulled out the shiny shoes. Taking off her old shoes, she shoved the new ones onto her feet, staring at the polished surface of the shoe.

Henry couldn't hear them over the sounds of other children meeting their parents, but whatever Bellamy said made her smile. She dived at him, hugging him around his waist, and for the first time since he met him, Henry saw Bellamy gave a genuine smile.

CHAPTER NINE
EMMY IN THE CAFE

Emmy understood responsibility well. She also knew how it could weigh a person down. She and Bellamy had clashed over many things, but she was wondering if that was because they were more alike than she realised.

Emmy remembered being told in a distant and fuzzy past that the qualities you dislike in yourself are amplified when you see them in other people. She was pretty sure that her mother told her that.

The things she disliked in herself were the same as she perceived in Bellamy.

He was a giant walking, talking mirror.

She could see all of her faults in him reflected at her.

His attention to the details in the cafe, the act he put on for the customers.

Even the way he accommodated her own demands reminded Emmy of herself.

He was trying to please everyone, and she was trying to please everyone, but somehow his efforts made her mad.

She hated how he told everyone what they wanted to hear.

But wasn't that what she always did?

The honeyed comments and apologies rolled off her tongue for her friends, her family, and her customers, and after so many years, she didn't know how to stop.

But with Bellamy, they didn't come. When she faced something that resembled herself, she couldn't pretend. And for that, she was grateful.

After their trip to the mall, she had spent the rest of the day tucked away in her room, thumbing through the history books on her bedside table and thinking about Bellamy.

One week later, just before she left for work on Sunday, Emmy walked into the kitchen, rehearsing the words she wanted to say. She turned them over, looking for the best way to ask.

She had been debating with herself for the entire week whether she should go through with it.

On the days she worked with Bellamy, she came up with reasons she should go through with her idea, and reasons she shouldn't. On her days off, she pretended to herself that she was getting to read her books, while her mind wandered to Bellamy, and her eyes read the same lines repeatedly.

She had doubted whether this was a good idea, or if she was just overcompensating for her behaviour because she felt guilty about how she treated him.

Emmy comforted herself with the fact that she was not feeling guilty because she had nothing to feel guilty about.

She was doing her job and making sure that the cafe ran without a hitch.

She used that train of thought to rationalise her internal debate and calm her mind.

Emmy convinced herself that she was doing it because of a burgeoning friendship and not festering guilt.

Fred was sitting at the kitchen table with a newspaper in front of him. He had a plate with crumbs next to a steaming cup of what she assumed was tea.

He raised his head when Emmy walked in. "Morning Emmy! Do you want some toast?" He lifted his cup and took a tentative sip.

Emmy shook her head at his question and sat in the chair opposite him. She folded her hands in front of her on the table, her fingers itching to pull at her sleeve.

"I'm fine. I just... was wondering... could you give Bellamy a pay rise?" She asked.

She glanced at him to see his reaction. He studied her while chewing his food.

Tilda told her that Bellamy supported his mother, but she hadn't believed it until she saw him buy school shoes for his sister.

She had seen him looking through the stores as they passed, but the only thing he bought was for his little sister.

He was again putting someone else before himself.

She wasn't sure if that was a conscious choice or not, but she thought it quite telling either way.

She met the small girl on Friday two days ago, and that was what had cemented her choice.

Henry had dragged Emmy out of her bed, forcing her to break in her new shoes. He took her jogging all around the park, from 12 pm to 2 pm, in the name of her health, he claimed, before he led her back to the car he had left parked outside her house.

Henry had already agreed to pick up Bellamy, to take him to collect his sister from school, since his mother had their car again.

To Emmy's surprise, he had made the offer to Bellamy the day of the trip to the mall after she left with Tilda.

Emmy had tagged along this time and saw first-hand Janey's love for her shoes.

And for her brother.

The little girl spends the entire time talking about her new shoes and thanking Bellamy, who was all too happy to please.

"Why are you asking?" Her uncle asked, drawing her attention back to him. Emmy raised her eyes to the ceiling, looking for an answer she could piece together.

Despite all the time she had dedicated to it, she still didn't know how to explain. Not one she wanted Fred to know, anyway.

"We've been getting along. I just... He's been working hard. I thought he could do with the extra money, or at least some extra shifts."

He nodded. "Fine."

She sighed in relief and sat back in the chair.

"Thank you." She breathed. She gave her uncle a big smile and rose from her chair and left to get ready for work.

After winning a fight with Lucy for the bathroom, she showered, dressed, and dashed back into her room to collect her things.

The last page she had been looking at the night before was the homepage of a university. She had been searching for details about enrolment, to see what she would need to apply.

It was only out of curiosity.

She closed the window, swinging her bag onto her back as she left her room.

The weather outside was balmy, so Emmy wore a light jacket. Since the weather was pleasant enough, Emmy walked to work, hoping it would be enough to calm her mind, if not her stomach.

She strolled into the cafe, feeling anticipation circle in her veins and settle behind her navel.

Bellamy was already busy wiping down a table.

He had already taken down half of the chairs and everything was shining and clean, even in the shadow of the unlit cafe.

He raised his head as she walked in, and the corners of his mouth lifted into a smile. "Morning. You're late."

Emmy looked at the clock hanging on the wall behind the counter. It was 7:40.

"I'm not late," she replied, as she took off her bag and her jacket. "You're just early."

He straightened up with the sponge in his hand. "At least I've been working. The last time you were in here early, you were too busy."

Emmy crossed the wooden planks on the floor to the opposite side of the table where Bellamy was standing, holding her jacket and bag over her arm.

"I was texting Henry. He still wants you to go jogging with us."

Bellamy laughed. "Good luck with that."

Emmy huffed, then walked into the backroom to put her things away.

She came back out and helped Bellamy take down the chairs and wipe the tables before they opened the cafe to the public.

Customers flooded in as soon as they opened the doors.

Parents and their children came in for a relaxing meal. Some customers sat down to eat, but most of them had takeaways, so Emmy and Bellamy were kept very busy during the rush hour.

They took the orders; Emmy serving the drinks while Bellamy handled the food.

Despite it being hectic, Emmy was content. She was getting along with Bellamy so well, and there hadn't been a disagreement between them all day.

A small twinge at the back of Emmy's mind suggested this change might have something to do with her change in attitude, but she soothe it with a smile to Bellamy.

She tried to keep the atmosphere calm between them.

She didn't know how it happened, but was pleased that she succeeded.

The rush soon died down, and the cafe was quiet again.

It was empty apart from a few stragglers scattered around, sipping coffee in the far corners of the cafe, away from Emmy and Bellamy.

She ran a hand along the counter, collecting crumbs, granules, and her resolve. "So, Henry still wants to go running this Thursday," she started.

Bellamy had been watching the cars pass outside the window as he leaned against the front of the counter.

At her words, he turned around to face her, leaning forward over the counter with a faint smile on his lips. "Yeah. He keeps dropping hints about that. I think he wants me to join the two of you."

Emmy's mouth curved into a smile and she shrugged, pushing away a curl from her face.

Henry had mentioned the idea on their jogs.

He thought the run would help Bellamy relax and get rid of his stress.

"Why don't you? You like early mornings, don't you?"

Bellamy shook his head, chuckling.

He hesitated for a second, studying her before he answered.

"No. I don't, I only do the extra shifts for the money. I've never enjoyed getting up early, so I guess that's why I was always late for school. I'd rather sleep in."

The honesty caught her off guard.

After spending months together, she still knew little about him.

She had accepted him as he was the moment she became comfortable with him working at the cafe. She had thought that she knew him well enough once she saw how he worked and didn't need to know much more.

Emmy gave a bitter laugh. "I was always early. Too early. I hated being late."

The memories of sitting in an empty classroom flooded her, and she shook them away. A glance to the side told her that Bellamy was gazing at the floor in front of him.

Bellamy raised his arm and plucked at the cuffs of his sleeves. "I did too. Though I don't think I liked school much. Uni was much better."

"You went to university?" The pang of jealousy she felt in her chest was like a punch to her stomach. It left a sharp and bitter taste in her mouth as she tried to swallow.

She had heard her friends talking about university and had wished that she was a part of it, but hearing Bellamy talk about it was different. She felt left out.

He had been out in the big wide world but still ended up here.

She had stayed, not growing at all, and here she still was.

He nodded. "Yep. That was much better than school. More time to sleep in and fewer subjects to worry about."

"And party, I'll bet."

He smiled. "Not all the time. But we had some fun."

Her eyebrows rose. "We?"

Bellamy nodded, still smiling. "Me and my friends, of course."

"Ah, those. I was wondering if they were imaginary, but now I guess I have to believe that they exist."

His eyes glittered. "You doubted me?"

"Of course I doubted you!"

Bellamy chuckled. "I didn't finish university. I was only there for a few months. Mum needed me at home. I would like the chance to go back, though."

He turned his head and his expression grew distant. His eyes were staring forward at a point Emmy didn't think she could see, and she allowed herself to think of going to the university with Bellamy.

The thought of focusing on one subject appealed to Emmy. So did going to university with Bellamy. It would be nice to have someone to go with her.

There was one thing she was worried about. Not fitting in yet again.

She tapped his arm with the back of her hand and his head snapped up to meet her eyes.

"So, what was your favourite subject?" She asked.

"Maths." He answered, his smile self-satisfied.

Emmy wrinkled her nose at him. "Yuck." That had never been her best subject, and while she didn't hate it, she couldn't believe anyone would choose to do it, especially at that level.

He pulled back in mock indignation, pretending to be hurt. And if she hadn't been looking, the blatant amusement would have gone unnoticed. "What's wrong with that? I liked it. I was good at it."

"Of course you would have to be. Only people good at maths like it."

Bellamy shrugged with little effort. "Oh, I don't know. I knew some people who liked maths and weren't great at it. Even at university."

"Huh. Strange."

"Oh, sure. They're strange." He said pointedly.

Emmy was all too aware of the emphasis in his words, and she pounced. "What does that mean?"

"Well, you're the strangest person I've met. You like to work."

Emmy laughed at that and raised her eyes to the ceiling. Despite it being an already open space, the cafe felt bigger now. She hadn't realised, but the cafe had felt smaller whenever she fought with Bellamy.

And now? The beams had never looked higher than they did now. The ceiling was sturdy and rustic and part of a home. Her home. It felt safe. It was sturdy. Dependable.

And predictable.

She folded her arms and turned to him. "And yet, you stick around. In this place. With me."

"It keeps the job interesting."

"Of course it does. Wondering if today will be the day that I kill you and stuff your body in the back... it's interesting stuff. I see why you come in early every day. The suspense must amaze."

"We all need some excitement in our lives. Since we work in a cafe, we need something to make it exciting."

Life at Marsh's could be too predictable, even for Emmy. But there was comfort in staying where she was, even if she wanted to do more.

There were things she kept to herself, things that she never did, that she wanted to do, but she was fine with that.

Or she had been.

Mostly.

But she wasn't like Bellamy. He was different. At least he tried to do more. That she could at least admire.

The door opened, ringing the bell above and drawing their attention away from their conversation.

Warm spring air wafted in through the door and Darcy walked in, fixing the hair that had blown into her face from the breeze. She smiled at the two of them and walked to the counter.

She flicked her hair over her shoulder. "Hey. I took your advice," she gestured to Emmy, "and came over."

Emmy folded her arms over her chest and smiled politely at her. Before seeing her at the mall, Emmy had seen her at the party over two months ago.

Bellamy placed his hands on his waist and smiled at her. "You and everyone else. You just missed the rush."

Darcy beamed. The movement made her nose crinkle. "Yeah, I did that on purpose. I have a day off and I intend to enjoy it."

"I don't envy your job." He answered, resting his hands on the counter.

Emmy watched as they exchanged words and felt heat creep into her cheeks. She had noticed that Bellamy and Darcy had been talking with each other like old friends at the mall, but she had thought it was because they were the two outsiders and had bonded for that reason.

"Why would you?" Darcy scoffed. "Mondays, Wednesdays, Fridays, and Saturdays, yuck. Who'd want to work like that?"

"At least you have Thursdays free. Unlike me."

The words kicked her brain into gear.

Emmy frowned and turned to Bellamy. "What do you mean? You don't work Thursdays."

Bellamy gave her the hint of a smile. "You haven't heard? Fred called me before you arrived this morning and asked if I wanted to do an extra shift on Thursday morning, from 8 to 12. I said yes."

His eyes said more than he did, and she wondered if he knew, or at least suspected, she had something to do with it.

Emmy tapped the side of her arm, not making eye contact.

As she stared down at her shoes, she remembered what he had just admitted to her and she grimaced. "But you aren't fond of early mornings, are you?"

"Not really. No."

Darcy hummed, drawing their attention back to her.

"How about I drop by and keep you company?" She suggested.

Emmy kept her eyes on Darcy, but out of her periphery, she saw Bellamy shrug.

"If you'd like."

Darcy smiled and Emmy busied herself with some non-existent tasks.

Darcy stayed at the cafe until after 1. She took a seat at a table in front of their counter, making jokes and telling a few stories that made Emmy raise her eyebrows.

Emmy had to admit that she was excellent at it, and she could see why Tilda enjoyed working with her.

Emmy had tried to join the conversation, but she never knew what to say, so she kept quiet and let them talk.

Talking to customers was fine, but talking to peers was excruciating.

As Darcy left, she promised again to drop by on Thursday. She waved goodbye, and Emmy watched her as she stepped back into the cool day.

"That's nice of her," Emmy said. She leaned forward and started straightening the packets of sugar behind the counter.

"I guess," Bellamy answered.

Emmy bobbed her head and moved on to the napkins.

"It's a shame that you have to work so early. Henry will be upset you can't come with us. At least you have a good excuse."

Bellamy laughed. "I'm sure you'll be fine without me. But I would like to know if you wanted me to come. Why did you tell Fred I should have an extra shift?"

The napkins fell from her hands, and she looked up at him. "What? I-"

Bellamy blinked, trying to look innocent. "Fred said you told him I was doing well, so I should get more responsibility. Finally, letting go of the reins, are we?"

"I didn't say that."

Bellamy raised an eyebrow at her. "Then what did you say?"

Emmy shrugged. "I just said you should get extra shifts..." She trailed off and frowned down at her feet.

"I didn't think you of all people would want that."

Emmy raised her head. "I think you do a good job."

He smirked. "Is that it?"

"It's all you're going to get," Emmy fiddled with her sleeve. "So, Darcy? She works at the gym, doesn't she? With Henry and... Tilda?"

Bellamy nodded. "She does. Tilda talks about how much fun she was at the gym. She's good at her job, too."

Emmy folded her arms over her chest. "Maybe she wants to lure you into the gym. Make you a member before you realise what's happening. Maybe she's working with Henry."

Bellamy laughed and straightened his spine. "That won't be happening."

"Well, you could always run with us. It's free. And you are... welcome to join."

Bellamy's eyes narrowed a fraction. If she hadn't been watching, she wouldn't have noticed. After a beat, he asked, "Are you sure we wouldn't just end up arguing?"

No, she was sure they would argue. But she wanted him there. She wanted to erase her mistakes and start again.

"It could be fun." She prodded.

"Alright. But instead of early in the morning, how about midday? And instead of running, we take a car?"

Emmy laughed out loud, and he beamed at her. "I think that defeats the point." She admitted.

"It's the only way I'll come along. Take it or leave it."

"I'll talk to Henry."

***

The next Thursday, Henry arrived at Emmy's doorstep in his running gear. She opened the door and pouted at the floor, fiddling with the hem of her hoodie. "I don't think this is a good idea." She muttered to her boots.

The day before had been Noah's birthday, and she had gorged a bit too much on cakes and sweets.

She and Noah had gathered in the cafe with Henry, Bellamy, and Tilda for a small party, where they passed out snacks.

It had been a lazy day since Noah had wanted little fuss.

Lucy, Katherine, Aiden, and Maelie had all been busy, and that left more snacks for the rest of them.

It made Emmy feel sick to her stomach to think about how much she ate. She blamed Tilda for egging her on.

Henry grinned and punched her shoulder, rocking her back on her heels with the momentum.

"Of course it is. Stretch and then we can go do some light jogging before the real run." He said.

Emmy groaned, and he began ushering her out of the front door. "Bye, Mr. Marsh." He called behind her.

Her uncle's goodbye drifted down from upstairs. Though Fred's leg was getting better, Emmy worried that his recovery was taking a long time.

She took her time crossing the threshold, dragging her heels until Henry grew impatient and hurried her through the front door.

She had already agreed to run with him, and it had seemed like a good idea.

In the store, with her fresh pair of boots, she felt it was possible to run with Henry every Thursday morning.

Now on the second Thursday, at 6:00 in the morning, the idea felt ridiculous. The birds hadn't even started chirping.

Henry did a few stretches and Emmy followed reluctantly before he jogged out to the main street. He looked back, waiting for her to follow.

She sighed, brushing her curls away from her face, and followed him.

They jogged from Emmy's house to the park. It was not as empty as Emmy had assumed it would be. People were hurrying through the path that led through the park, but there were already some people walking on it.

"So, let's talk about Bell." Henry stated.

"What about him?" Emmy sulked. She did not want to talk about Bellamy at all. She had thought they could just talk about something else. TV shows, books, or just anything else. But Henry seemed determined to keep the subject from changing.

Henry shrugged with an ease that she envied as she huffed beside him. "I was just wondering if you like him. Do you?"

Emmy stumbled to a halt, tripping over her feet. "What? What do you mean? Like him, how?"

Henry stopped jogging and shrugged, his hands resting on his hips.

"Well, Tilda seems to think you like him. As maybe a little more than a friend."

Before she could help herself, she scoffed out loud, causing Henry to pull back at the sound.

"I don't," she protested.

"I have no idea why Tilda would even think that."

That Tilda was even discussing something she hadn't even thought about herself with Henry made her want to scream. And plug Tilda's mouth.

The outburst did nothing to deter him from continuing. In fact, it seemed to egg him on. A smile broke his face and his eyes creased at the corners. "Well, do you care if he was going on dates with pretty girls? Like Darcy?"

Emmy's head whipped up to look at him. "No." She denied. She had a sinking feeling in the pit of her stomach, making her ill. "I don't-. Is he going on a date with her?"

Henry's smile dimmed, and he patted her on her shoulder. "No... not yet. But it's nice to know you won't care if he does."

He jogged off and left Emmy to stare after him. Her cheeks felt hot as she took a deep breath and trailed off behind Henry, wishing she was still in bed under her covers, hidden away from embarrassment and the eyes of prying friends.

They jogged for fifteen minutes, and walked for an hour, before they ended up playing a one-sided game of hide-and-seek for another forty-five minutes, when Emmy tried to ditch him by hiding inside of the bathroom in another cafe.

They were both fed up with the sight of the other by the time they stalked into the cafe, sweaty and agitated.

Henry was usually even-tempered, but after two hours of her complaining, he'd had enough. He was irritable and ready to squash their entire arrangement. He was sure that Emmy wouldn't fight him on that.

Henry pushed open the cafe door and stormed in ahead of her. Emmy trudged inside after him, sighing gratefully at the interior, and collapsed into her usual seat in the cafe's corner. Henry followed behind and sank into the seat next to hers. He dragged a hand through his hair, tousling it and making it stand up in different directions. "Maybe this wasn't the best idea. The gym might have been better. I should have just given you to Tilda."

Emmy was about to say something to squash that idea, but laughter coming from upstairs interrupted her. She raised her head and saw Darcy coming down from the upstairs, followed by Bellamy. Darcy spotted the two of them and waved.

Emmy lifted her hand and waved back. Out of the corner of her eye, she saw Henry observing her.

She tried to ignore it, but she felt a familiar emotion creep up inside her whenever she sees Darcy with Bellamy.

Jealousy.

Against her will, her legs carried her towards the two of them. Sweat dripped down her back and she could only imagine what she looked like after the run. She smiled insincerely at the two of them.

Darcy grinned back at her, her pearly teeth flashing. "The cafe queen herself."

Emmy blinked. "Sorry?"

"We were just talking about you." She gestured between her and Bellamy.

"Good things, I hope."

"Of course," Bellamy said smoothly. "Before you came in, a trainee of Darcy's came in and she was talking about salads and stuff."

"Yeah," Darcy chimed in. "And he," Darcy waved a hand at Bellamy, "just flat out said he knew nothing about healthy foods, he just knew what tasted good."

"And we were just saying that you would have handled her better. You would have known what to give her. I'm sure you know the menus inside out." Bellamy finished.

"Oh." It was a compliment, she guessed, but it made her sound so...

Boring.

As if she only ever talked about the cafe, went to the cafe and thought about the cafe.

And that she couldn't argue otherwise upset her more than anything else.

CHAPTER TEN

TILDA IN THE CAFE

It wasn't often that Tilda had time to lounge in the front room of her house. For years, it had been her brother's domain, filled with his toys, his imaginary friends, and video games. Or her father and his paperwork dominated it. But her brother had gone to school and her father was sitting at the dining table, sipping on his coffee as he scanned a fresh newspaper.

Sensing an opportunity, she edged into the living room. She tiptoed over the threshold to the middle of the room and slid onto the couch.

Just as she reached out her hand for the remote resting on the coffee table, her father's voice rang out in the room. "Are you planning on staying here all day?"

Her hand dropped in defeat and hit the floor with a dull thud on the carpet. "Not all day... just some of it."

Will Myles lowered his newspaper and glowered over the top of it. "Matilda, there are better things to do than lazing around the entire day."

Tilda reclined against the armrest of the couch and stared at the ceiling. "Dad, I've been doing everything but lazing around. I'm at the cafe with my friends most days... socialising. Then, I'm at Matty's school picking him up. And then I'm at work... you know... working. Why can't I just relax? Just for a minute? Please?"

She heard the rustle of the newspaper and her father's chair legs scrape across the tiles. "Because it wouldn't be just for a minute, would it? You'd be here for the rest of the day, and then the next. Besides, you rest all the time. You sleep in late and lounge around all the time."

Tilda folded her arms and pouted at the ceiling. "Not in the living room."

"No," her father insisted, "you go out, call your friends. Do something with them. I'll pick up Matt. We'll have dinner later. Together."

Tilda rolled onto her stomach and her hair spilt over her face. She peered up at her father through her curtain of dark hair. "Why? What's wrong?" A family dinner in her house wasn't that unusual, but it wasn't common for her father to announce one. Her dad would cook and all three of them would sit at the dining table to eat. They would fill their stomachs, talk about their days, and leave whenever they finished. The gathering was natural, not forced.

Will shook his head and stared down at the floor, away from her eyes. "I just think it would be good for all of us to spend some time together."

Tilda nodded once to let him know she had heard, but she wasn't sure she understood.

What could her father say to reach Matty during a ride home she hadn't tried before? She had been a part of many drives with Matt since the divorce, and she could safely say that they had never bonded during them. She doubted their father would get any more out of him at dinner.

Despite her doubts about him bonding with Matt, Tilda was reluctant to debate it with him. She didn't want to talk about her mother, not with her father.

She stood up from the chair, huffing out loud. "Fine," she blurted, "I'll go... I'll go see Emmy."

Will nodded at that, his eyes concerned. "Good." He said.

"Good." Tilda echoed. She turned and ran out of the living room, escaping her father and a meaningful chat.

***

Tilda slowed her pace as she approached the stone path that led to the Marsh's front porch, hoisting the bag in her hand higher.

It was the start of May, about four weeks after the shopping spree, and she had seen little of Emmy, Noah, or anyone else. Now seemed as good a time as any to visit.

She had been shopping with Katherine, trying on different outfits, but Tilda wasn't sure why. Katherine had an entire wardrobe of clothes that would be enough to impress even the most sophisticated clients.

Tilda had seen a new side to her friend that day. Katherine was always calm and elegant, with a grace that would make a ballerina throw a tantrum in envy, but as she stepped out of the dressing room in her first outfit, Tilda saw her as the panicky mess that she really was, under a mask of indifference. Her eyes were bright, and her cheeks flushed under her make-up. She kept smoothing down her blouse every few seconds, as she took a deep breath and exhaled quietly.

Tilda had never seen her so excited.

Tilda sighed as she knocked on the navy-blue front door of the Marshes and waited, shifting her bag from one hand to the other. The sound of feet thundering downstairs drifted past the door, and a moment later, the door was unlocked and swung inward. Lucy peered out from around the door and smiled when she saw Tilda. She opened the door wider and stepped back to let her into the hallway. "Hey. You here for Emmy?"

Tilda nodded and reached her hand into her bag, pulling out the muffins she had brought with her. She had decided it was best to bring food when barging into someone's house.

"I brought these too. Here, you can have one. Aren't you supposed to be in school?"

Lucy shook her head, eyeing the bag. "I'm off for exams."

A door creaked, and Noah rounded the corner, still wearing his pyjamas. He dragged a hand through his hair, making it look even messier.

Lucy took the muffin and bit into the top with care. Noah leaned against the bannister, yawning in the crease of his elbow. "Are these for us?" He asked, his voice slurred.

Tilda nodded and handed one to him. "Did you just got up?" Tilda asked Noah as he shovelled the muffin into his mouth.

"There's nowhere I've got to be," He mumbled back, around his food.

Lucy raised her hand to the staircase. "Emmy's upstairs in her room. She's in a bit of a mood. Has been for a while now. I think you can just go up. I'm sure she'll be happy to see you."

Tilda handed the rest of the muffins to Lucy and began the climb upstairs. "Yeah, thanks. I'll do my best not to tick her off."

She slid past Noah and walked up the stairs to the second-floor landing. Emmy's room was to her left and the last door in the corner of the house. She walked down to the end and knocked on the off-white door. Emmy's muffled voice drifted out from behind it. What she said wasn't very clear, but Tilda took her reply to be an invitation to come in. She pushed the door open and entered.

Emmy was standing in the middle of her room, ripping her forest green sheets from her bed. Fresh sheets sat folded on the desk situated under a window. She picked up the duvet cover and unfolded the fabric. It was a mint green, decorated with dark green swirls near the bottom of the cover. She snapped the clean bed sheet through the air once before stretching it over the mattress.

Tilda looked around at the rest of the room. She couldn't remember being in Emmy's room for some time, but from a glance, she could tell that not much had changed.

The elegant wooden bookshelf which stood at the opposite end of the room was the same. There were many more books stacked on the shelf this time that Emmy had stacked them on the top of the case. Regardless, the books on the case were lined up precisely. No clothes were lying on the floor or across the chair like in Tilda's room. It was... tidy, but Tilda was pretty sure that Emmy's solemn mood might have something to do with it, though, with Emmy, it was hard to tell.

Emmy raised her head from her task. "Hey, Tilda." She scanned the room with a wry smile. "It's been a while, hasn't it?" She gestured a hand at the room. "When's the last time you've been in here? A while?"

Tilda nodded, picking a bottle of lotion from Emmy's dresser. "That sounds about right. I figured I would come to see you." She took off the lid and inhaled the sweet scent. It smelt like cake. She squeezed out a pea-sized amount in her palm and rubbed her hands together, the smell wafting up to greet her.

Emmy nodded at her bed. "Sorry about the mess. I wasn't expecting you." She finished smoothing down the bedsheet over her mattress and went for the pillows and duvet next.

"It's just an impromptu visit, as Kat would say." Tilda chirped as her stomach rumbled for cake at the smell. She glanced around the room again, eyeing the crisp lines of the furniture. Her own room had looked nothing like that, even when she tried. "Are you ok?"

Emmy looked up from tugging a pillow out from its case, her face puzzled and her eyes wary. "Course, I am. Why?"

Tilda waved her hand around the room. "You're cleaning."

Emmy scoffed at the statement and returned her full attention to the pillows. "So?"

That made Tilda pause. She had her assumptions about Emmy's behaviour... and also Bellamy. She had watched them long enough to see them gravitated toward each other. That they were both more comfortable with each other than in a group. But she wondered if that was just speculation. "Well, I thought it might have something to do with Bell..."

"Oh, no. Not this." Emmy groaned. She threw the pillows down at the head of her bed. "Henry said you think I like him. Bellamy."

Tilda sat down on the bed and looked up at Emmy. "Do you? It's ok if you do. I'm not judging."

Emmy placed her hands on her hips and frowned down at Tilda. Her hair was in a messy bun on her head, strands curled around the edge of her face, but it did nothing to soften her expression. Her large brown eyes narrowed in annoyance and her lips pressed into a thin line. "But I don't. So, I would like to know why you would even think that."

Tilda shrugged and crossed her legs. "You two have been getting along better. Talking."

Emmy bristled, and Tilda could tell that she had struck a nerve, so she pressed forward. "Even Bellamy says so."

"So, because I talk to him, I like him."

Tilda wasn't ready to just back down. "No. But I think you like him. And he likes you."

"I doubt that." Emmy snapped. She turned away and picked up her duvet from her chair. She tapped Tilda's thigh and ushered her away from the bed.

Tilda moved and perched herself against Emmy's bedside table, picking up the large shiny book lying just under her lamp. "What do you mean? Of course, he likes you. You're one of his friends," she responded, as she turned the book over in her hands.

It was a book about the French Revolution. Aiden had waved it in front of Tilda's face just before Christmas, asking if she thought Emmy would like it as a present.

Emmy dropped the duvet over the bed and stood back with a huff. She prised the book out of Tilda's hands and stared at the cover. "He seems more interested in Darcy." She muttered. She put the book back in its place and folded her arms over her chest. "I suppose I could have been nicer to him. And I could have done it sooner."

Tilda didn't have an answer to that. Emmy tried to slip past her out of her own room, but Tilda jumped up and grabbed her arm, trapping her. "How about we go out? Just go for a walk?"

A line appeared between Emmy's brows as she looked up at Tilda. Her eyes narrowed in suspicion.

Tilda knew that look too well. That was the look Emmy always had when she wanted to dig her heels in about something. Tilda sometimes felt that this was the only look Emmy had.

Tilda grabbed Emmy's other hand and swayed them. "Come on. Just a walk. No running. Henry told me you didn't like that."

Emmy rolled her eyes to the ceiling. "He tells you a lot of things, doesn't he?"

Tilda ignored her and began tugging her friend to the door. "Let's go."

She towed Emmy downstairs and past the living room where Lucy and Noah sat. They stayed to talk with them for an hour before they left, with Tilda towing Emmy behind her.

It was a day off for her and Emmy both, so they didn't have anywhere to be. Emmy's mood disturbed her, so she did something she thought might help. She wasn't sure how successful she would be in cheering her up, but she thought she'd try. The cafe seemed like the best way to do that.

They walked to the cafe, babbling about work and friends as the wind rustled the trees scattered around them. They talked about university and the books that Emmy had left on her table.

When they had arrived at the cafe, they were talking about Maelie and Aiden's film. As they stepped through the door, Tilda spotted Katherine at a table in a corner staring at a notebook, while Maelie and Aiden both sat opposite her.

Emmy spotted them too, and they walked over to the table. Maelie's woolly hat was not on her head, as usual, but on the table in front of her as she slouched in her seat, with Aiden sat next to her.

As Emmy and Tilda grew closer, Maelie and Aiden both looked up at the two of them.

The sound of chairs scraping across the wooden floor made Katherine look up from her notebook, startled.

Emmy took the seat to Katherine's right and Tilda sat next to Maelie. Katherine relaxed once she realised it was Emmy and leaned back against her chair.

"Oh, hey. I was just talking with Maelie and Aiden, and we decided it would be a good idea one evening to have a viewing. You know... to watch their short film. At my house." She tucked a strand of hair behind her ear.

"Yep." Aiden agreed sourly. "We'll be showing our masterpiece at her house. Not at mine, or Maelie's, but Katherine's. That makes sense."

Katherine didn't even bother to look at him. "My house is bigger. The computer can connect to the TV in the den."

Maelie exchanged a look with Aiden. She picked up her hat and shoved it in her coat pocket.

"Whatever. When is this going to be, anyway?"

Katherine shrugged. "I must think of a day."

"All that, just to watch our stupid movie?" Aiden scoffed. "It's good, but it's not that good."

Tilda shrugged. "We'll be the judge of that. Em and I were just talking about it. I believe you think you're some cinematic genius."

Aiden puffed out his chest. "I know I am."

Tilda drummed her fingers against the table, eyeing Katherine's notes. "We'll see. Either way, I'm ready to see this thing whenever you are."

She reached out a hand to pick up Katherine's notebook. Out of the corner of her eye, she saw Katherine's hands twitch toward it before she planted them down on the table. Emmy eyed the movement before she glanced at the book. Tilda looked down at the page. It was covered in Katherine's elegant scribbles. Tilda tried to read it a few times before she realised it was a list.

"It's for our little private screening," Maelie grumbled, watching Katherine. "All that, and she doesn't have a date for it. We tried to tell her it was too much, but she won't listen."

Tilda propped her chin on her hand and gazed at Katherine. "Don't you ever relax?" she asked.

A part of her wondered why she was surprised. It's not like Katherine ever did. Katherine treated everything like work, or even worse, turn fun things into work.

Katherine placed both of her hands on top of the paper and scowled at her. "Yes, I do." She looked at Tilda up and down. "Why are you two even here?"

"What? You mean, in the cafe that Emmy's family owns? Where we always come to relax?" Tilda shrugged and waved her hand at Emmy. "I'm trying to cheer her up."

Katherine raised an eyebrow, turning to look at Emmy. "Why?"

Emmy bowed her head and stared at the table, scratching it with her fingernail. "Ask her," she muttered, pointing at Tilda.

Tilda rolled her shoulders and rubbed Emmy's back. "She needs some fun. And so do you, apparently. So, let's do something. Something fun!"

She stood up out of her chair and motioned to the rest of them to follow her. No one moved.

Tilda sighed and motioned to them again. "Come on!"

Maelie shook her head and picked up her hat. "I've got some sleeping to do. The only reason I'm only out here is because Katherine called us. I am going straight back to bed." She pointed a finger at Tilda. "Don't you dare try to stop me!"

Tilda's shoulders slumped, and she twisted to look out of the window. Outside, the day was still bright. "It's not even night." It was around midday.

Maelie shoved her hat on her head and folded her arms over her chest. "Who says it needs to be night to sleep?"

Aiden rose from his chair. Katherine and Maelie did the same. "Yeah, I have somewhere to be, too. But you two have fun." He gestured to her and Emmy. "Don't kill each other." All three of them slipped away from the table and out through the front door before Tilda could say anything else.

Tilda turned back to Emmy and sank into her chair. Emmy watched her sceptically, and Tilda beamed back at her. From the look on her face, Tilda could tell that she could not convince Emmy to go anywhere right now. Tonight, however...

"So, I've been thinking," Tilda began. "Do you want to go to the park? Tonight? Not right now. I hear there's a fair. Or we can do whatever you want. Stay here, even. What do you say?"

The answer was a resounding no. Emmy didn't want to go to the park, but despite her refusal, Tilda wasn't taking no for an answer. She emphasised the need for Matt to have fun and mentioned her father's efforts to pick him up from school, and that was when Tilda knew she had Emmy. Sympathy and concern etched her face, though she tried to hide it.

It took a few hours to convince her, but Tilda made Emmy agree to go to the park with her and Matt despite her protests. In return, Tilda bought Emmy a cup of hot chocolate and agreed to let her drink it in the cafe.

Tilda and Emmy were in the middle of drinking their hot chocolate when the cafe door opened again and Bellamy walked in. Emmy's spine straightened the moment she saw him. She looked away, staring at her mug while attempting to disappear into her chair.

It occurred to Tilda that it would be for the best to do like Emmy and ignore him too, so she waited for him to see them. Emmy was having a rough day, and she didn't want to make it worse by forcing her to sit opposite Bellamy. But it also occurred to Tilda that this situation would become more awkward if no one said anything at all and left things to fester.

So, like a good friend, she took the leap for Emmy.

Tilda raised her hand in the air and waved at Bellamy. "Hey." She called. She heard Emmy inhale sharply next to her.

Bellamy walked over, smiling at the two of them. "Hey."

"Hi," Emmy whispered to her mug.

Tilda gestured to the chair next to her. "Come sit with us. What are you doing here on your day off? You're as bad as her." Tilda pointed at Emmy, who shrank even smaller in her seat.

Bellamy sat down in the seat, looking curiously at Emmy. "I'm meeting Darcy."

"Ah, a date," Tilda remarked, resting her chin on her palm. From the corner of her eye, she saw Emmy's hands clutch her mug with both hands, her head still bowed.

Bellamy shook his head, and his smile faltered, then disappeared. He leaned back in his seat and crossed his arms over his chest. "It's not." His voice was sharper this time, and Tilda's eyebrows raised in surprise. "Darcy said she'd be coming here and asked if we could have a chat. I was already in the area, so I agreed."

Tilda nodded. "Did she say what it's about?"

Bellamy shrugged and shoved his hands in his pockets. "A gym thing, maybe."

"Are you sure she's not declaring her undying love?"

Bellamy's eyes flickered over to Emmy, but she was busy giving the cup in her hands her undivided attention. "No... No. She just needs help with something."

Tilda nodded again, then was silent for a moment. Emmy had not uttered a word since she greeted Bellamy. The quiet hum of the cafe took over as Emmy and Bellamy continued to avoid making eye contact.

"Just as well she hasn't," Tilda continued. "Your work wife might've had something to say about that!"

The words came out of Tilda's mouth before she realised she was going to say it.

Tilda should have seen it coming, and in a way, she did. She just didn't realise that Emmy was quicker. The searing pain in her shin almost made her cry out loud, but it came out as a whine. Emmy's foot had the power of a bowling ball behind it, and Tilda knew that would hurt much more in the morning.

Emmy glared at her as Tilda rubbed her injured leg. Bellamy stared at the two of them, his gaze moving from Tilda to Emmy and back again.

"Joke." Tilda hissed. "Just a joke."

Emmy looked up at Bellamy, her face flushed. "I don't have a problem." She stated and glared back at Tilda, then she tapped her hands on the table in a way that told Tilda she was itching to wrap her hands around Tilda's neck. "And I'm not... his... his work... wife!"

Tilda held up her palms in surrender. "You argue like a married couple."

Bellamy chuckled. "She has a point," he said, good-naturedly. "We argue a lot."

Emmy glowered at the table. "Not that much."

"It's what we're known for."

"But we don't do that anymore."

Bellamy rubbed his hands on his knees. "Some things stick."

Tilda took another sip from her mug; her eyes were mischievous as she glanced from Bellamy to Emmy over the rim. "Spoken like a true married couple."

The scrape of the chair across the floor made Tilda jump.

"I have things to do. I'll see you later." Emmy snapped. She pushed away from her hot chocolate as she stood up from her chair and stormed out of the cafe without another word.

"I'll pick you up for the fair." Tilda called out to her as Emmy rushed out of the cafe's front door, waving over her shoulder in acknowledgement as the bell overhead jingled.

Bellamy seemed uneasy, but he said nothing.

In hindsight, Tilda realised that should have kept her mouth shut.

Tilda smiled and turned to Bellamy, clearing her throat. "So, Darcy mentioned she dropped by to see you yesterday."

Bellamy's face was expressionless. "Yeah. I told her I had an extra shift, and she thought she'd come over."

Tilda waited for him to say more, but he didn't, so she continued. "She told me about it. I can't get her to wake up so early for me."

Bellamy stared at her, and after a second, he gave her a feeble smile. "She's just being nice."

Tilda put her hands on the table in front of her and observed him. "At least she's nicer than Emmy."

Tilda saw something flashed behind his eyes, and he shifted back in his seat. "We're getting along a lot better now." He said, nodding his head after Emmy.

"She was the one who asked Fred if I can have an extra shift."

Tilda's eyes widened in surprise, and she leaned forward.

"Just like that? When? Did you ask her?"

Bellamy shook his head. "I didn't tell her anything. Last Sunday morning, I got a call from Fred and he said she suggested it."

Tilda nodded. "I saw her this morning, and she didn't mention it at all."

"I'm not surprised. She seemed embarrassed when I mentioned it. It's like she doesn't want to be nice to me. Or she doesn't want me to know when she's being nice to me."

Tilda hesitated a second before answering. "Maybe she's embarrassed about how she was and she's trying to warm up to you. Maybe she did always like you and it was just an 'Emmy' thing she was working through."

Bellamy turned to look at her, his eyes searching hers. "Did she say something?"

Tilda shook her head. "No."

Bellamy did not seem convinced. "This morning when you went to meet her, did she say anything?"

Tilda sighed. "She was just wishing that she had been nicer to you." Before he could ask her any more questions, she brought her mug to her lips and swallowed the rest of her hot chocolate, wondering if she had said too much.

They sat in silence for a few minutes before the bell over the door chimed and Darcy walked in to settle down into the seat that Emmy had vacated.

Tilda drifted in and out of the conversation until she realised Darcy's concerns- her hectic work schedule- were not Bellamy's concerns.

She thought about her agreement with Emmy, about finding herself a boyfriend. She had forgotten it since Bellamy's arrival had proven to be a great distraction.

It didn't seem so important now when she had Matt to worry about, too. He needed her attention. Even Emmy had put her issues aside for Bellamy. And he had put aside any issues he had with Emmy for his mother and Janey.

She could do that for Matt, couldn't she? He had to be her priority. She had to put her brother first.

"Hey, Bellamy?" She started. "Would you and Janey like to come with me, Matt, and Emmy to a fair this afternoon?"

CHAPTER ELEVEN
EMMY IN THE CAFE

A warm morning air stroked Emmy's face, pushing strands of hair away from her eyes. The sun burned against the back of her head and neck as she walked to the cafe, and cars sailed past her as she marched along the pavement.

She had gotten past the night before with Tilda and Bellamy and their siblings. It had gone better than she expected, and now it was behind her.

It would be a good day. Saturdays were fun.

Emmy knew that whatever happened, she would have the heat of the sun to warm her mood.

She liked to walk, but Emmy knew that someday she would have to get a car of her own. She would have to learn to drive, though. Noah had tried to teach her, but she had given up too soon. The only places she ever went to were within walking distance, and if she needed to travel further, Noah would drive her, or she would take public transport.

She watched as more cars glided by her, and her longing for one of her own became stronger.

She arrived at the cafe, with her T-shirt sticking to the middle of her back, still thinking about cars as she walked along the pavement.

Sunlight lit up the front of the cafe, but the inside was still and empty, with shadows and slivers of sunlight trailing across the tables and chairs.

Emmy fished out her key from her bag, unlocked the front door, and flipped the sign from 'closed' to 'open' before nudging the door shut behind her.

There was no sign of Bellamy. That, and the clock on the wall, told her she had arrived earlier than usual. This relieved her.

Ever since she had asked Fred to give Bellamy extra shifts, she had been less likely to attack him and his ideas for the cafe, and Bellamy had warmed up to her even more. She supposed that was because he no longer had to worry about her being bad-tempered anymore.

They would still bicker, but it was less life-or-death and more like old friends.

Or even, as Tilda said, a work wife/husband relationship.

Emmy dropped her bag on the table in front of her with an alarming rattle. She took down one of the wooden chairs that belonged to the table in front of the counter and sat down on it. The wood groaned a protest as she leaned back against the backrest.

It had become far too familiar to her over the years. She ran her hand along the grooves in the wood, digging her nails into the marks. Some of them had been ones that customers made over time and others she had made herself while waiting in the cafe. They curved around her nails and she dug in harder.

Her mind felt numb, but there was a buzzing behind it, gnawing at the peace it gave her. She allowed her mind to wander to the buzz and she let the thoughts drift back into her head.

The evening before, Emmy had gone with Tilda and Matt to the fair. Tilda had matched back to her house with Matt in the car, demanding that they all go to the fair. For Matt's sake.

They invited Bellamy and Janey to come along with them. Emmy was still embarrassed about what Tilda had said earlier in the cafe, but neither she nor Bellamy said a word about it.

She had to spend the entire time avoiding him, for other reasons.

She thought of the wind rushing past her as she and Janey ran through the fair. The bright, colourful lights were flashing everywhere. There were crowds of families in line for the rides. Janey clung to her, dragging her forward with her sweaty little hand. Tilda and Matt followed them, encouraging Janey's enthusiasm.

Emmy, Janey, Matt, and Tilda went on every ride, even getting Bellamy to join them on a few. He had even seemed to enjoy himself.

Emmy couldn't think of the last time she had gone to a fair. She remembered seeing the rides looming above her as she passed through the park with her mother on the way home from school, watching as the other children dragged their parents, begging to go on the rides.

She wondered what those kids were doing now. In a university far from home, parents, and supervision. They must have even begged their parents to go to ones far away from home.

She would have to thank Tilda for hauling her to the park.

Once she got home from the carnival, she had hidden away up in her room with her books spread over her bed. The books Aiden bought her were still sitting on top of her dresser, taking up most of the space.

Emmy had almost finished the trio of books, but she hadn't packed them away on her shelf. Along the edge of the book, she could see where she had folded over the corners of a few pages.

Reading was different when done for enjoyment, not as schoolwork. A thirst for knowledge and a need to know what happened next, and not because she was told to drive her. She could decide what to read for herself. There, she guessed, she was lucky.

Maelie and Aiden had been pulling their hair out from the roots, and they were only working on a short film for their class. Writing thousand-word essays for a university-level history class would be much harder than school-level essays, but she didn't think it would be this hard.

Emmy rose from her seat and walked around the counter as the bell above the door tinkled behind her, signalling Bellamy's arrival. The door swung in with a dull creak of wood and metal, and Bellamy strolled in, the sun framing his head in a halo of light, turning the edges a light brown.

His cheeks were flushed from the journey and his hair looked like a strong wind had come along and tousled his hair.

He scanned the room, then smiled as he spotted her. He closed the door behind him and shrugged off his coat.

It was almost summer, and it had warmed up considerably. Bellamy was suitably dressed for the weather. He wore jeans and a dark blue t-shirt with an olive jacket over it. His shirt looked new and had a pattern on the breast pocket, and Emmy was pretty sure that she had never seen him wear it before.

She looked up at the clock on the wall behind her. It read 7:35. "You're late. What happened? I was worried. I thought last night must have tired you out." She joked.

Tilda's 'work wife' comment floated through the air between them, but neither of them addressed it.

He gave her a boyish grin. "Sorry to disappoint you. I'm sure you'd have been just fine if I didn't show up." He glanced at the clock on the wall. "Anyway, I'm here now."

He wasn't late for his job; he was just later than usual for him. She had grown accustomed to walking into the cafe and seeing Bellamy already in the middle of a task. They had worked together more, and they had been arguing less.

"Well, anyway. Morning to you." She smiled.

Bellamy paused at her tone and raised his head, his eyes puzzled. It was too perky for her and they both knew it.

"Morning to you, too." He hesitated, glancing around the rest of the room. There were several chairs between them, still stacked on top of the tables. Emmy hadn't yet made a move to open the shop, besides flipping the sign to show they were opened for business.

She stood, her head rising just above the seats, taking off her own jacket. "How are you?" She began.

Bellamy frowned and stared at her in confusion. He continued to gaze at her for a moment longer before he moved closer to stand on the other side of her table. He folded his arms over his chest and his expression grew more puzzled as he watched her. "Good. How are you?" His tone was light, but everything else about him seemed tense.

Emmy nodded. "I'm good." It was a common exchange between them, but it had always felt hollow when he asked her, and it felt just as hollow when she answered. It was a reflex for them both.

She hooked her jacket in the crook of her arm and opened her mouth again, but paused. Bellamy noticed the movement, and he raised an eyebrow.

"What?" He asked, his voice apprehensive.

She stepped away from the table and walked to the counter. She wanted to say more, but she didn't know what.

Emmy went behind the counter to fetch her apron, fiddling with the strings and trying to build the courage to do something that she had been dreading. She wanted to apologise but closed her mouth, with her apology still on the tip of her tongue. "Nothing," she replied. "I was just thinking."

He nodded and walked past her and into the backroom to put away his coat. Before he reached the door, she took a deep breath and let all of her words fly out in a rush. "I'm sorry. I know I haven't been the nicest person to you. And I know I could have done better, but a part of me didn't want to. I am sorry, and I want to know if... we... could we start again?"

Emmy finished speaking and put her hands on her hips, mustering all the confidence she could, and waited for his reply. He slumped his shoulders and slouched as he stood staring at her. His eyes were intent, but the rest of his face was passive as he observed her.

After a few seconds, he cupped a hand around his ear and leaned toward her. "Pardon? I didn't catch everything. I think I heard an apology, but I can't be sure."

Emmy fought a smile, took another deep breath, and tried to give her apology again, slower and shorter this time. "I'm sorry."

Bellamy was silent for a minute as he looked at her. Emmy's chest tightened, and she felt the heat from her chest radiate out to the rest of her body and taint her with unease. His face contorted into a frown before straightening back out. "Thanks."

Breath rushed out of Emmy, leaving her optimistic.

Bellamy folded his arms over his chest and leaned back on his heels. "Though I thought we were already getting along."

She smiled. "Even with all the arguments?"

"I just thought that was you. Just the way you were with people."

Emmy's mouth dropped open in shock, and she heard herself make a strangled squeak.

Bellamy smirked. "So, you know you were being difficult? You were doing it on purpose?"

Emmy averted her eyes and shrugged. "I might have... given you a harder time than you deserved."

Bellamy uncrossed his arms and rubbed his chin. "Well, there's a surprise."

"So," she continued, "how are you?? Because I know we say it, but I guess it's more of a reflex than anything."

He grimaced and frowned at the floor. When he looked up, he looked hesitant. He hooked his jacket over his forearm. "My mum and I argued. It was a few days ago. It's not even an issue anymore but... Darcy keeps... asking about it."

"And you don't want to talk about it?" She asked. He shook his head, his eyes still trained on the floor.

Emmy wondered what she could say to that. She fiddled with the sleeve of her top and focused her gaze on Bellamy's face, examining his expression. The only notable sign of his distress was the corners of his mouth turned down and his brows frowned over his eyes.

Bellamy stepped forward, holding his coat in his right hand, and held out his left hand toward her. She held up her jacket to him and he took it.

Emmy gazed at a spot next to Bellamy's shoulder. "Well, I can't do anything about that, but I just want to say that... I promise that from now on I will...... allow you to do more around the cafe... and other things like that."

Bellamy scoffed. "I think your first apology was better." He walked to the back room and disappeared behind the door for a moment.

Emmy huffed and folded her arms over her chest. "I'm trying to be nice, you know." She called after him.

Bellamy walked back out, smiling at her. "I know. And I appreciate the effort you're making. I get how tough it is for you. What changed your mind?"

Emmy ran her hand along the edge of the counter and shrugged. "I think I could do with a break."

He gestured to the chairs still stacked on the tables. "Is that why you haven't started opening up?"

Emmy glanced around at the room in surprise. It hadn't occurred to her to take down the chairs. It was always the first thing that she did when she entered the cafe and had become a reflex, but when she walked in that morning, she didn't want to get to work. She felt too tired and distracted to do anything.

"I guess I was waiting for you." She joked. She looked over to stare at Bellamy. He was staring at the door to the cafe.

"Alright then. Now I'm here. Let's work." He walked forward and started taking down the chairs from the table. Emmy joined him and helped him with the chairs.

"So, do you really like Maths?" Emmy asked suddenly. If they were going to start afresh, she should understand him more.

Bellamy raised an eyebrow. "Yep, and you don't. You're terrible at it. How are you able to give the correct change?"

Emmy hit him on his arm before she could stop herself and Bellamy danced away, laughing, pretending to fear her small hands.

"I can count just fine, thank you! No, but seriously, it's horrible. Maths is the worst thing." The subject wasn't something she or anyone she knew would do if they had a choice, and not for fun.

Bellamy approached her, resting his palms on the table. "Alright, what do you like?"

Emmy crossed her arms over her chest and proudly stated her choice. "History. Aiden even got a few history books for my birthday."

"Your birthday!" He scoffed. He stood up straighter and shook his head in disbelief. "Aren't you supposed to get something that you want? Like clothes or jewellery, or toys, in my sister's case. Even the odd potted plant or ornament. Not schoolbooks. You're not even at school!"

"It's not schoolwork! And I did want the books." She pouted.

"Besides, I got him a hard drive, so it would have made my gift look terrible."

Bellamy pinched the bridge of his nose and shook his head again. "Why?" He wailed.

"Why, what?"

"Why did you give your friend a hard drive for his birthday?"

Emmy folded her arms as she stifled down her laughter. "He needed one."

"For his birthday?" He stressed the last word as if she couldn't see the argument he was making.

Emmy shrugged a shoulder. "He didn't mind. He kind of had a meltdown when the last one broke. It was at the cafe and people were watching, so I offered to buy him a new one. That cheered him up."

"So, you bought him a hard drive for his birthday, and told him before that you were going to buy him a hard drive? Do you understand how presents work? You buy the person something fun and you don't tell them what it is."

Emmy narrowed her eyes in mock annoyance. That was more real than she would admit.

"I know how they work! But Aiden wanted nothing else!"

"Oh? All he wanted was a piece of hardware?"

"Not just any hardware. Hardware that holds 1 terabyte of space."

"What?"

"I don't know, but he was happy, so…"

Bellamy laughed. "Well, if you got me a present like that, I'd never talk to you again."

Emmy rolled her eyes. "I'd never get you a hard drive."

"Good."

"I'd get you a calculator."

"As long as it's a good one." He sighed. "So, have you seen Maelie and Aiden's film?"

Emmy shook her head. "No., I haven't. Not yet. I heard that Henry's in it."

Bellamy paused before he rested the chair he was holding on the floor. "I didn't know that he could act."

Emmy laughed. "Neither did I. I'm pretty sure that Maelie and Aiden pushed him into it, so he had little choice."

"Do you know what it's about?"

Emmy shook her head again. "No, but they're going to have a mini viewing for all of us and they'll let us know when it is. Aiden keeps going on and on about how great it is and how professional everything looks. But from what Maelie was saying, he was getting fed up with editing it, and almost gave up near the end."

Bellamy moved to the next table and took down the chairs there. "Doesn't have a lot of patience, does he?"

"He didn't with us. I mean, we were just trying to help." Emmy joined Bellamy at the table. "He doesn't have any subtlety, either. I think that's why he and Katherine always clash."

Bellamy went to the kitchen, took out a damp plaid cloth, and wiped down the tables. "I think he cares. About her."

Emmy crossed her arms over her chest. "You think so."

He stared off toward the door. "Just because they argue, it doesn't mean he doesn't care."

Emmy fidgeted with the folds of her skirt and tried to change the conversation. "I have heard little about her new job. Has anyone told you anything?"

Bellamy straightened, dropping the cloth on the table in front of him. "I think you're more likely to hear anything before I do."

Months had passed since Bellamy arrived and, to be honest, she hadn't gotten to know him on a personal level. They were getting on better, but that didn't mean she knew him much better than the day she met him.

She thought her friends may have bonded with him quicker than she had, but she didn't know what Bellamy thought of them. He always appeared reserved with them, but apart from his interactions with Janey, Emmy wasn't sure if he was close to anyone else.

"How is everyone treating you? Has the novelty of you worn off yet?"

Bellamy shrugged as he folded the towel in half and rested it on top of the counter. "Everyone's still fine. Everyone's great. Funny. Interesting."

It was a sign of how far they had come in their relationship, that Emmy knew that there was more that he wanted to say and that what he said was just a hollow sentiment.

"Still, it must be difficult. We all know each other. We've known each other for years. You can't be expected to make new relationships with a bunch of people in a few months."

Bellamy didn't answer, and she wasn't sure if she should say anything, but she couldn't shut up. "Have you seen your friends since you started?"

"No. I haven't had time. Between work and Janey..." he trailed off.

"Well, how about Darcy?" She kept her eyes trained on him, waiting for more than just his verbal answer.

He tilted his head to the side as his eyebrows knitted together. "What about Darcy?"

Emmy shrugged. "I thought... you liked her. I thought you two were... friends. You two are... close, aren't you?"

Bellamy's eyes remained fixed on her. "I like her as much as I like Tilda and the others., Of all the people I've met here, I would say I'm closest to you. I feel like I can be... open with you. I mean, it's not like it made things worse with us."

Emmy felt her cheeks heat again and smiled to herself as Bellamy walked away to finish making the shop presentable for the customers.

While she knew it was a simple statement from him, it changed how she perceived his behaviour and his words from the day she met him.

Ever since Bellamy had arrived, she had only thought about what his presence meant for her and not what it meant for him. For the first time in her life, it had been difficult for her to pretend that she was happy, so she had taken it out on him.

His words meant nothing because she refused to accept him, even when he was honest and helpful. She had seen him as an obstacle when he saw her as a friend.

Emmy hovered for a second before she went behind the counter to grab his apron, feeling a pang of guilt spread in her stomach, twisting her insides.

She was pretty sure that out of everyone she knew; she was closest to Bellamy, too.

CHAPTER TWELVE

BELLAMY IN THE CAFE

The door swung open for what felt like the fiftieth time that day, disturbing the small bell above it. The shrill tinkle echoed through the room, announcing the departure of another customer and sending in a stale wind through the door, stretching out the ring of the bell.

Bellamy rolled his shoulders back as he stood behind the counter and exhaled heavily.

He shifted on his feet and prepared for the next customer to enter.

It was a generic thing, the bell. Small, brass, and ancient. It matched the rest of the room, with all the wooden furniture, the fireplace, and pale colours.

The fireplace wasn't something Bellamy had expected. He had seen nothing like that in a cafe before. It was like he was standing inside a living room. Initially, that had attracted Bellamy. And the warmth of the cafe. But the charm of a new place could only last so long.

As a customer, it was inviting, a place for conversations, meals, and games with friends.

But as a worker, it had its... difficulties.

He did not know why Emmy enjoyed working here after so many years. He had tried for weeks to see the job the way she did, but he just couldn't see the appeal.

Emmy bustled past the counter, keeping busy tidying things while pretending not to notice him.

She had promised to let him have more responsibility at the cafe and gifted him with the counter and all the work it entailed.

Astonishingly, Emmy had kept to her word while she had taken to tidying the cafe and cleaning the dishes from the table as he served the customers at the counter.

She was slowly warming to him, and he was grateful. She had even loosened her grip on the reins of the cafe. What he didn't expect was for her to let him run things, even if it was for a weekend.

While he appreciated the sentiment, this wasn't what he wanted. He had expected them to work together. To banter and to play and maybe even argue, occasionally.

She thought this was what he had wanted.

And it wasn't.

When he first met Emmy, it didn't take him long to realise that she wasn't all that happy to meet him. He thought it must have been something he said, but as time passed, he realised that Emmy just wasn't happy with his presence there.

Since there wasn't much he could do about that, he stopped trying. After a month of arguing, she suddenly got along with him. They talked and listen to each other, instead of assuming the other's motive.

He never felt that he could speak openly with anyone, but she was someone he could be honest with, and that was mainly because they had gotten to a point where there wasn't much left to say that would permanently damage their friendship.

They had said enough already.

There was a lull of half an hour before the next customer arrived. Bellamy, who was watching Emmy talk to an old man, turned toward the ding made by the chiming of the doorbell as another customer entered.

An older, wiry woman with greying hair and large sagging eyes barged in through the door, battling with a tattered bag hanging on her arm. Her hair came to a blunt end at her chin, curling in at the ends and her eyes were like sludgy ice. Her eyes landed on Bellamy and she pursed her lips.

The pleasant expression he had plastered on his face when he walked into the cafe that morning had worn off since he arrived. Bellamy forced a smile to his lips. It had been genuine enough throughout most of his shift, but it had slipped as he dealt with the next customer.

It was a young woman, a little older than him, maybe over twenty-five. A student, he suspected, grabbing a late breakfast on her way to uni.

She changed her order four times while she complained about the times of the trains while holding up the queue. He served her, which gave him five seconds of peace.

EMMY IN THE CAFE

Bellamy smiled at the new customer in front of him, but the woman didn't return it. She hobbled to the counter and shoved her hand inside her tattered black bag.

"Coffee, one sugar, a bit of milk. To go." She demanded.

Bellamy nodded. Emmy appeared at his side and began making the coffee while the older woman waited, her eyes cold and narrowed.

If Bellamy had to say what he hated most about the cafe, he would say dealing with the customers. They would drift in once in a while, forcing him to paste a pleasant expression on his face to greet them. No matter how they treated him.

Emmy handed him the coffee, which he gave to the woman who handed him the exact change with a mumble, before shuffling out of the cafe.

He kept his smile in place, though it made his cheeks ache to where he thought the corners of his mouth may tear. Emmy crept away to some other part of the cafe he probably hadn't seen yet before he could say anything to her.

He pushed his sleeves further up his arm and fixed his apron around his waist for the second time that day. His eyes followed Emmy as she strode away. She pushed a chair under a table as she went and after a second; she glanced back at him, tugging at her sleeve. Her eyes flicked down at the counter and he could see that something distracted her.

It was as if she didn't know what to do next and was looking at the counter for guidance. When she saw him watching, she jerked her hand up in a wave, then turned away to walk upstairs.

Emmy was probably trying to fight the urge to take control again. A part of him wished she would. He knew that if he asked her to, she would happily take over. She would deal with everyone that came in, and he could wash the dishes, wipe the tables, and wish that things were different. That he was the one complaining about the late trains taking him to a faraway university.

But he couldn't do that. It wouldn't be fair. Not to Emmy. Not to Janey or his mother.

It was just a job. A job he wouldn't have to do much longer once his mother started her job. She had promised he could finish at the cafe when she did.

He wiped down the counter and waited for the next customer to arrive. After a few minutes, he wished for the end of the shift. It would thrill him if no other customer came in for the rest of the day. But he wasn't that lucky.

The day was busy. Emmy had to join him again at the counter a few times to serve the people that ducked in, hiding from the sun and the rising heat. After a rush of customers, things slowed down and Emmy retreated to the kitchen.

An hour later, the door swung open again, and a man walked in. He was older than Bellamy, in his thirties, with sandy hair.

He strolled up to the counter, not bothering to look up from his newspaper at Bellamy. "Um, can I have tea and a tuna melt?" he said absently, flicking through pages.

Bellamy cleared his throat, but it did nothing to gain the other man's attention. "Are you... eating here or..."

The man was silent for a moment as he read. Bellamy folded his arms over his chest and waited, exasperated.

The man finished reading and glanced up at him. "Er, no, I'm going."

"What kind of tea?" Bellamy asked quickly before the man became lost in his newspaper again.

Bellamy was trying to stay patient, but he had enough of waiting on people who acted like the world revolved around them.

"Regular, two sugars, almond milk."

Out of the corner of his eye, Bellamy saw Emmy slip back in behind the counter beside him, her own eyes fixed on the customer. "I'll get it. You take the tables." She raised a hand and patted Bellamy on his arm, nudging him out of the way.

He took a step away and went to work sorting the tables and collecting the dishes. When he looked back, Emmy was smiling at the man, though he did not know what for, since the situation was hardly amusing as far as he saw.

As the man left, the bell rang, and a family tumbled into the cafe. A mother, father, their two adolescent daughters, and a baby boy in a stroller.

Bellamy did everything he could to not groan out loud at the sight. Thankfully, Emmy waved him away as soon as the baby screamed.

There were now only a few people remaining in the cafe focused on themselves, though some kept glancing at the family with the screaming baby.

Bellamy retreated upstairs to the second landing, but the yells of the children and their parents' feeble attempts to keep them quiet followed him.

He was pretty sure neither he nor Janey ever caused their parents this much trouble. He thought of his own mother and the way he had always tried to make life easier for her whenever he could.

He looked around at the landing, at the stuffed pale cream couches lined along the wood-panelled wall, and he comforted himself with the thought that he wouldn't be working here much longer once his mother started her new job.

A part of him thought that the time couldn't come soon enough. The customers were a handful, and having to wake up early in the morning to serve self-centred people wasn't what he wanted.

Another part of him, a smaller, but more insistent part, dreaded the day he would have to leave.

Because, although he hated almost everything about the cafe, he knew he would miss Emmy, as absurd as the idea was.

About fifteen minutes later, the bell rang again, but this time, the sounds of the family faded out into the street. Bellamy looked out of the window and saw the parents wrestling their kids down the street.

When he walked back down the stairs, he could see that the cafe had emptied, which left only Emmy.

The air rushed out of him as he deflated, and this time Bellamy sighed in contentment.

"Finally." He huffed to the empty interior and his voice rattled around the room. He felt relief wash over him, in a refreshing wave from his neck and down his spine. He dragged his hands over his face and glanced at the clock. It was almost time for them to close. No one else would come in so near to closing.

He crossed the room to the cafe door and flipped the sign to say 'closed'.

He turned around and saw Emmy looking at him from behind the counter. Her brow furrowed, and her eyes narrowed in confusion. She opened her mouth as if she wanted to say something. If someone walked in right now, they would have thought that he insulted her, and perhaps he had.

She glanced toward the door and then back at him. "W-what's wrong? I... You...?" She pointed to the door. "You don't...? Today wasn't that bad, was it?"

Bellamy dragged out one chair from under the table and collapsed into it. "No. It was just a regular day at the cafe. But this," he motioned to the rest of the room. "is not my idea of fun. Especially with customers like that." He pointed at the door. "I know it's yours, but then again, you are strange."

Emmy walked around the counter and stood opposite him. She placed her hands on her hips, her mouth open in indignation. "I thought you were enjoying it here. That you were... you know... having fun working here."

Bellamy leaned back in the chair, stretching his legs out in front of him. He dropped his head onto the back of the chair and sighed.

"I try." He mumbled. "And sometimes, I do. When it's just us and we don't have to deal with any customers, it's fun. But not when we have a large group of hungry people yelling for our food and attention. I know you love it because you like to wait on strangers who might say something nice to you. But I just don't see this place like you do."

He raised his head in time to see Emmy pull back, and he regretted the words that fell out of his mouth.

It was an insult to her. He could see the self-consciousness in her eyes at his dismissal of the place she loved. Her relationship with the place was more complicated than he could work out.

She was having trouble understanding how someone could dislike working in the place that she loved. He wondered for a brief second if she thought he disliked her.

He didn't.

She was his favourite thing about the place.

They always argued, but that was because they both had strong opinions and he liked that. Emmy was responsible and determined and always true to her word. She can be stubborn, but will admit when she was wrong. She also noticed details about other people and cared enough to remember them.

Marsh's was more than a cafe to her. It was a home, a place she belonged, an extension of her.

It wasn't just the people she cared about. It was the sense of satisfaction she got from being in control of this small space. There was safety in the routine, and in seeing the same faces every day. The safe excitement of meeting a new customer every once in a while.

They would always need her at a cafe this small. It was the centre of her world, a haven for her, and a lot more.

It just wasn't like that to him.

She shook her head in disbelief. "But you've been so involved in everything-"

Bellamy stood up and pushed his chair back under the table. "Like an excellent manager, you mean?"

Emmy shook her head again. "Yeah, but you're always on time. You even come to work early."

"Like an outstanding employee?"

"And you picked me up that morning when you showed up for the keys. You didn't need the keys, you suggested it."

Bellamy stared at her. "Well, I did promise to be an excellent employee and a good friend. I didn't want to be a liar. But you thought I was trying to one-up you, didn't you?"

Emmy stepped away. "That's not true. I did not say that."

Now that he was being honest, he couldn't seem to stop. He knew it sounded like he was attacking her, but everything he had wanted to say came pouring out of his mouth. "But it's not far off from what you're thinking, is it? You were afraid I'd steal your job, but I never wanted it." Bellamy stood still, watching her.

"You're assuming quite a lot." She hissed. She turned and marched to the kitchen. "You know nothing about me. You're just assuming."

Ever since he had arrived, Emmy always had been transparent with how she felt, whether she meant to be. The latter was probably true, but her emotions showed up on her face, in the crease of her brow and her wide, expressive eyes. She would sulk when she thought no one saw and smile too brightly when everyone was watching.

Bellamy followed behind her, his frustration growing. He had enough of the job and pretending to be the best manager. It didn't come naturally to him as it did to Emmy. Taking charge was second nature to her, while he had to take on another persona to be that person.

He wanted her to understand that. He wanted her to understand him.

"And you don't know me, but you were happy to make assumptions instead of just talking to me?

I have been watching you. You act like you're forced into working hard, but you like it when people need you. That's why you do whatever your friends need. Whether they ask you to."

He knew he had pushed too hard when she stopped and turned to face him.

Emmy scowled up at him. "You know nothing about my friends. Or me! You haven't even been here that long!"

"Long enough to know that you need people to need you. You need to be here because you don't have a life outside of this job."

"I do!"

"You worked here on the weekdays, you hung out here on the weekends, then even when your shifts changed, you hung out on the weekdays and you worked here on the weekends!"

"With my friends! Who likes it here!"

"Is that all? Or is there another reason? Because you didn't want me here! You didn't want to change. I tried! I really did, but it's not like I can do anything about that, because you need to be in charge, and you hate that I am! Even now, you're trying to fight it, but you couldn't help yourself today."

Emmy barked a harsh laugh and folded her arms over her chest. "I thought you didn't mind. You just said that the customers were too much for you."

"You didn't know that!" He didn't mind what she did, but it proved just how addicted to the cafe she was.

Emmy lowered her eyes to the floor, and her shoulders slumped with them. "Fine! Fine!" She relented. "That might be true. I do like it here, and yes, I like to be in charge, and no, I don't like change. I just don't see the need to change things if they work. Is that so bad? That I'm comfortable?"

"No. But, are you? Comfortable? Happy? Because you don't relax. Ever. You worry and complain."

"I was happy before..."

Emmy's words died in her throat, and she swallowed them. "Before I showed up." He finished bitterly.

Emmy faltered. "I... yes, but it's not like that. It's not you. I know that. I felt like that once... that it was you... before everything. But, I don't hate you. I like you."

Emmy's words were heavy in the air. Bellamy's chest rose and fell four times before he responded. "Is that true?"

Emmy looked down at the floor again, and her hands pulled at her sleeves. She sighed. "I was thinking it was... interesting to compete with someone." She shrugged. "Besides, what's wrong with wanting people to need you to you help them? People barely noticed me at school, and they do here. No, I don't have a life outside of this, but I'm happier here."

"I thought you wanted to go to university. History, right? What about that?"

Emmy shrunk back. "What about it?"

"You don't want to go?"

"Yes... No. I- No, I said I'm fine here."

"No, you're not. You're happy to bend over backwards for everyone else but yourself."

"Do you want me to admit it, then? Yes, I want to go, but I'm happy here, as I am. I don't need this."

"You don't know how lucky you are. At least you can leave. Because you're wrong. No one needs you here. They want you here, they're your friends, and they will miss you, sure. But you get to leave. Your family can cope without you."

Emmy stared up at him. Her eyes widened, and he realised he had said too much.

He turned away from her and walked to the front door, grabbing his jacket.

"Are you done? I need to get home."

Emmy nodded once and collected her own coat from the back storeroom. They stepped outside the cafe and stood in silence as Bellamy locked the door behind them.

They paused for a moment on the pavement, afraid to make direct eye contact with the other, before they turned and started walking down the road.

He had been wrong before. He had told her too much, and it had ruined whatever friendship they had. They hadn't been through enough. They still didn't know each other.

"Bellamy! There you are." Bellamy looked up and saw his mother towing his younger sister along the street toward him and Emmy. He glanced down and saw Emmy watching the two of them with curiosity.

Olivia smiled at Bellamy. "Finished your shift?" She asked as Janey dropped Olivia's hand to pick up Bellamy's. He squeezed her hand, and she grinned up at him.

Olivia noticed Emmy and turned to her. "Hello. Are you Emmy?" she questioned her with a smile.

"Yes," Bellamy answered before Emmy could. He didn't think now was the best time to put her on the spot. He extended his hand to his family. "Emmy, this is my mother, Olivia, and you've already met my sister Janey."

"Nice to meet you. And to see you again, Janey." Emmy greeted, raising her hand to wave at Janey.

Janey smiled shyly and rested her head against Bellamy's leg.

"You too, dear." His mother responded, smiling back at Emmy. "Janey hasn't stopped talking about you since the fair. And Bellamy's said lovely things about you, too."

Embarrassed, Emmy glanced at Bellamy out of the corner of her eye. "Did he?" she asked Olivia.

Bellamy cleared his throat before Olivia could say more. He had mentioned Emmy a few times in passing when talking about his day, and she had picked up on it.

"Let's go. I'll see you later, Emmy." Bellamy tugged his sister's hand and steered her away from Emmy and led his family away from her cafe.

True, he wanted to get along with Emmy and earn his pay, but he hated his job.

Emmy thought of the job as some kind of paradise, while to him it was just his hell.

CHAPTER THIRTEEN
BELLAMY IN THE CAFE

Bellamy dodged out of his mother's way just before she collided with him. She had finished dusting the cabinet in the living room and turned to leave just as he walked into the room.

Olivia barely noticed and continued past him into the hallway. She came back a few seconds later and bustled around the living room, fixing the cushions on the chair. Bellamy collapsed on one of the dining chairs, resting his head on his palm.

"We need new curtains." Olivia sighed. "And new tables, chairs. Maybe some new sheets for the beds."

Bellamy nodded and closed his eyes. His mother continued talking, and he tried to follow her words, but they were all blurred together.

His eyes felt heavy, and he struggled to keep them open. He had collapsed into his bed after he came back home on Sunday evening. There had been more customers than the day before, and he was grateful since they acted as a buffer between him and Emmy.

Olivia kept talking, fluttering around the room, fluffing the pillows, and talking a mile a minute. He smiled and tried to say something, anything positive, but it came out as slurred nonsense. His mother didn't notice and kept going.

He closed his eyes for a second and when he opened them, his mother was in the kitchen asking questions and answering them in the next breath.

"I'll pick Janey up from school today." She said, looking through their cupboards. "But I'll need you to get some groceries for me. And then you can have a sleep."

Bellamy nodded and yawned. He drifted in and out of the conversation a few times before she finally left the kitchen, still chattering.

Olivia sat down in front of her laptop at the dining table. When she had gotten up that morning, she had paid bills and checking accounts.

His mother's new job at the council meant they had more money to spend. She had taken up other jobs but had not earned enough for them to live on, so Bellamy got a job when his father left. For the past year, Olivia had been at home while Bellamy worked. Now that they were both working, they would have to take turns looking after Janey. Bellamy was optimistic that things will be better soon.

"We must figure out something for Janey." She continued. "I'll be working long hours, so we need to know who'll pick up Janey on what days. I'll get the times and days I'll be working soon. It'll be official. You can pick her up on the weekdays. Oh, but I'll need the car... I could take her. But what about the weekends? You're still working those, and I..."

"I've been thinking about that." Bellamy yawned as he sat forward. Olivia raised her eyes from the screen to look at him. "I think I know someone who might be interested in looking after her on the weekends."

"Oh,..... really?"

Bellamy nodded. He dragged himself out of the chair and stretched. "Her name is Tilda, and Janey's already met her and Matt. She has a brother, and she wants him to have a friend or two. We took them to the cinema, and they took us to the fair."

Olivia nodded. "I've heard about Matt. Janey wouldn't stop talking about him and his sister."

"Yeah, I can ask Tilda."

Olivia hesitated, her eyes wary. "Do you think she'll want to look after two kids on the weekends?"

Bellamy ran his hand over the arm of the chair. Tilda had talked about Matt and Janey getting together more often, and he had agreed. Tilda would do it for her brother's sake.

"Their parents just divorced, and I think Tilda would think that this would be good for Matt, too."

Olivia's shoulders stiffened, but she nodded her head. "Oh, yes, that would be a relief. Tell her we'll pay."

"Alright then." He answered. "I'm having a shower."

He left the room and headed to the bathroom. When he had showered and dressed, he went back into the living room. Olivia was contemplative. She stared at the couch, brushing her hand along the worn arm.

"We need new furniture." She whispered. "Maybe we can get some in a few weeks."

She started chattering again and began moving around the space, imagining the new furniture as she'd done for years.

"Well, you can look for some furniture online while I get the shopping and we can talk about it later."

She smiled at him and shook her head. "I'll wait for you to get back."

Bellamy shrugged on his new jacket. "No, you'll know what to pick. Just make sure you measure the place first. The tape's in your top drawer."

Olivia smiled. "So, you won't mind whatever I pick?"

Bellamy shook his head. "Why would I? It's your flat."

"It's yours too."

"Not for much longer, Mum. I've got to move out soon."

Olivia smiled. He walked over to her and leaned down to hug her. She wrapped her arms around him and gave him a tight hug.

"Still love you." He mumbled against her shoulder.

She sniffed, tutted at him, and fixed his jacket and hair. "No son of mine is going out looking like that." She picked up a brush lying on the table in the centre of the carpeted floor and began brushing his hair.

He leaned down and let her brush his hair back, but soon he realised she was going over his hair, with no intention of stopping. "I've got to go, Mum." He mumbled.

She relented and put down the brush.

"I love you." She whispered.

"Love you too."

He kissed her cheek and walked out of the front door. He walked past the doors of their neighbours, then out of the main gate of their flat and down the ramp.

It should have been a much shorter trip than it was. Olivia expected him back in about forty minutes.

It didn't take him long to get to the cash machine and get the cash. He should have taken half an hour to shop, but he had to travel to the supermarket and that was just over half an hour for the round trip.

He took the car, but he would have to bring it back so that Olivia could use it to pick up Janey.

He drove down the street and made a detour down the road to a store that sold new household ornaments.

The first time he walked outside of the antique store with Emmy, he had hated it. More than any store he had ever walked in. For years, his mother had gone on and on about buying new furniture for the house, so he got something for her, something she didn't have to buy, something new.

The problem at first was he didn't have any idea what to buy.

He trudged over to the displays to see what he could find.

Small ornaments and pillows and other things filled the shelves. Bellamy saw nothing worth buying, but maybe his mother would. Having one little knick-knack for her to display, something she could say was a gift from her son.

He picked up a ceramic bird and turned it over. On the bottom, it had a sticker which labelled the price as £43.99. He placed it back where it came from with much more care than he had when he first picked it up before moving along the aisle to continue his search.

He stopped when he saw a silver candle holder. Olivia didn't use candles much, but it would be nice enough to decorate the table.

Bellamy moved further down the aisles and found curtains and sheets neatly lined up. He picked up a pack of curtains spotted with faint green flowers. Turning it over, he checks to see the price. It cost £12.99, so he figured it was something Olivia would like for the house.

He walked down the aisle a few steps and found bedsheets. After picking out sheets for Janey, Olivia, and himself, he paid for the sheets, the curtains, and the candlestick and left the store.

He checked his list as he entered through the sliding doors of the supermarket. His mother had written out a list of groceries to get on his way out of the door. It was most of the same things that they bought, but he checked the list all the same.

He was standing in the middle of one of the frozen foods sections, trying to remember the brand of frozen vegetables Olivia preferred, when he heard a voice over his left shoulder.

"I didn't think I'd see you here. Don't you live further away? Why are you shopping here?"

Bellamy turned around and saw Emmy standing behind him, bouncing on the balls of her toes. She stood next to a trolley that was filled high with groceries. She had stacked boxes of cereal precariously on top of packets of biscuits, cartons of apple juice, orange juice, and milk. Fruits were mixed with fresh vegetables, covering assortments of household spices, and an assortment of tinned and dry foods.

She pushed the trolley back and forth and gave him a small, reserved smile. Bellamy returned it. He hadn't seen her since their last exchange at the cafe.

"Oh, yeah," he answered, slowly. "My mum usually does the shopping here. We've been coming here for years."

Emmy looked surprised. "Oh. I thought you didn't come from around here."

"I wouldn't have taken a job too far from home."

"Uncle Fred's exact words were that you didn't live near, but 'local'."

He was silent for a few moments. He shifted his basket to his other hand and scratched his head with his free one. "I'm sorry for what I said to you at the cafe. This job isn't exactly what I would have picked if I had a choice, but I don't want to sound ungrateful. Or insult you."

Emmy shook her head, rocking forward onto her toes. "You didn't. And I'm sorry too. I think I might have overacted a bit. It's a stressful job. I get it. It gets me a little fed up sometimes, too. But I thought you did like it, like me. At least, a bit."

Bellamy noticed the double meaning of her words but ignored it when she turned her head away and chuckled. "To be honest? I never really liked it. The cafe, I mean."

Emmy wilted where she stood and glanced around as a shopper ambled past them in the aisle, a basket dangling from his hand. She watched him leave before she turned back to him. "What... what do you mean?"

He lowered his head. "I think any fun I got out of it had less to do with the job. I like working with you."

Emmy cocked her head to the side and took a deep breath. "Well, I've had fun too. I guess you've made me more outgoing. I have something to tell you, too." She whispered.

"What?"

"I can't tell you right now. But, I'll let you know. I have to... finalise things first." She smiled mischievously, swinging her arms around her.

She looked away and let out another deep breath. "All that time I spend thinking you were trying to outdo me... Tilda tried to tell me, but Tilda says a lot of things. Strange things that you shouldn't always believe." She stared down at the floor.

Bellamy raised his eyes to the ceiling. "You mean, like when she said that you don't like Darcy?"

Emmy folded her arms. "I never said I didn't like Darcy! I... I love Darcy! I think she's fun and sweet. I have nothing against her." Emmy's voice had risen in pitch, and neither she nor Bellamy believed what she had just said.

She sighed. "I just... you get on with her better. And I felt left out, that's all."

Now that they were talking, he wasn't ready to stop. "What about when Tilda called you my work wife?"

Emmy blinked uncertainly. "She was just joking. She thought that I... She just said it because we work... together."

Bellamy nodded. The first day that he started at Marsh's, she had complained about a lack of sleep. He had asked her if it had anything to do with him, and she had lied. He knew it was a lie.

And perhaps he wanted it to be.

"Why would she think you have a problem with Darcy?"

Emmy shrugged and ran a hand along the handle of her trolley. "Not Darcy... Not, really. Not specifically. She just thought I was jealous of you and Darcy."

Bellamy started walking along the aisle, and Emmy followed, pushing her overflowing trolley ahead of her. "Are you?" He whispered, not looking at her.

Emmy nearly steered the trolley over his foot, but she swerved at the last second. "No. No, you're... we're not even... and I don't have a problem. Tilda's just exaggerating things. If you wanted to date Darcy-"

"Who said I wanted to date Darcy?"

Emmy froze. "Henry." She intoned. "He might have suggested that the two of you were getting close. He keeps trying to tease me because he thinks that I... That I like you. Which I don't, so don't worry about that. Tilda's been talking to him too... and..."

He didn't believe that as much as he would have a few months ago.

"You don't?" He asked.

Emmy scoffed, and she looked around to see who else had heard. "No! I mean, I like you just fine, as a friend. But I don't want..."

"Ok." Bellamy passed his basket from one hand to another. "I like you too, you know, as a friend. And I like Darcy, as a friend."

There was a difference in their friendships, but the overall message was true, and it was enough for Emmy to relax. She tilted her head. "Really? Do you think so? Because I wasn't sure we were. Officially. We have had difficulties."

He wouldn't disagree with her about that. "At first. But you bark more than you bite."

Emmy turned her trolley into the bakery aisle. "I'd bite if I had to."

Bellamy chuckled and followed behind her. "It won't matter soon. I don't think I'll be at Marsh's much longer."

Emmy stilled and brought her trolley to a wobbly stop. "Why?"

Bellamy rubbed the back of his neck. "I'm thinking about leaving the cafe."

Emmy's face dropped, and he wanted to change his answer, but it was too late.

"My mother got a new job. She'll be starting soon, and I won't need to take so many shifts, because she'll be making a lot more money so... And there's Janey. She needs someone to help look after her."

Emmy nodded her head. "Well, when are you thinking of leaving?"

Bellamy shrugged. "I don't know yet."

Emmy nodded again, taking more interest in her trolley. "So, I'll see you this Saturday?"

She picked up a packet of crackers that was teetering on a bag of apples and started reorganising her trolley.

Bellamy wanted to say something else, but Emmy seemed preoccupied with stacking her shopping. "Yeah. You still need to tell me about how I've made you more outgoing."

She nodded stiffly. "Yep. Well, then... I'll see you then." She looked up at him from her trolley and, giving him a sad smile, she pushed her trolley in the opposite direction. Bellamy wanted to call her back and say something, but he did not know what he wanted to say, so instead, he returned to his shopping.

Bellamy wandered around the rest of the supermarket and threw the rest of his shopping in the basket, paying less and less attention to the brands.

He knew them by heart, so double-checking them made less sense.

As he passed through the aisles, Bellamy looked for Emmy, but she had disappeared completely. He scanned the checkout, but she wasn't at any of the tills.

When he returned home, Bellamy would have liked nothing more than to go back to sleep, but his mobile rang, dashing his hopes.

He took out his phone and glanced down at the screen. Tilda had left him a message. She had texted him to come down to the gym to talk about Matt and Janey.

He had texted her about taking Janey to stay with her and Matt on some evenings before he walked out of his house that afternoon.

Tilda herself had mentioned wanting them to spend more time together so that Matt would have a friend. Bellamy agreed it was a good idea for them to make friends, even if Matt was a little older.

He dropped off the bags in the kitchen, leaving his mother to unpack them before he slipped back out and headed to the gym. The rain poured, but he just flipped his hood up to deflect the water.

Bellamy arrived around twenty minutes later, soaking wet and grimacing as he entered. He didn't like the gym. It just wasn't something he was interested in.

He thought about Emmy running with Henry on the early Thursday mornings and how well that had gone between them. They had come back after, flustered and silent with one another. Bellamy had assumed that it was just the run, but he had noticed that Emmy had always been much quieter in Darcy's presence.

Bellamy walked in through the glass door and almost ducked right back out when he saw Henry talking to Tilda at the reception counter. Henry had clarified that he was still up to training him, though Bellamy had repeatedly declined.

But before he could even take a step back, Tilda looked up and waved at him, beaming. Bellamy took a step forward and out of the corner of his eye, he saw Darcy coming to join them.

He never wondered if Darcy liked him more than a friend. He didn't think she did, and she hadn't acted as if she did.

Despite what Emmy said, she was jealous. He could always tell when she was upset, but not always why. Emmy never liked to be very open with her feelings.

Neither was he, so he couldn't judge. He had hoped that she would give him some sign of what he could do to help, but that was the one thing she was good at hiding.

The why.

Tilda rushed over to him and clasped her hands together. "So, I'd love to babysit Janey, and Matt would love to have her over. It's perfect!" Tilda beamed.

"I'm glad. I wasn't sure that you would."

Tilda's face fell. "Why wouldn't I? Your sister is so sweet, and it's good for Matt to have some friends. My dad's been trying to get us all to talk, and it might work, but Matty's happiest with friends, so thank you."

Bellamy dismissed her thanks with a wave of his hand. "It's fine. My mum's willing to pay you."

Tilda shook her head and made a face at the idea. "No! It's fine, I'll do it. No need to twist my arm."

A weight lifted from Bellamy's shoulders, and he exhaled. They joined both Henry and Darcy at the counter, and he relaxed with the group.

Bellamy listened to Tilda, Henry, and Darcy as they all chatted with each other, only making vague sounds of agreement whenever they asked his opinion.

There was only one concern on his mind.

As they continued to talk, he wondered how right his speculations about Emmy's genuine feelings were and what would it take for her to admit them.

EMMY IN THE CAFE

CHAPTER FOURTEEN
EMMY IN THE CAFE

Sunlight glittered across the room as a car sailed past the cafe window, the only thing in motion on such a quiet Saturday morning. Emmy followed the car with her eyes and returned her focus to the couple curled away in the corner.

She tapped her fingers on the counter while her other hand propped up her chin, watching with mild curiosity as Eric and Lianne cooed over one another next to the window. The rest of the cafe was empty, with a few stray people sipping from their mugs, their heads down, and their attention elsewhere.

Emmy couldn't believe that Lianne and Eric's meeting at Katherine's party would end with them as a couple. She had known little about Eric herself, but knew Lianne. Or at least, she knew enough about her from Katherine to know that Eric wasn't her usual type.

A shadow loomed over Emmy as Bellamy came to stand next to her, following the direction of her gaze. He tapped her on her arm, breaking her concentration. "It's rude to stare." He chided, resting his elbows on the counter next to her.

Emmy looked up at him and dragged herself from the top counter, yawning. She hadn't yet talked to him about the idea of him leaving the cafe, and she didn't want to.

She stretched her arms over her head as she stood up straighter, determined not to discuss the issue. "I wasn't. Well, not really. I just... saw... them." She gestured in Eric's and Lianne's direction. "I thought they might've needed me."

She turned her back on the couple to make her lack of interest a point, but Bellamy's eyes were sceptical. He said nothing to that. He just pulled at the cuff of his sleeve, unbuttoning it and rolling the sleeve up to his elbow.

Emmy squirmed, even though he wasn't looking at her. "I'm serious." She insisted. "They might have wanted something to eat, or something-"

He finished his task and let his arms fall to his sides. "I'm sure they'd say. So, no need to keep staring. Why were you staring?"

"I was not." Emmy waved him away.

"Were you trying to hear what they were saying?" Bellamy demanded.

"No, I wasn't doing that either." Emmy insisted.

"Then what were you doing?"

"I was just thinking."

"If you were just thinking, then you can help me move the boxes in the back."

Emmy heaved a sigh as she followed him into the storeroom, craning her neck to watch Lianne and Eric. "I didn't think they'd be a thing." She whispered to Bellamy as she passed him a box, leaning in close so that the couple didn't hear them. Though that didn't seem to be a problem, since they didn't appear to notice that anyone else was there, let alone watching them.

Bellamy leaned down next to her and took the box from her, chuckling, his voice rumbling in his chest. "Neither did I. Strange couple. Still, it hasn't been that long. Any minute now, they could start fighting."

The couple nuzzled closer to one another. Emmy scoffed as she picked up another box. "I guess not every couple is us."

"No? I thought that's what people did." He said, his voice heavy with sarcasm. Emmy's hand brushed against his as he took the box, but Bellamy barely seemed to notice as he continued. "What do you think they see in each other?"

Emmy lifted a shoulder. "They must have something in common. A hobby or something."

"Maybe, but not necessarily," Bellamy said absently as he picked up another box and moved it to sit with the others.

"Then, what?" Emmy asked.

He shrugged, his expression pensive as he watched them. "Well, Emmy," he started, standing up taller, "maybe they just like each other's personalities."

Emmy frowned. "And how long will that last?"

"You sound cynical."

"And you're not?"

Bellamy chuckled. "Who, me? I'm a romantic."

"Since when?"

"Since always. I think they just liked each other as soon as they met."

"What, in the two seconds that I was looking the other way?"

"Sometimes you can be very observant, and other times you're as blind as a bat."

Emmy shrugged her shoulders. "Maybe you're right."

The couple in question suddenly broke apart from each other and then realised that other people existed inside the cafe. Lianne raised her hand to wave it in their direction. Emmy took a step to the counter to wait on them, but Bellamy stretched his arm out and Emmy came to an abrupt stop. She looked up at him, puzzled, but he shook his head.

"I'll go." He said. "If that's okay with you. Can't have you meddling in their love affair. Again."

"I didn't know I was meddling the first time. And you didn't either."

"But at least I brought them together."

Emmy raised her hands in surrender, smiling at the memory, and went back to the counter at a slower pace, watching the couple as Bellamy joined them.

She ran her hand over the counter, feeling the stray sugar granules on the counter, and her mind drifted to her sleeping computer laying on the middle of her bed.

She spent the rest of the day wondering about both Lianne and Eric, and her unfinished university application, even as she sat in Bellamy's car as he dropped her home.

****

Evening light bled in through the window to spill on the floor of Emmy's room, staining everything golden yellow. It was just gone past seven in the evening and the sun was only just setting. Emmy had been sitting in her bedroom at the end of her bed with her forms and her books on the bed next to her.

An hour ago, she had completed a university application for a course in history. She still couldn't believe that she had gone through with it. Ever since she had gotten Bellamy more shifts at the cafe, she had worked on her application.

She tried to keep herself from thinking too hard about what she was doing. Fill out the profile. Ask an old teacher for a reference. Write a personal statement. It was a lot easier than she had thought it would be.

She had been afraid of what would happen if she went through with it, but she realised she was more afraid of what would happen if she hadn't.

The sounds of laughter floated up to her from downstairs as she lay on her bed. Her mother, Lisa, had arrived at the house three hours ago to visit Emmy and the rest of the family.

The last time she saw Lisa was after dinner. Lisa had cooked for the family and together they had sat around the table discussing recent events. Emmy had told no one about her decision just yet. She hadn't wanted to until it was final, when she couldn't back out of it. She had hesitated even as she clicked to send in her application, but she did it before she had gone downstairs and joined her family for dinner.

Since Bellamy's arrival was announced over dinner, it was only right that his departure was discussed at another one.

After dinner, Lisa had gone into the living room with Fred to watch a movie. Noah and Lucy had gone straight to their rooms. As Emmy passed Noah's room, she could hear him snoring loudly, a sign that he was in a deep sleep. Lucy's room was quiet, and so Emmy could only assume that she was studying for one of her exams.

Lucy had complained for most of the evening about needing a job. She pestered Fred about his offer for a job, but now that he was in better shape, he had taken on more responsibilities.

It reminded her of what Bellamy had told her. She couldn't imagine the cafe without him. She had become so accustomed to having him there and bickering with him.

She supposed that was the push that she needed to send in her application.

Emmy arched her back as she stretched her arms up to the ceiling. She dragged her hand over the covers of the books. She would tell them all tomorrow, she decided, before she got ready for bed.

The next day she trudged down the stairs, the sounds of downstairs became louder as she did. She supposed it was the best time to tell her mother, anyway, after breakfast and before her leaving for work.

Lisa and Fred were once again sat on the couches that Emmy had last seen them on. Once she stepped into the room, they turned their attention to her. She knew what that would say about her decision, but she was annoyed at proving them right. She sat down in front of them and told them her news.

It went as she expected. Lisa and Fred were both pleased for her. Lisa went on and on about how she always knew that Emmy would go and that she should have listened to her sooner.

Forty minutes later, Emmy finally escaped her house and her family. Lisa had declared Emmy's news a cause for a celebration and she had dragged Lucy and Noah back downstairs for breakfast. Lisa had wanted to go on and on about it, but Emmy slipped away out of the front door to the cafe.

Emmy shifted her bag on her back once she got outside and walked down the street. She had been so stuck in her own thoughts she didn't notice when a dark blue car drove up beside her as she walked along the pavement. She recognised the car before it came to a complete stop. It was Bellamy's.

He rolled down the window, and she crossed the pavement and leaned down by the passenger door so they were on eye level.

"Where are you headed?" He joked.

Emmy shrugged and adjusted the strap of her bag. "You know, around. I wasn't really going anywhere. I was just out for a walk." She answered lightly.

"So just a stroll, then? Nowhere in particular?" Bellamy asked. "So, I won't take you to the cafe then."

Emmy shook her head, feigning disinterest. "Nope." He nodded indulgently. "What are you doing here?" She asked.

Bellamy shrugged, not quite meeting her eyes. "I dropped by to tell you that you've got a day off. Andrea's taking you shift today."

Emmy raised her eyebrows in surprise. "Oh, that's nice of you." Once, the idea of time off would have annoyed her and she would have refused to take it, especially if Bellamy had been the one to tell her. But now, all she felt was relief.

"It's an apology. Kind of." He drawled, his eyes lowered and fixed on the door handle. "How about we go somewhere?"

Emmy leaned forward, tempted by the idea. The destination wasn't important to her, but she asked anyway. "Where are we going?"

Bellamy shrugged as his fingers drummed on the steering wheel. "Anywhere you like. Completely your choice."

She thought for a moment before she opened the door. "I want ice cream." She declared.

"Done."

Emmy climbed into the passenger seat, throwing her bag on the backseat of his car before she buckled up her seatbelt as Bellamy pulled away from the curb.

She rubbed her eyes as she stared out of the windshield at the road and cars ahead of them. "So, my mum is at the house, visiting. I just told her and Noah, Lucy, and Uncle Fred about me... applying for university."

Bellamy was silent for a second, and Emmy wondered if he had heard her. Before she could say anything else, he chuckled.

"To be honest, I never thought that you would do anything like that."

Emmy raised an eyebrow at him. "And why's that?"

He shrugged halfheartedly, his eyes on the road ahead. "You hate change."

Emmy rested her head back against the passenger seat and stretched out her feet. "Yeah, well, maybe I had some expert advice about doing things for myself."

Bellamy chuckled again. "Really? That changed your mind? A few months ago, you would have dug in your heels harder about staying. Now, look. You're ready to take my advice and do something for yourself."

Emmy smiled to herself. "Well, I definitely have to do that now I have a day off."

"Oh, you poor thing," Bellamy uttered with mock sincerity. "What will you do with all of your free time? We must find something for you to do."

"We?"

"Yes, we. If we're not going to the cafe, then we have to go somewhere else, don't we?"

Emmy grinned. "An ice cream parlour?"

"Done."

"You could have told me before I left the house, you know, and we wouldn't have to go anywhere." If Bellamy wanted to give her a day off, all he had to do was call her the day before and tell her, but he showed up in his car.

"And where's the fun in that?" He stated and Emmy hummed her agreement.

They drove to the nearest ice cream parlour in the area.

It wasn't anything like Marsh's.

Instead of the warm, natural, and rustic atmosphere, it was generic and stark, its only purpose as an eating establishment. He had to admit that's what most eating places did. Not everyone placed as much emphasis on where they ate as she did.

Bellamy paid for them both and they sat down at a small table by the store window, with their small tubs of ice cream.

"So? What is it?" Emmy sighed.

"What?" Bellamy answered, staring down at his ice cream.

"You want to talk about something, don't you? Come on. Tell me."

Bellamy took in a deep breath and raised his eyes to look at Emmy. "I won't be the manager for much longer. Mum's getting her new job soon and Fred's going to be back to take care of things-"

Emmy clasped her hands in front of her. She kept her eyes focused on them to avoid looking at him. "Really? He said that?"

Bellamy nodded. "He didn't tell you? He mentioned it yesterday when I called him to talk about my job. It was short term. Just to get you through everything."

That came as a bit of a surprise to her. She did not know that this was all arranged or why no one thought to tell her.

"And with you going to university... well, I don't want to leave you in the lurch or force you back in your job by leaving so soon. So, I wanted you to know what was going on and to say that I will stay here for as long as necessary until you find a decent replacement. Next week, I've switched our shifts with Andrea and Tania, since Fred's coming back."

Emmy didn't know what to say to that, so she just nodded. "Well, thanks, I guess."

They sat in silence for a few seconds before Emmy opened her mouth again.

"Are you planning to visit? Have you even told Tilda, or Henry, or everyone else?"

Bellamy shook his head. "Nope. The only person I told, besides Fred, is you?"

That made Emmy shift in her seat. She didn't dare to look at him and kept her eyes on her melting ice cream.

"Where would you like me to drop you off next?" He asked. He had barely touched his tub of ice cream, choosing instead to poke at it with his spoon.

Emmy hesitated for a second before raising her eyes to Bellamy.

"Can we stay here?" she smiled sadly, swirling the ice-cream in the container.

Emmy didn't like the thought that Bellamy could just leave and never come back.

She wondered what was the point in him coming to their cafe and disrupting everything if he was going to turn around and leave them, just as things were settling down. What was the point in getting to know him, if, in a few months, it would be as if he was never there?

"Sure." He answered. "We'll stay as long as you want."

She opened her mouth again, but it was only to swallow down the ice cream sitting in front of her, that had suddenly had no taste.

CHAPTER FIFTEEN
KATHERINE IN THE CAFE

Katherine paced the length of her room, unsure of what she was going to say to her mother. It was just past midday and the June sun was blazing in through the windows. Both her mother and her father had gone to work, leaving her all alone in the big, empty house.

This will give her time to find the perfect words to tell her mother about her new job to convince her to let her go. Katherine did not want to work with her mother at her estate agency.

Soft pale light bled in through her large bedroom windows and she stopped to admire how it lit up her room. The room had changed drastically in the past year and a half. She painted the pale lilac walls with cream and traded in her childish furniture for more sophisticated fittings.

Her mother, Caroline, picked out most of the decorations, which was why most of Katherine's furniture was different shades of silver or grey. Her headboard was a grey monstrosity that dominated her room. Opposite her bed was a large metallic desk. It was immaculate, well organised, like her wardrobe, shelves, and the rest of her room.

Caroline liked it, so Katherine liked it, but sometimes the room felt too big for her. Too austere.

She was just a cub following in the two big tracks of her lioness of a mother. If she strayed, she'd be lost.

Katherine smoothed her dress down as she walked and took a deep breath, shaking back her freshly curled hair over her shoulders.

Her hair and make-up were well-groomed, even though there was nowhere that she needed to be, though her feet were bare. They sank into the thick, wool grey carpet every time she took a step.

She knew she was going to have to tell her parents soon, but she had wanted to tell them after she had a few months at the job. That way, they wouldn't drag her away from it if they saw she was a success.

The doorbell rang loudly in the middle of the calm silence. With a sigh, she wrenched open her bedroom door and trekked downstairs to the hallway. She opened the front door and found Emmy twitching on the porch, looking dishevelled but brimming with excitement. Katherine appraised her and Emmy smiled, waiting patiently for Katherine to let her into the house.

"What are you doing here?" The question hadn't sounded so bad in her head, but as soon as it slipped out of her mouth, she realised how harsh she sounded.

Emmy's smile faltered like the flickering of a lightbulb, but she fixed it back in place. "That's always nice to hear from your friends." She joked. "I was in the area and thought we should talk. I haven't seen you in a while."

Katherine raised an eyebrow. "Is that so?" she wondered.

Emmy's enthusiasm dimmed to a fleeting smile, though this one was genuine and more like herself. "No. Bellamy dropped me off. He changed our shifts with Andrea and Tania so we can have today off. Again. Fred's back and he's been insisting on giving me and Bellamy more time off."

That surprised Katherine. She had heard a lot of speculation from everyone else about what had been going on with Bellamy and Emmy, but she wasn't sure how they had been getting along.

"Oh, alright." Katherine stood back and held the door open to allow Emmy to step inside. Emmy slipped in, keeping her arms firmly at her sides to keep from knocking over a vase that stood a foot away.

"So, I applied for university," Emmy announced to the hall.

"You did what? When did you apply?"

"A month ago. I had been working on it. And now, I've done it."

Again, Katherine was surprised. Emmy was one of the most predictable people she knew, but this was not her typical behaviour. "That's great. I'm honoured that you would think to tell me first."

Emmy looked bashful. "I only came over here because I had nothing to do, and then Bellamy asked where I wanted to go and your place was my first thought."

"You haven't yet told Tilda?"

Emmy frowned. "I'll tell her later. I still don't trust her to keep a secret." She joked.

"Why?" Katherine inquired. She didn't recall Tilda and Emmy ever fight with each other.

"She didn't tell you?" Emmy hesitated. "It was a while ago."

Katherine shook her head again, and Emmy nodded. "She made a... joke about me and... and Bellamy."

Katherine's brow furrowed as she waited for Emmy to continue.

"In front of him."

"Oh."

Katherine could acknowledge her own shortcomings and recognise the importance of becoming a better friend. She thought about the times she hadn't been a good one to Emmy, or the rest of her friends.

Katherine pushed her hair back from her face and breathe deeply. "I'm sorry for how I acted."

Emmy smiled. "It's fine. I'm guilty of being a terrible friend, too."

Katherine placed a hand on her hip and tilted her head to the side. "I never said I was terrible."

There was a pause between the two of them. "Didn't you?"

"No, I didn't."

Emmy shrugged. "Well, you kind of have been."

Katherine had to agree to that, too. She wasn't proud of the way she had treated her friends, but everything she said only made things worse between them. That might have something to do with the fact that of all the things she ever said to her friends, very few of them were apologies.

She had a problem admitting when she was wrong, and also with sharing things with the rest of them.

"I have something that I want to tell my mum." She admitted.

Emmy's brows creased as she leaned closer to hear better. "What's that?"

"You remember when I told you about the job I got?" The question was rhetorical and just to start the conversation, but Emmy raised her eyebrows higher and nodded.

"Of course, I do." She drawled. "How could I forget?"

"Well, now I need to tell my mother." There was silence, and it scared Katherine. Telling her mother was a big deal to her, but the lack of response from Emmy confirmed the relevance of her fear.

"What are you going to say?"

Katherine dragged her hands over her skirt. "I don't know."

"Well, what are you going to do?"

Katherine marched to her front door and grabbed her coat and keys. "I don't know. First, I need dessert. I'll worry about everything else later."

They left Katherine's house and headed for a dessert shop at Katherine's insistence, despite Emmy's protests, that she had already had dessert.

As always, it would be Katherine's treat. Emmy ordered a chocolate-covered waffle, but Katherine added on a chocolate milkshake. Emmy would never want to expense her. She was too selfless and unwilling to accept the gifts her friends offered her.

Emmy had turned around, stopping mid-sentence as they stood by the counter. Katherine raised her head to see why and saw Bellamy standing by the front door, accompanied by Darcy and Henry.

Someone brought their order to them and Katherine took it with a smile, handed Emmy's order to her. Bellamy, Henry, and Darcy walked over to the two of them, drawing their attention.

"Hey, what are you two doing here?" Henry asked.

"For dessert, Henry. I'm sure you're here for the same." Katherine quipped.

"Yes, we are, but you're so sweet. I wouldn't have thought you needed anything else," Henry answered.

Katherine rolled her eyes as her phone beeped. She checked the screen. It was her mother. She texted to tell Katherine that she would be home soon and would Katherine be wanting dinner. Katherine texted back a hasty reply. This was her chance.

She turned to Emmy. "I'm sorry, I have to go. It's my mum. Will you be okay getting home?"

"We'll take her," Bellamy answered. Katherine looked at Emmy for confirmation and gave him a curt nod. She waved goodbye to them and went home to meet her mother.

As she was leaving, she saw Bellamy move to stand closer to Emmy and wondered once again what was going on between them.

She hurried along the pavement to her car. She heard someone call her name, and as she turned, she almost ran into Aiden directly behind her.

He grabbed her by her forearms to steady her, then raised an eyebrow at her, annoyed. "Careful. Where are you going?"

"Home." She stated as if it was obvious.

To her surprise, Aiden looked concerned. "Is everything alright?"

"Yes. I just have to speak to my mom about something."

Aiden folded his arms, and his eyes narrowed. He had the same posture as her father when he interrogated her about her credit card balance last week. "Is it about your job?"

"Yes." Her voice wasn't as strong as she would have liked. She didn't want Aiden to think her weak.

Aiden dragged his hands over his face. "Do you want me to come with you?"

Katherine shook her head, surprised. "No... but thanks. I'll let you know how it goes."

Aiden had never been sympathetic, so it surprised her he was being so nice to her. She appreciated it, even if it was strange and misplaced.

Aiden turned to walk in the opposite direction, but at the last moment, he turned back to her.

"You throw the best parties. You'll be great at the job. Your mum will realise that and your dad too. It's all you do, so why not make a career out of it?"

Katherine smiled gratefully at him. That was the nicest thing that he had ever said to her. "Thanks... I'll see you later."

His mouth twitched as if he wanted to smile before he turned and walked away down the street.

***

When she arrived back home, she realised that she had arrived first. She marched back up to her room to wait as the sky outside darkened.

Katherine paced for half an hour before she heard a car pulling into the driveway. Katherine flicked back her hair over her shoulder and prepared herself for what would come next.

She went downstairs, smoothing down her blouse. She hurried to greet her mother as she opened the front door.

Her mother crossed the threshold in her pressed suit, her hair coiled on the top of her head. Her face scowled at the floor as she juggled shopping bags with the keys in her hands.

Katherine rushed forward and took them.

"Oh, thank you, darling," Caroline said absently, as she closed the front door.

Katherine stood awkwardly in the hallway. Caroline raised her eyebrows as she waited for her daughter to speak.

Katherine cleared her throat. "Mum, I've... I have something to say to you. Some news."

As her mother waited for Katherine to speak, the words got stuck in her throat.

"Yes?" questioned her mother.

"I... I've got a job."

Her mother frowned, and Katherine wanted to run away and hide in her room. "I thought you were going to work with me."

"Well, yes, but I applied for a job to work as an event organiser, and I got it. I'll be starting in a few weeks."

Caroline put down her purse and keys on the table by the door. "We didn't know you felt this way."

Katherine lifted her shoulders in a feeble shrug. "I thought that you... that you wanted me to work with you. But if I got the job already, you would be fine if I did that instead. If the job was a certainty and not speculation."

Her mother sighed. "If you didn't want to work with me, you should have said."

Katherine smiled feebly and her mother walked towards her to hug her. Her father was more understanding than she thought he would be. Her confession surprised him, but he was ultimately pleased for her.

Both of her parents were far more understanding than she had thought they would be. She had imagined worse, and the reality was nowhere near it.

As she went upstairs, after dinner with both of her parents, she sent a text to Emmy to thank her for listening. She took a moment before she sent another to Aiden.

She would have to thank the two of them later for being loyal friends. And maybe bribe Aiden to keep quiet about being some kind of good luck charm.

CHAPTER SIXTEEN
EMMY IN THE CAFE

The lights in Katherine's den dimmed to where Emmy could barely see the outline of anybody else in the room. It was already late in the evening when they arrived at the house. She could just make out Katherine's silhouette, sitting next to the computer, with Aiden hovering over her shoulder. She kept swatting his hand away every time he pointed to the screen.

Katherine had invited her, Tilda, Noah, Bellamy, and Henry over to watch Maelie and Aiden's movie in her den.

Katherine was in a much more cheerful mood than the last time Emmy had seen her. The message she had sent Emmy told her things had gone well between her and her mother, and the lilt in Katherine's voice also confirmed it.

Before the lights went out, Emmy had been sitting between Tilda and Bellamy on one of Katherine's plush couches. Next to Bellamy sat Henry and Maelie. They were busy talking about the movie with Noah.

There were a few moments of hushed whispers before the video popped up on the screen and played on the large tv that had taken centre stage.

They sat huddled in silence as the video continued. It was a short horror film with Henry as the chief character. It lasted less than ten minutes, and when it finished, the group remained silent. Aiden got up from his chair beside Katherine and raised his arms out to the rest of them.

"So?" He asked.

"I'm surprised at you, Aid. I didn't think you would ever put any effort into anything." Tilda sighed. She crossed her legs and turned to the rest of them. "I thought it was great."

Emmy nodded. She didn't know what else she could say. She thought it was brilliant. Everyone else chimed in their praise, and Aiden soaked it up like a sponge. He took a bow.

Maelie rolled her eyes at him. "I helped too, you know."

Aiden stood back up. "Oh yeah, Mae helped." He added.

Tilda and Henry chuckled.

Noah stretched his legs out in front of him. "You're a talented actor, Henry. I'm impressed."

"So am I," Henry replied.

"Yeah, your acting was good," Bellamy said to Henry. He turned to look at Aiden. "And who came up with the plot?"

Maelie and Aiden both put up their hands, then scowled at each other before they started bickering again.

Everyone laughed while Maelie and Aiden argued. Emmy stood up and left the den to slip into the kitchen. As she opened the fridge, she heard someone step into the room behind her. She turned and saw that Bellamy was standing behind her in the doorway.

"Oh, hey. Do you want a drink?" She waved her hand at the fridge in front of her.

He smirked at her. "Always the hostess, even at someone else's party."

"It's not a party." She closed the fridge door behind her. When Katherine left her alone with Henry, Darcy, Bellamy, and her waffle the day before, Emmy had spent most of her time staring at her plate instead of talking to either of them.

She kept thinking about what things would be like once Bellamy left the cafe.

She wondered if things would be the same.

Of course, they wouldn't. If Bellamy had taught her anything, it was that things have a way of changing quickly. She couldn't force him to stay. She wanted him to choose to come back because, as soon as he finished working at Marsh's, she wouldn't see much of him again.

"So?" He asked.

"So what?" She answered.

"Are you going to tell me why you're avoiding me?"

"I'm not."

"So you're not going to tell me?"

"No, I mean, I'm not avoiding you."

Bellamy shoved his hands in his pockets. "Do you think I know by now what you look like when you're avoiding me, or when you're sulking? I swear, it's like you have only three faces."

"Oh, yeah? What's the third face?"

"A 'happy' face."

"You've seen me happy? Around you?" She knew he had. She could remember being in a good mood around Bellamy, but not happy. Though that didn't matter now.

"Yes. I like you when you're cheerful. It's the nicest you."

Emmy didn't know what to say to that. She fiddled with her sleeve. "I thought you liked the sulking me the best."

"Well, yeah, but I like you when you're happy."

She felt like he was trying to say goodbye, but it was the one thing he wouldn't say. "I hope things go well for you... away from the cafe." She mumbled. She turned again and opened the fridge, picked up a bottle of water, and walked past Bellamy out of the kitchen.

As they arrived back in the den, they heard Aiden announce a toast to the group to celebrate his genius.

"To my genius and to my friends." He announced, raising a glass to the rest of them.

Emmy looked at Bellamy as they drank.

After the non-party dissolved, Bellamy drove Emmy and Noah home, the same way they had arrived. Even before he had asked, she gravitated towards him as the night neared its end.

After Bellamy parked outside her house, Noah jumped out of the car, but Emmy remained in the car for a second longer. She told Noah that she would come in a minute as he went on ahead of her. She saw Bellamy gazing intently at her. Another second passed before Emmy leaned over and pressed her lips to Bellamy's. He leaned in to her and returned the kiss. After another beat, she pulled away and got out of the car without looking back.

CHAPTER SEVENTEEN

BELLAMY IN THE CAFE

As Emmy and Bellamy closed the cafe, golden summer light filtered in through the windows, casting long, lazy shadows across the floor. Emmy had spent the entire day dodging him in the cafe, which was an impressive task considering how close they worked together. Not that it wasn't obvious, because it was.

The cafe felt as big as a shoebox. The more she tried to avoid him and the closer the time came for him to leave the cafe.

Janey was spending more time with Tilda and Matt so she could get used to them and his mother had already started at her new job.

He had tried, over the course of the day, to continue the conversation he had been having with Emmy from the week before at Katherine's house, but Emmy wasn't in a mood to listen. But though she kept her distance, she was in no rush to leave.

Neither one of them moved to leave, even after they had stacked the tables and chairs for the day, their belongings in their hands. There were so many things he wanted to say, but he wasn't sure how to start.

"What took you so long this morning? You're usually here before me." Bellamy asked. He couldn't think of anything else to say and he knew if he wasn't careful, Emmy would run away.

"I was thinking about things again. You know, Katherine apologised to me. She explained what was going on. She was afraid to speak to her parents about her new job. It ended well, though."

"Oh, good." He said.

Emmy reached into her bag and pulled out a wrapped parcel and handed it to him. It rattled as he took it, the contents heavy in the box.

"It's for Janey." Emmy explained. "I got her a doll."

He held the parcel carefully, feeling the weight of the box. "Thank you."

They stood in silence for a few seconds as he stared at the box. "I like you, Bellamy. I just didn't want to admit it." Emmy whispered.

Bellamy kept his eyes on the wrapped package. Wrapping paper was meticulously folded to cover the box. He placed it down on the table in front of him. "I like you, too."

He looked directly at Emmy. She tucked a stray curl behind her ear, then admitted what she had on her mind.

"I... I'm so tired. I'm tired of trying to be everywhere and everything in this place. I wanted to be the best employee I could be because I loved it here."

She closed her mouth abruptly, and Bellamy stepped closer to her.

"What?" He pressed.

She shook her head, but she opened her mouth, anyway. She didn't want to say what she thought, but Bellamy wanted it out in the open.

"I think... I want... I want to..." She cleared her throat. "I don't know." She whispered.

Bellamy was silent. He shifted closer to her and put his arm around her as he stood in front of her, their heads touching.

"You don't know what?"

"I just... I don't know if I should say. If I can."

Bellamy didn't move. If he moved again, he might scare her, and she would never admit her feelings.

"I think you can."

She froze and for a second; he thought she would leave and walk away, but she didn't. Instead, she reached up on her toes and pressed her lips against his again. His arms wrapped around her and pulled her closer.

***

The following Friday, Bellamy spent most of the morning lounging with Emmy in the cafe on their day off.

They sat and talked about random stuff before the rest of the group joined them. Noah and Lucy arrived before Henry and Aiden. An hour later, Katherine, Maelie, and Tilda all walked in together.

None of them had places to be for the first time in ages. Noah and Lucy fought between themselves as Henry, Maelie, and Aiden bickered about their movie again. Aiden was already planning a sequel and wanted Henry to agree to take part, while Maelie demanded that she got recognition for her part of the project. Katherine sat opposite them, unconcerned even as they rose their voices.

She waited for them to stop talking before she cleared her throat. She told them about what happened with her mother, then Tilda talked about her brother and Aiden continued to brag about his film.

Both Emmy listened to everyone else's stories, sitting side by side, as a couple with Bellamy, who wasn't paying attention to what was being said.

CHAPTER EIGHTEEN
EMMY IN THE CAFE

Even in the middle of summer, the air was too humid. Not even passing under the shade of the buildings and trees helped with the blazing heat.

Taking one step felt like taking ten. Emmy's legs were heavy logs, and she was just glad that she chose that day to wear shorts and a light baggy top.

Not that it did much to help.

Emmy fanned herself with her hand as she readjusted her bag on her shoulder. The strap had caused a patch of sweat to form and she irritably pulled her top away from her skin.

She had walked from her home since it seemed like a nice day, but she regretted it once she had gotten a quarter of the way there.

It was a scorching day, but every once in a while, a strong blustery wind blew past her to keep her going.

She sighed in relief as she entered Marsh's, only to find the air inside the cafe stifling.

Someone had propped the door open along with all the windows, hoping to encourage a cool wind in to ease the thick atmosphere.

From the sweaty faces of the people inside, it didn't appear to make much of a difference.

Emmy spotted her friends next to the window, sprawled across their usual couches. Tilda, draped as usual over her armchair, was fanning herself from the heat.

She had her hair was tied in a messy knot on the top of her head and away from her neck. She kept fidgeting, pulling at her shorts and her damp T-shirt away from her skin every few seconds.

On the couch next to Tilda's armchair, Maelie sat in between Aiden and Henry.

All three of them looked equally miserable. Maelie's beanie was absent from her head, and she had her hair pulled in a tousled ponytail.

Aiden leaned forward in his seat and grabbed his glass from the coffee table, grimacing all the way.

Henry brought his bottle to his lips and gulped down the iced water.

Katherine, Noah, and Bellamy sat opposite them. Katherine was the only one who looked relaxed, though her forehead was covered in sweat.

Emmy walked over to them, dropping her bag beside the chair, and sank into the couch next to Bellamy. She moved in closer to his side, feeling the heat radiating off him.

Despite her sweaty skin, he put his arm around her, shifting his position to accommodate her on the couch.

Tilda stretched out her legs, sweat shining on them as they moved. "It's too hot." She complained. "We need to find a pool or something to soak in."

"Or a fan or, you know, air conditioning. That might be easier to find," Maelie grumbled, picking up her glass from the table and bringing it to her cheek.

Aiden stretched his arm along the back of the couch behind Maelie and sipped from his cup.

"Don't complain. It's better to have this stifling heat roasting us, instead of cold, damp weather."

Maelie took a large gulp from her glass, and gave him a withering glare, before pressing the glass back to her head.

"Is it? Because, and, this may just be my opinion, but cold damp weather doesn't make me want to cry every time I have to go outside. I mean, I assume I want to cry, but there's never enough moisture for me to be sure about that."

Emmy had to agree with Maelie, but Aiden was adamant. "The cold makes me want to curl up in bed and never move. And it's always wet. It's never just cold."

Katherine rolled her eyes. "When was the last time you went out? You don't even go anywhere!"

Aiden shrugged. "It doesn't change the way I feel. Anyway, hot or cold, at least we don't have to go anywhere now."

"Speak for yourself." Henry groaned.

He grabbed his water bottle from the table. The ice rattled around as he took a swig. "Some of us have to work."

He placed the bottle down, and when the water settled, it only covered the chunks of ice at the bottom.

Katherine tapped on her cup, looking at the rest of them lounging on the couches. She crossed her leg and sat up straighter. "Speaking of work. I'm... going to have another party."

Everyone groaned out loud and Katherine rolled her eyes at the rest of them, holding up a placating hand to the group.

"This is for my birthday. But this is more for us than anything. I'm just going to invite all of you, no one else, so relax."

Aiden scoffed. "What, you mean we're guests this time and not Katherine's little assistants? Because you made us think that the last time you had a party and that was a lie."

"It's not a lie! It's just going to be us. We can have time to celebrate everything we've done and everything we're going to do."

"On your birthday?" Aiden asked.

"Well, it so happens that it will soon be my birthday." Katherine countered innocently.

"I'm not buying that. Is anyone buying that?" Aiden asked, looking around at the group. Everyone shook their heads.

Katherine puffed out her chest and took in a haughty breath. "We'll have a party for Bellamy, too. Your birthday is after mine, right?"

Bellamy hesitated. "Yeah, the 18th. But we don't have to do anything for it."

"No, no, we are having a party." Katherine protested. She folded her arms over her chest. "I've got too much to celebrate not to. We all do. We've had a good year, so far."

"Did we?" Noah asked.

Katherine raised her chin and scowled at him. "Yes, we did."

Aiden stretched his arms over his head. "Well, can we do that at the end of the year? You know, when we can definitely say that this was a good year. We can just have a party for you and Bellamy."

"Hey, will I be having a party too?" Maelie interjected. "My birthday's in September."

Henry raised a hand. "Mine, too."

Aiden took another swig from his glass. "Keep going, and we'll be celebrating Emmy's birthday next. We'll celebrate your birthdays when they get here. If we're not busy." Aiden turned back to Katherine. "Besides, your parties aren't as much fun for us as they are for everyone else. Not when you make us set them up."

"I told you! You won't have to do anything. But I could do with some help." Everyone groaned again.

"Emmy?" Katherine turned to her. "Please help me out? Just a little. I need some help with the catering. We can work next week on Friday and you can choose what to make. This time I won't interfere, and I'll even help you if you need me to."

Emmy's first instinct was to say yes to Katherine. Things were different now, and she understood Katherine better. She knew she valued her as a friend and not a workhorse, but a small part of her didn't want to let Katherine down.

Another part admitted that she was tired. Not physically, but the thought of preparing food for a party made her feel drained.

Emmy inhaled and smiled at her friend. "No. I'm sorry."

Katherine raised her eyebrows. "No?"

"I'm not doing it. I can't. I'm sorry, but I need time to relax and get ready."

The words spilt out of her mouth, and they scared her. Bellamy was right. She worked herself too hard, and she let Katherine push her around too much.

She neglected herself because she was more concerned with what everyone else wanted. It scared her to say it out loud, but it felt good.

"Get ready for what?" Katherine questioned.

Out of the corner of her eye, Emmy saw Lucy walk through the front door, dragging her feet as she walked.

Emmy turned back to the group as Lucy sat down next to Noah. "I have something to tell you." Everyone turned toward her. "I'm quitting the cafe."

She felt Bellamy take a deep breath next to her, and she felt everyone's eyes fixed on her, all of them showing varying degrees of surprise.

Tilda leaned forward with wide eyes. "Why?"

"I've decided that I should try something else. I should look for something I'm interested in. Something other than the cafe. I spoke to my parents and decided I'm going to go to university."

Maelie raised her brows. "What are you going to study? English or something?"

Emmy shook her head. "History. I loved it in school, so..." She shrugged.

"Finally." Noah sighed, pushing Lucy's bag off his leg. "We've been trying to get rid of you for so long."

Katherine frowned. "Oh, um... fine. That's fine. Congratulations. Bellamy? Would you help me?"

Emmy patted Bellamy's leg. "Bellamy needs to rest, too. But Lucy would be happy to do it. Wouldn't you, Lucy?"

Lucy's eyes widen, and she pointed at herself. "Me?"

Emmy nodded. "You wanted a job, right? I'm sure she will be fantastic," she said to Katherine, "especially since you'll be paying her pretty handsomely." She grinned at Lucy.

Lucy smiled tentatively at Katherine. "I'd love to."

Katherine smirked at her. "Ok, then. I guess I can use you."

Lucy crossed her arms over her chest. "So... what about here? Noah and Bellamy can't work here on their own. Can I get a job here, too?" Lucy asked.

Bellamy shifted in his chair. "I won't be working here for much longer, either. Today's my last day. I told Fred."

Everyone froze for a second. Aiden and Tilda leaned forward. Aiden cleared his throat, but Tilda spoke before he could. "You're leaving?" Tilda asked, clearly upset.

"When were you planning on telling us?" Maelie mumbled.

"You could have given us some warning," Henry added.

Bellamy held up his hands to placate them. "No! Well, yeah, I won't be working here, but you'll still see me. Don't worry."

Emmy smirked at their faces. "I'm sure that they'll manage without you here." She said, leaning toward Bellamy.

Katherine turned to Emmy. "Are you moving?"

Emmy shook her head. "No. I'll commute."

"Well, I'm sure everyone'll look after things here for you. You'll have a lot of fun. I did." Bellamy added.

"I will." Emmy smiled up at him.

They all spent the rest of the day at the cafe.

Both Emmy and Bellamy had agreed to take the late shifts and close up the cafe.

Since it was Bellamy's last day, they closed early and ate a slice of cake each. They laughed and joked with each other as they ate.

Golden light filtered in through the glass in the cafe, spilling across the floor and furniture like honey as they sat upstairs in the cafe.

"So, what's your plan?" Emmy asked before she took a last bite of cake.

Bellamy raised his eyebrows. "What do you mean?"

"After you leave here, then what?"

Bellamy tapped his chin thoughtfully. "There are... things I'd like to do."

Emmy's interest peaked. "Oh, yeah. And those are?"

"I'll let you know."

"Well, before you do, how about a trip?"

"Where?"

Emmy shrugged. "I don't know."

"As long as it's not a museum or something like that."

Emmy blushed. "No, more like a trip or something."

"And is this with or without Tilda, Maelie, Aiden, and everyone else?"

Emmy shrugged again. "But they might end up tagging along, anyway." She smiled at that. "Let's just start with the cinema and go from there."

That would be a nice, relaxing thing for the two of them to do as a couple. And if the rest of their friends came along, at least it would get them out of the cafe.

THE END